CALL OF THE WRAITH

Also by Kevin Sands

The Blackthorn Key
Mark of the Plague
The Assassin's Curse

THE BLACKTHORN KEY

CALL
OF THE
WRAITH

BOOK 4

KEVIN SANDS

ALADDIN
NEW YORK   LONDON   TORONTO   SYDNEY   NEW DELHI

ALADDIN

An imprint of Simon & Schuster Children's Publishing Division
1230 Avenue of the Americas, New York, New York 10020
First Aladdin hardcover edition September 2018
Text copyright © 2018 by Kevin Sands
Interior illustrations on pages 41, 61, 79 copyright © 2018 by Jim Madsen
Interior illustrations on pages 13, 26, 47, 374, 378 by Greg Stadnyk
copyright © 2018 by Simon & Schuster, Inc.
Interior images on pages 201, 204, 212, 250 from *Dictionnaire infernal, ou Bibliothèque universelle* by Collin de Plancy, courtesy of Wikipedia.com
Jacket illustration copyright © 2018 by James Fraser
All rights reserved, including the right of reproduction in whole or in part in any form.
ALADDIN and related logo are registered trademarks of Simon & Schuster, Inc.
For information about special discounts for bulk purchases, please contact
Simon & Schuster Special Sales at 1-866-506-1949 or business@simonandschuster.com.
The Simon & Schuster Speakers Bureau can bring authors to your live event. For more information or to book an event, contact the Simon & Schuster Speakers Bureau at 1-866-248-3049 or visit our website at www.simonspeakers.com.
Interior designed by Karin Paprocki
The text of this book was set in Adobe Garamond Pro.
Manufactured in the United States of America 0818 FFG
2 4 6 8 10 9 7 5 3 1
Library of Congress Cataloging-in-Publication Data
Names: Sands, Kevin, author.
Title: Call of the wraith / by Kevin Sands.
Description: First Simon Pulse hardcover edition. | New York : Simon Pulse, 2018. | Series: The Blackthorn key ; 4 | Summary: Christopher Rowe is shipwrecked in Devonshire, where children are disappearing and a ghost is suspected, but even Tom and Sally's arrival may not cure his amnesia in time to help.
Identifiers: LCCN 2018012451 (print) | LCCN 2018018884 (eBook) | ISBN 9781534428478 (hc) | ISBN 9781534428492 (eBook)
Subjects: CYAC: Adventure and adventurers—Fiction. | Amnesia—Fiction. | Missing children—Fiction. | Supernatural—Fiction. | Friendship—Fiction. | Secret societies—Fiction. | Devon (England)—Fiction. | Great Britain—History—Charles II, 1660-1685—Fiction. | Mystery and detective stories. |
BISAC: JUVENILE FICTION / Mysteries & Detective Stories. | JUVENILE FICTION / Action & Adventure / General. | JUVENILE FICTION / Historical / General.
Classification: LCC PZ7.1.S26 (eBook) | LCC PZ7.1.S26 Cal 2018 (print) | DDC [Fic]—dc23
LC record available at https://lccn.loc.gov/2018012451

CALL
OF THE
WRAITH

?

I'M SO COLD.

I shiver, but this does nothing to fight the chill. The frost grips me like vines, creeps under my skin. My flesh, my bones, my veins turn to ice. Even my thoughts cannot escape. The wisps of vapor that rise from my head freeze, fall, and shatter on the plain.

The cold surrounds me, envelops me, swallows me. I try to move, but I can't. I look down from the slate-gray sky and see I am buried to my waist. My hands, my legs are stuck in ice, endless ice: deep, eternal white.

I scream. "Help me!"

My words echo back, twisted, mocking. "Help me," not-me says, and laughs.

There is no other sound. The giant is gone, his body lying bleeding in the valley, pierced by a thousand arrows. The princess is gone, locked in the tower, no one around to hear her cries. And warmth is gone, the hands that once held me ripped from my heart. Nothing remains.

Except the bird.

A branch rises from the ice, crooked and twisting. The bird perches at its end, watching me. Its feathers are . . . not black, for black would mean they were made of something. These feathers are nothing. The bird is a hole in the universe. And beyond that hole is nothing at all.

It looks down at me. Its eyes, like its feathers, are black, but not the deep empty black of nothingness. These eyes are glittering onyx. There is intelligence behind them, and it sees my pain.

"Let me go," I plead.

The bird answers. THIS PLACE IS YOURS. THIS PLACE IS ETERNAL. NO ONE LEAVES. EVER.

I'm so cold. Yet it isn't the chill that makes me shudder. "I don't belong here!"

BUT YOU DO.

"I betrayed no one!"

BUT YOU DID.

"Please," I say. "I don't deserve this."

YES, *the bird answers, but now another voice answers underneath. It's the faintest of whispers, so soft, it's not even sound, just the memory of it. It echoes inside me, and its words fight against the cold.*

Hold on, *it says.*

Hold on to what? I ask. I am lost. I am alone.

No, *the voice says.* I am with you. Always.

And that's when I begin to fall.

CHAPTER

1

MY HEAD SLAMMED INTO THE FLOOR.

I lay there, dizzy, stunned, my legs wrapped and bound above me. I couldn't move. I couldn't think.

My *head*.

My head ached with a deep, throbbing pulse, every thrum a promise to split my skull. My stomach roiled, rebelled, and when I could stand it no more, I turned over and retched.

Nothing came out. My muscles strained, but there was nothing in my cramping stomach to throw up. When the spasms finally stopped, I rested my head on the floor, the packed dirt cool against my cheek.

I coughed, then swallowed. My throat burned, scratched,

dried with hollow spit. I groaned and opened my eyes.

I saw tarred wooden beams above me. Confused, it took me a moment to understand: I was looking at the ceiling. I'd fallen out of bed. Now I lay upside down, half on the floor, half hanging from the mattress. The bonds that held my legs were the bedding: a sheet of cool white linen, a heavy wrap of deerskin on top.

I wriggled free. My body slipped from the blankets and thumped against the floor. I lay there, waiting for the world to stop spinning.

The light, as faint as it was, was still enough to make me squint. It came from a fire of wood and peat, burning low in the hearth opposite the bed, filling the air with the smell of smoked dirt. The room itself was unfamiliar, and nearly empty: just the bed I'd fallen from, a rickety wooden table and chair, and a palliasse in the corner near the fire, a second deerskin blanket crumpled behind it. The mantel over the fireplace, a plank of sagging cedar, was empty. The walls were made of cob: smoothly packed clay and straw, washed with lime. A single door offered an exit, one step up from the floor. Beneath the handle, a rusted iron plate covered its keyhole.

Where was I?

I tried to remember how I'd got here, but tasking my

brain made my head spin again. I crawled back onto the bed and lay there, breathing, letting the whirling subside.

At least it was warm. The fading dream of the icy plain made me shiver, and I pulled the deerskin up to cover me. As I did, I noticed what I was wearing: a plain gray shirt, breeches, and hose. All simple, undyed wool, all too large for me.

These were not my clothes. Where had they come from?

Where *was* I?

Again I tried to remember, and again the world began to spin. I groaned and covered my eyes until the queasiness passed.

I stayed like that for a while, resting against the mattress. It was soft—goose down. The comfort struck me as oddly out of place, considering my surroundings. Not that I was about to complain.

Complain to whom?

I sat up, startled. The motion made my head throb.

The question I'd heard wasn't a thought. It was a voice, a man's voice. Deep, the strains of age beginning to weather it.

"Hello?"

My own voice came out ragged. I was so thirsty. I looked around and spied a ceramic jug at the foot of my bed. My fingers ached as I picked it up, grateful to hear sloshing inside. I pulled the cork from its neck. The jug's mouth had already reached mine before I smelled the horror.

I recoiled just before it touched my lips. The jug slipped from my fingers, bounced off the mattress, cracked on the dirt below. The liquid splashed from the broken bottom, and the sharp tang of urine filled the room.

I stared, shaking, at the mess on the ground. Underneath the shards, soaked in the waste, were a handful of stones, a half dozen nails, and short strands of something tied in a knot. It looked like hair.

I gagged, the stink choking my throat. Why would someone leave me that to drink?

It's not for you to drink.

That voice again. "Who are you?" I said.

No answer came. I made to call out once more, then stopped when I realized: The voice was right.

The jug. Ceramic, filled with urine, stones, nails, and hair. It wasn't meant to be drunk. It was . . .

The room tumbled, and this time I couldn't control my nausea. I leaned over the side of the bed, retching, my skull throbbing with every heave.

The spell finally passed. I rolled over, gasping.

You need to get up, the voice said.

I heard it clearly. The voice . . . it wasn't coming from inside the room. It was inside my *head*.

I lay there, breath caught in my throat, and responded in kind. *Who are you?*

Get up, the voice said.

My mind swirled with questions, but the voice wouldn't answer them. I crawled to the edge of the bed, then stood. My legs wobbled under my weight, the dizziness overwhelming.

Give it a moment.

I steadied myself against the wall. The roughness of the lime-washed cob made my fingers sting. I looked at them; they were red and raw. Blackened skin peeled away from the tips.

"What's happened to me?" I whispered.

The voice in my head spoke, soothing. *Calm, child.*

But I couldn't stay calm. I tried to remember how I got here, and the room spun faster than ever.

I fought it, searched for the memory. I tried to remember. The walls swam. The walls melted.

I tried—

I opened my eyes.

Timbers. I saw tarred timbers over thatch.

The ceiling. I was looking at the ceiling again.

You passed out, the voice said.

I pushed myself up. I didn't try to remember anything this time. I just stayed hunched over, head between my knees, until the dizziness subsided.

That's it, the voice said. *Good.*

What do I do now? I said.

Go to the door.

Slowly, I stood, then staggered over. When I touched the handle, I jerked my blackened fingers away.

The handle was freezing. I could feel the cold beyond the door, seeping through the wood. The nightmare of ice returned to my mind, and all I wanted to do was run. But there was nowhere to go.

I took a breath, trying to calm myself. Then I knelt and pushed the iron plate covering the keyhole out of the way. It swung upward with a squeal of rusted metal.

Light winked through the keyhole. I squinted and peered into it.

Snow.

The door led outside, to a world covered with snow. Some thirty feet away was a line of trees, branches swaying in the wind, weighed down by heaps of white. The sky above was a dull gray ceiling of clouds.

I pressed closer, trying to see more. To the left, I could just make out the corner of another cob house. I could smell something, too: charred wood.

I saw no fire through the keyhole. The smell wasn't coming from outside; it was closer. I pulled back, blinking away the spots the brightness had left in my eyes. Then I saw: There were symbols, burned into the wood of the doorjamb.

There were five of them. Four were circles, arcane markings within. The fifth was a *W.*

No. Wait. It wasn't a *W.* It was . . . conjoined *Vs?*

Yes, the voice in my head said.

I knew these symbols. I looked back at the broken jug, and once again my stomach began to tumble.

Yes, the voice said. *Those go together. Think.*

But thinking made me dizzy. The only thing I could remember

no, not remember—feel

was that those symbols meant nothing good. A sudden, desperate wish gripped me: Be anywhere but here.

I grabbed the handle again, ignoring the pain in my fingers. I pulled. But the door only rattled. It was locked.

I was a prisoner.

CHAPTER

2

I COULDN'T FIGHT THE PANIC ANY-
more. I shook the handle, shouting.

"Hey! Let me out! *Let me out!*"

The door wouldn't budge. All my calls did was make
me dizzy again, so I stopped, resting on my knees, waiting
to recover.

Calm, child.

That was the second time the voice—I'd begun to think
of it as the Voice—said those words. They were familiar, in
a way I couldn't place. Someone had said them to me a long
time ago, and they'd made me feel safe.

I listened to the Voice, and his words stilled my heart,

my panic fading with my breaths. It returned when I heard a sound outside. The crunching of boots in snow.

Someone was coming.

I crawled from the door, but there was no place to hide. I looked about the room for a weapon, any weapon. All I could find were the broken shards of pottery—and the chair.

I stood; I hefted it. It was a flimsy thing, creaking under its own weight. A single blow would likely turn it to splinters.

Fortunately, one blow might be all I'd need. The door wasn't tall, so whoever came in would need to bend over to enter. If I surprised them, hit them on the back of the neck, even this rickety chair would leave them dazed.

The crunching footsteps reached the door. A key rattled in the lock. I pressed my back to the wall, the chair overhead.

Daylight spilled in as the door creaked open, and the figure stepped inside. I spun around, heaving the chair back to slam it down. I stopped myself just in time.

It was a girl. She looked to be about ten years old, wearing a long sheepskin overcoat and heavy boots, hands weighed down with a pair of bowls. She shrieked as I jumped out at her. Her heel caught on the step, and she fell backward into the snow, sending the bowls bouncing off the door frame. I ducked as carrots, leeks, and steaming chunks of meat splashed gravy everywhere.

The girl scrambled to her feet and fled, screaming, "Daddy! Daddy!" The bowls dripped the last of their stew into the snow. The smell of it made my stomach growl, and my heart sank to see it wasted. I suddenly realized how desperately hungry I was.

I could hear the girl running, calling for her father. She'd left the door open. Cold air blew inside, daylight promising escape. I rushed toward it.

Then a man stepped into the doorway, blocking my path. He was tall and awkwardly lanky, and though he was bundled in the same sort of sheepskin coat as the girl, he couldn't have been her father. He was too old, the lines of countless decades etched into his face.

He froze when he saw me. Unlike the girl, he wasn't carrying stew. He held a longbow.

I stepped back, chair held high. "Get away from me!" I said.

He held a hand out. Moving carefully, he rested his longbow against the wall, then backed away, hands open so

I could see them. A quiver of arrows remained slung behind his neck.

I studied his face, trying to place him. Besides the marks of age, there was a bruise on his cheek, a deep, angry purple, and the corner of his mouth was cut. Sometime recently, someone had split his lip.

"Where am I?" I said. "What do you want from me?"

He didn't answer. He just held out his hands, as if asking me to keep calm.

I tried again. "Who are you? Why am I being held prisoner?"

The old man looked puzzled. He shook his head, then gestured. I couldn't understand what he was trying to tell me.

"Why won't you speak?" I said, fear raising my voice to a shout.

He hesitated. Then he opened his mouth, and I understood.

Someone had cut out his tongue.

The chair drifted downward as I stared in horror. "Who did that to you?"

He just shook his head. I was about to ask him more, but then I heard someone else running through the snow.

I brought the chair up again as the new man arrived. He was heavy, a burly sort, and, unlike the others, he wasn't wearing a coat. His sleeves were rolled up, stained at the cuffs with what looked like blood. He was shaggy—shaggy head, shaggy beard, shaggy forearms, covered in hair—and he reminded me, as much as anything, of a bear.

He skidded to a stop when he saw me. He held out his hands, like the old man had, and spoke, low and soothing, his voice a rumble. "Please, my lord. You'll hurt yourself."

I kept the chair right where it was. "Where am I?"

"On my farm, my lord." His accent was pure West Country: *On moy fahrrm, muh'larrd.* "My name's Robert. Robert Dryden." He motioned to the old man beside him. "This is Wise. We've been looking after you. No one means you any harm, I promise."

The strain was too much. My knees wobbled. "Why am I being held prisoner?"

"Prisoner?" The farmer looked confused. "You're no prisoner."

"Then why was I locked in here?"

"Oh," he said, surprised. "Oh, no, my lord. The lock wasn't to keep you in. It was to keep the bad things *out*."

CHAPTER

3

I STARED AT HIM. "WHAT BAD things?"

He hesitated. "Will you let me explain? Put the chair down? Please?"

I wasn't sure what to do. Despite his wild appearance, the calm in the farmer's manner made me feel he wasn't much of a threat. "I . . ."

My body gave my answer. I collapsed.

Wise sprang forward, catching me before my skull cracked on the floor. Gently he disarmed me, pulling my fingers from the chair. Then he lifted me with ease, the man much stronger than I'd have guessed.

I didn't try to resist. I couldn't, in any case. Wise carried me to the bed and sat me at its edge. He and Robert waited, hands on my shoulders, until the world righted itself.

"What's happened to me?" I said when I could finally speak.

"You've been very sick, my lord," Robert said. "Right worried about you, we were. We kept you here, in the cob house, so you'd be safe. You and the girl."

Safe? I thought. *What girl?* "The one who brought me stew?"

"No, that's my daughter, Margery. I was meaning to speak of the little one."

He nodded toward the corner, where the empty palliasse rested. I looked at him quizzically.

"She's hiding under the blanket," the farmer said. "She's a shy one, that."

They steadied me as I stood, until they were sure I wouldn't fall again. Then I stepped closer to the palliasse. As I did, the blanket behind it moved. Surprised, I took a corner and lifted it.

A little girl, four, five years old at the most, lay curled beneath the deerskin. Her hair—blond, it looked like, though it was hard to tell, so matted as it was with dirt and grime—stuck with oily gumminess to her cheeks. She was wearing an odd mix of togs: a torn and filthy lemon dress with brand-new sheepskin boots and a coat far too large for her draped over her shoulders.

She slid away from me, big blue eyes round with fear. She curled up in the corner, an animal trapped, watching me through strings of tangled hair.

"Do you know her, my lord?" Robert asked.

I shook my head. The motion made the girl twitch. I realized that I probably looked as monstrous to her as Wise had to me.

"It's all right," I said to her. "Don't be scared. I won't hurt you—"

She bolted. She tore her blanket from my grasp and scrambled over the palliasse. The coat fell from her shoulders as she slid into the opposite corner, where she crouched, trembling, behind the deerskin.

"Best not to press her, my lord," Robert said. "She won't let anyone touch her, not even my girls."

I was beginning to understand why. When her coat had fallen, I'd seen the marks of violence on her arms: red, scabbed scratches and huge purple bruises, already turning an ugly yellow. "What happened to her?"

Robert hesitated. "Couldn't say for sure, my lord. Wise found her by the river three days ago, dying in the snow, poor thing. Still tried to run when he picked her up. Screamed blue murder the whole way, too, until he brought her inside and let her go. Since then, she just hides behind that blanket we gave her. Hasn't said a single word."

He sounded troubled. *There's something he's not telling me*, I thought, and the idea nearly made me miss what he'd said.

He'd found her three days ago. But then . . . "How long have I been here?"

"Thirteen days."

My jaw dropped. Thirteen *days*?

How . . . how had I got here?

Calm, child, the Voice said.

But I couldn't stay calm. I was nowhere. I remembered *nothing*.

And the harder I tried, the more the world spun. Before I knew it, Robert and Wise were holding me again, lowering me to the bed.

"What am I doing here?" I croaked.

"We think you were in a shipwreck," Robert said.

A shipwreck?

"A fortnight ago," Robert said, "the snow came. A terrible storm—a fury, the like I've never seen. Wise found you the next day, down at the beach. You were practically buried in ice."

Now I began to shake. My dream

my hands, my legs are stuck in ice, endless ice: deep, eternal white

returned, and it made my stomach quiver. I fled from the memory, flexing my fingers, just to prove I could still move.

The farmer saw that. "Your hands were very badly frost-bitten. I feared you might lose them. Luckily, we warmed you in time."

Not without cost. My fingers stung, their blackened tips aching. Still, the pain was better than the dream. "Thank you."

Robert looked troubled as he continued. "Kept drifting in and out of a dark sleep, you did. Skin was so hot, I thought your fever would boil your insides. Then you had . . . fits. You were babbling—it was tongues, my lord. And you got violent. Had to tie you down so you wouldn't hurt yourself."

I looked over at Wise. His bruises, his split lip. "Did I do that?"

Wise nodded.

I slumped. "I'm sorry."

"No one blames you, my lord," Robert said. "Wasn't your fault. Was the demon."

"What demon?"

"The one that had hold of you." He looked at me seriously. "You were possessed."

CHAPTER

MY MOUTH WORKED,
barely able to speak. *"Possessed?"*

The Voice cut through my thoughts.
Now do you see the signs?

And I did.

The marks on the door. I knew
them now. Those were witches' marks,
inscribed to bar the way against evil spirits. The circles warded the entrance, and
the conjoined *Vs* were an appeal to the
Virgo Virginum: the Virgin Mary.

And the jug. The one by the foot of

the bed, now broken. It was another charm against evil. Unbidden, the recipe burned across my mind. *Take the urine and hair of the afflicted. Immerse protection stones and iron nails within, to ground the soul to the body. Then seal it tight with a spell.*

They said I'd been having fits—seizures—and babbling in strange languages. All were common signs of possession. But I remembered none of this. Just my dream. The dead plain.

And the bird.

"My lord?"

Robert and Wise were watching me. I'd been so lost in thought, I hadn't been paying attention.

Careful, the Voice said. *If they think a demon still holds you . . .*

"Thank you for caring for me," I said quickly. "Not many would shelter one held by evil."

Robert folded his arms. "No one will ever be turned away from my farm." He said it as a point of pride. Yet there was something—his brief downward glance, the way he avoided my eyes—that made me believe someone had, indeed, made that very suggestion.

"If you're feeling better, my lord," he continued, "perhaps now we could appeal for your help."

My help? I could barely stand unaided. What could they possibly need from me?

"I was wondering if you'd be willing to speak for us," the farmer said. "Because of your standing."

"What standing?" I said.

"I mean to speak of your lordship, my lord."

I frowned. Robert had been using that honorific from the beginning. I'd assumed he'd meant it as a general mark of respect to an unknown guest. "Why would you think I'm a lord?"

"Aren't you?" he said, surprised. "I mean . . . your clothes."

I looked down at the simple peasant wool I was wearing.

"Not those, my lord," Robert said. "We gave you those. I meant the clothes we found you in. And the money."

"I have money?"

"In your coin purse. It's all there, I promise. We haven't touched a farthing."

I just stared at him.

"Do you not remember that?" he said.

I shook my head.

He and Wise exchanged a glance. "What *do* you remember?"

I tried to recall something—anything—that had happened before today. The room began to spin.

"Could you tell us your name?" Robert said.

"My . . . name?"

Robert's body seemed . . . strange. It stretched and bent, like he was made of caramel.

I'm dreaming, I thought. *I'm still dreaming.*

I shut my eyes, and the world stopped whirling around me. But I was still in that terrible nightmare. I had to be. Because I remembered nothing. Nothing at all.

"Who am I?" I whispered.

CHAPTER
5

THEY STEPPED BACK, EYES WIDE.

"The demon," Robert gasped. "He's stolen your *soul*."

My panic finally overwhelmed me. I sprang from the bed. The girl in the corner flung her blanket over her head, huddling underneath, as Robert and Wise spread their arms, trying to stop me from bolting into the snow.

"Now, my lord—" the farmer began.

This dream. It was madness. I had to get out of this dream.

I slapped myself. My cheek burned, flushed with warmth and pain.

"My lord!"

I slapped myself again, harder. I swung a third time,

but suddenly Wise was there, his fingers wrapped around my wrists like iron bands.

"Let me go!" I screamed. *"Let me go!"*

The old man twisted my arm. I lost my balance, my whirling head doing much of the work for him. Robert took my shoulders, and together they lowered me to the bed.

"Shhh," Robert said. "It's all right. We're here. We have you."

"Let me go," I whispered.

They did. I lay there, staring at the thatched roof above until it stopped spinning. Robert and Wise hovered, afraid I'd try to flee again. But I had no more fight inside.

Who was I? I pleaded with the Voice to answer. *Please. Please tell me who I am.* But it had nothing to say. If I could have remembered anything, I doubt I'd have recalled ever being so scared.

Wise placed a gnarled hand on my shoulder. Gentle this time, comforting. He sat me up.

"Are you better, my lord?" Robert said, genuine concern in his voice.

The panic had gone, leaving me feeling ashamed—of my outburst, of the bruises I'd left on Wise's face. "I'm sorry," I said, and the words seemed so small.

They understood. "It's no trifling thing, to be attacked by evil," Robert said. "You won't try and hurt yourself again now, will you?"

I shook my head.

"And you won't run?"

"Where would I go?"

I said it in despair. But Robert scratched his chin, thinking. "Well, now. We might help you with that yet. Come to the farmhouse. We've cleaned your clothes, and your coin purse is there, and your other . . . thing."

"My what?"

He pursed his lips. "I'm not certain. Never seen anything like it. Perhaps you'd best come and see."

Wise pulled a pair of knee-high boots from under the bed and handed them to me. The leather was supple, the buckles were silver, they were lined with soft, plush wool— and they didn't match my clothes in the slightest. What's more, they fit me perfectly.

I looked at Robert, and he nodded. "You were wearing those when we found you."

He said he'd get me a coat—he didn't want me catching cold in the snow—but Wise saved the time by draping his over my shoulders. It was so long, it hung more like a cape, but the warmth of it was a comfort.

The girl in the corner watched us, peeking over the deerskin. "What about her?" I said.

Robert turned to her. "What do you say, moppet? Would you like to see my girls—"

She disappeared beneath the blanket.

Robert laughed good-naturedly. "Guess not. We'll leave her be. She can join us in her own time."

I felt like I'd walked into a painting.

A farmhouse of weathered stone lay to my right, snow blanketing the thatch, the straw beneath black with age. A pair of smaller cottages stood opposite, a trail tramped between them, with a second cob house, identical to the one I'd just left, beside it. Smoke curled from the chimneys, disappearing into the gray overhead.

Behind the cottages rose an enormous barn, cracked wooden planks painted with the same white lime-wash that stained the cob. A cow stood in the door, poking her nose into the snow. From beyond her came a soft lowing.

The land around the farm rolled gently with the hills. A leafless forest covered half the horizon; from that direction I heard water, trickling in a stream. On the other side, the hills dropped away, and I saw a vast expanse of blue: the ocean. And with it all came the scent of the country: crisp, frosted air; the earthy smell of livestock; the tang of ocean salt.

"Where is this place?" I said.

"Devonshire, my lord." Robert motioned toward the sea. "That's the Channel."

Devonshire. So I was in southwest England. A name came to me.

"Exeter," I said.

Robert nodded. "That's our county town. Lies twenty miles to the west. Seaton's our closest village. It's a few miles east, at the mouth of the River Axe."

I didn't recognize those places. All I knew was where Devonshire was, and that Exeter was the shire's town. "You don't suppose I'm from there?"

"Wouldn't think so, my lord," Robert said. "Your speech marks you from the east, I'd say. London, maybe?"

Of course. My accent would mark my home. I didn't speak West Country like Robert, so perhaps my voice was the key to discovering who I was. I searched my mind, but the more I tried to remember, the more the dizziness returned. Reluctantly, I let the thoughts go. I didn't want to end up face down in the snow.

My boots sank into it two feet deep as we walked the path to the farmhouse. Wise followed us, longbow slung over his shoulder. The sight of so much snow was almost magical, though its depth made the short trek a slog. "Is this normal for Devonshire?"

"Not a bit," Robert said. "Even half a foot would be strange. And never this early in the season. Be a hard winter for any who didn't prepare fodder."

"What day is it?"

"Sunday. The twentieth of December."

I hesitated. "What year?"

Robert raised his eyebrows. "The year of our Lord, 1665."

I flushed, embarrassed. I knew where Devonshire was, I knew its county town, I knew about accents . . . but I didn't know the year? How could this be?

"So you keep cattle?" I said, just to change the subject.

Robert nodded. "And a few goats for the extra milk, though we don't really need it. I keep them mostly because my little ones like them. They'll take in anything with four legs."

"And you'll take in anything with two?"

He laughed. "So I will. There's a place for everyone, God grant them rest."

As if heeding his words, a bird flew down to join us.

Its salt-and-pepper-speckled wings flapped furiously—as it landed right on my shoulder. I stood motionless as the bird marched across my coat, then hopped up and poked its beak into my hair.

Robert and Wise watched, grinning.

"There's a pigeon on my head," I said.

"So it appears, my lord."

"A friend of yours?"

"Actually, I believe she's a friend of *yours.*"

Mine?

Slowly, I reached up. I expected the bird to shy away, but she walked right into my hands and let me hold her. She nuzzled her head into my thumbs, feathers soft and warm.

Wise pointed at her, then me, then at the ocean. I listened, barely able to believe it, as Robert told me how I'd been found.

Wise had been hunting in the forest when the pigeon landed nearby. He'd drawn his bow to shoot her for the pot, but she'd run straight up to him. It seemed clear to him the bird was domesticated, and it kept flying away, as if trying to get him to follow.

"So he did," Robert said. "And that's when Wise found you on the beach."

I held the bird up. She cooed.

"A blessed event, my lord," Robert said seriously. "The shoreline's mad with coves, and there are hundreds of caves in these hills. If that bird hadn't led him there, you'd have died, your bones washed into the Channel. That pigeon saved you."

It was a strange thing, to owe one's life to a bird. But there was no denying she was friendly, and holding her felt so natural, I could only believe she was mine. I scratched gently under her feathers, and she closed her eyes in contentment.

It made me wonder: If this pigeon had been with me, what about people? Did I have family? Friends? Had they been on board with me, too?

I couldn't remember anyone. Not a name, not a face. And yet the more I imagined a ship breaking apart in a storm, the more my stomach churned. The rest of the passengers . . . where were they? Everyone I'd loved . . . were they dead?

The thought left me feeling so alone. I stroked the pigeon's feathers, trying to find some comfort.

"She's been living in the barn," Robert said. "The children have been feeding her. Come, let's meet them."

We pushed on, and as we approached the farmhouse, my stomach rumbled at the scent wafting toward us. Behind the house, Robert had set an entire side of beef to seethe in the skin—that's where the blood on his shirt had come from, he explained. A cow's freshly skinned hide had been staked over a low fire like a hammock. Then it had been filled with chunks of beef, vegetables, and herbs and left to simmer, the fat bubbling under the skin, infusing the stew with its sweetness. The sight of it alone left me wobbly; the smell nearly made me collapse. I couldn't hold on to my manners anymore.

"When your daughter Margery came," I said, "she was carrying some stew. I'm afraid I scared her—"

He understood. "Course, you must be starving. I'll bring more food right away."

Wise gestured toward the cob house.

"For the moppet, too," Robert said. "Right."

He welcomed me into his home. There was no entrance hall, just a long, broad room that took up the entire length of the house. Heat radiated from the fire, filling the place with warmth.

A woman hunched over one end of a long table, a girl and boy of around ten helping her scrape the inner skin of a cowhide. On the opposite side, a younger girl, hands pink with foamy blood, scooped handfuls of salt from a bucket and rubbed it into slabs of freshly cut beef. By the fire, an older girl stood on a chair, stirring a shallow lake of cream in a flat iron pan suspended on chains above a pot of steaming water. The nutty, buttery smell of heated cream was incredible.

Margery, the daughter I'd scared in the cob house, entered the room from the back as we came in. She gasped when she saw me, dropping her stack of linens.

Everyone stared. The woman's eyes flicked from me to the pigeon in my hands to her husband.

"Children," she said. "The fire needs more wood. And the cows need tending."

The oldest girl pulled her spoon from the cream and took the hands of the younger ones, who gawked over their shoulders as they were led away. The boy remained, looking me up and down with naked curiosity.

"What did I say?" The woman reached across the cowhide and grabbed him by the ear, dragging him, protesting, from the room.

Robert flushed, embarrassed. But I understood. The witches' marks, the protective charm, my seizures, Wise's bruise . . . she was afraid of me. She believed I'd brought evil to her home. I wondered: Had I? I recalled the look on Robert's face when I hadn't even known my own name. *The demon. He's stolen your soul.*

I shuddered. Was that true? To some, it wouldn't matter. I needed to be very careful about what I said. People even *thinking* I was possessed could be enough to see me burned.

Wise drew a set of clothes from the drawers near the door and laid them on the chairs, carefully avoiding the cow's blood that dripped from the table. They were a far cry from what Robert had given me. The shirt was blue silk, with a baize-backed waistcoat and a patterned leather belt to match. The breeches were wool, but of the finest kind, soft and thin. The hose, too, were finely made, and I was amazed: I might not have felt like a lord, but these clothes were unquestionably tailored to fit one.

Robert used a key to open a small lockbox, tucked away in the back of the same drawer. "You weren't wearing a coat when Wise found you. But you had this."

He held out a coin purse. I put the pigeon down to take it; when I did, she flapped up to perch on my shoulder, as if as interested to see inside as I was. The purse, of smooth and supple leather, jingled in my hands. Though it was only half full, it was heavy. I opened it.

The coins. There were so *many* of them inside. And more than half of them were gold. The rest were mostly silver, with just a few coppers mixed in.

I was *rich*.

"You see, my lord?" Robert said. "All there, just as you left it."

I dug into the coins, let them flow through my fingers. Then I noticed something peculiar. I took one of the gold pieces out and examined it.

On one face was an intricate design of four crowns, four fleurs-de-lis, and eight *L*s arranged to form a cross. The letters around it said *CHRS REGN VINC IMP*, which stood for *Christus regnat vincit imperat*: Christ reigns, conquers, and commands. The reverse showed a handsome young king with a laurel wreath and long, curly hair. There was an inscription here, too. *LVD XIIII D G FR ET NAV REX 1653: Ludovicus XIIII Dei gratia Franciae et Navarrae rex.* Louis XIV, by the grace of God, king of France and Navarre.

"This coin is French," I said. I dug through the purse, turning the coins over. "Most of them are."

Robert studied it, curious. "Maybe that's where your ship was coming from. You were returning to England, and you got caught in the storm."

Or maybe it was the other way around. I'd known what the coins were immediately: gold *louis d'or*, silver *écu*, copper *sou*. I also clearly spoke Latin; which meant at some point I'd had some education. But what if . . . ?

I tried thinking in French. *Et tout de suite, je me suis rendu compte que je parler couramment.*

My breath caught in my throat. Was I *French*?

I didn't *feel* French. Then again, I wasn't sure what being French should feel like. Really, I didn't feel like much of anything at all. Just . . . blank. On a whim, I tested other languages in my head and found to my surprise I spoke several: Spanish, German, Italian; the classical languages of Latin, Greek, and Hebrew; and a smattering of words in others.

Robert had said that during my fits, I'd been babbling in tongues. Was it possible my ravings weren't caused by an evil spirit? Was it just me after all?

I wanted to believe it. But knowing other tongues wouldn't have accounted for my seizures. And none of this told me who I really was. Regardless, seeing this purse filled me with gratitude. What I held in my hand was a fortune. Robert and his family hadn't just nursed me back to health, they'd passed up enough money to feed their family until Margery was an old woman. And, judging by the plainness of their home, it wasn't as if they didn't need it.

"Thank you," I said.

Robert smiled, satisfied. "You also had— Mary! Where's his lordship's . . . belt?"

I motioned to the chairs, where Wise had placed my clothes. "It's there."

"No, you had something else. Mary?"

His wife called through the door. "It's in the barn."

"Why would you . . . ?" He shook his head. "A moment, my lord."

He left the room. In hushed voices, he and his wife exchanged words—not entirely peaceably—and then he hurried outside.

I looked more closely at the clothes. The pigeon flapped down to march across them. I ran my hands over the cloth in her wake, hoping I'd feel . . . something. Anything. Anything that might tell me what my broken mind couldn't. But nothing came.

Robert returned, shutting the cold behind him. "This was with you, too," he said, and I moved to see what he'd brought.

CHAPTER 6

IT WAS THE STRANGEST THING I'D found yet.

Robert had called it a belt, but it looked more like a sash of some kind. It was broad, made of leather, stitched with dozens of narrow pockets. Inside most of them were glass vials, stopped with cork. They held a dizzying array of powders, grains, liquids, herbs, and pills—all the colors of the rainbow.

I pulled them out one by one. Each vial was labeled. On some, the ink had smudged, but to my surprise, I found that even for those half-illegible, I recognized what was inside. Some were basic ingredients: sugar, salt, charcoal. Others were more exotic. Sulfur powder. Oil of vitriol.

You remember them, the Voice said.

"Remember" wasn't quite the right word. I couldn't recall ever having seen them before. But I knew these ingredients: what they were, what they could do. Aloe was good for healing burns. Oil of vitriol had many uses, the most remarkable of which was to dissolve metals. Colts-foot, mixed with honey, would make an effective remedy for congestion.

There were other things in the sash, too. Not ingredients, but tools: a silver spoon, a knife, a magnifying lens, a pair of iron keys.

And a mirror.

I paused, holding the mirror between my fingers. Slowly, I turned it toward me.

A stranger stared back. Hollow—that's how I felt as I looked at my own reflection. It was a boy completely unfamiliar. I studied his face, and I'd have said he looked friendly, if he hadn't looked so scared.

I put the mirror away, unsettled. Trying to shake off the empty feeling, I focused on the one thing in the sash whose purpose I didn't know.

I held up the keys. "What are these for?" I asked Robert.

He shrugged. "Don't know. This was all you had. Any of it familiar?"

"No." The sash had two long straps with buckles; it was obviously intended to be worn. *A belt,* Robert had said. I wrapped it around my waist, but somehow that felt wrong. Light-headed, almost dizzy, I lifted my shirt and buckled the sash on, the leather soft against my skin.

"That's it!" Robert said. "That's just how you were wearing it. Under your shirt. You remember."

I didn't. Yet this *felt* right. I couldn't explain it. It was almost like . . . as stupid as it sounded, it felt like a hug.

I unbuckled the sash and looked it over again. On the back, I spotted two initials scraped into the leather.

B. B. Was that me? My name? I tried to recall, but all that got me was the same old dizzy spell. The pigeon flapped over to the table while Wise steadied me.

"I'm all right," I said. "Just pushed myself too far, I think."

"You should rest," Robert said, and he pulled the chair out for me to sit.

His wife's voice came from behind us. "You'll have these in the cob house, then?"

Mary stood in the doorway, lips tight, holding a pair of steaming bowls. She kept looking at the pigeon.

"He can eat here," Robert said sternly.

I didn't want to start a fight. "The cob house is fine. I should lie down, anyway. And we still have to feed the girl."

Wise took the bowls from Mary while Robert grabbed mugs of ale. As we turned to leave, I saw the woman cross her fingers and flick them—not at me, but at the bird. Robert noticed it, too. He flushed, and we returned to the cob house in silence.

The girl huddled in the corner as we came in. Wise placed her lunch on the floor beside the palliasse. She waited until the old man backed away. Then she stretched a hand out, hooked a finger over the edge of the bowl, and dragged it under the blanket. I heard slurping.

Sounded like a good idea to me. I slurped my own dinner down, and when Wise went to collect more, Robert's smile faded. "I apologize, my lord," he said.

He meant his wife. That gesture she'd made: She'd thrown a ward against evil at my pigeon. "She's worried it's a familiar," Robert explained.

Now I understood. A familiar was a demon spirit that took animal form. They were said to be companions of witches. The bird marched along the table, pecking at stray drips of gravy. She saw me watching her and cooed.

Did demon spirits coo? "You're not afraid of her, are you?" I said.

"No," Robert said, hesitant. "The way she is with you, I'm sure she's just a pet. But strange things have been happening here of late, my lord. Dark things."

He'd said something like that before. It made me think of Wise. "What happened to him?"

Robert looked at me blankly.

"His tongue," I said.

"Oh. That." He scratched his chin. "Been that way my whole life—it just seems normal. It was corsairs what did it."

"Corsairs? You mean . . . Barbary pirates?" They'd

plagued English shipping for centuries, taking ships, raiding coastal towns.

Robert nodded. "My grandfather told me the story. When Wise was twelve, he signed on as a deckhand on an English merchantman bound for the colonies. After he served his two years, he found another ship—English, Dutch, Spanish—didn't matter. He just wanted to sail around the world. Never made it, sadly."

Robert sighed. "Happened when he was sixteen or so. He was on a Venetian silk ship when they were attacked near the Barbary Coast. Their boat was captured, and the crew sold as slaves. Wise tried to escape, but he was caught. As punishment, they cut out his tongue."

I shuddered.

"Wise did get free, eventually," Robert said. "Stole a small boat and made his way north to Spain. An English spice merchant found him, ragged and starving, in a market in Madrid. He took pity on him, and arranged for passage back home.

"When Wise returned, there wasn't anything left for him. The Lord High Admiral granted him a permit to beg in Exeter, but Wise didn't want to be a beggar. So he went looking for work. Most turned him away, but my grandfather gave him a place at our farm."

"That was kind of him," I said.

"He was a kind man. Though he liked to pretend he wasn't. Claimed he took Wise in so he'd finally get a farmhand that wouldn't yap in his ear all day. Said he'd be fine tending to the cattle—'Yer dinna need ta converse wi' a cow, do yer?'" He laughed. "Wise helped raise me. Now he helps raise my children. He's a good man."

I had as much reason as anyone to believe it. "It's a miracle he found me."

Robert looked at me speculatively. "Maybe for us, too. I'd asked you before . . . I know you're not yet well, but could we plead for your help?"

This time, I understood why he asked. As a lord, I'd have the power to make his life easier. "What can I do?"

"Just speak for us."

"Is someone giving you trouble?"

"Not someone. Some*thing*," Robert said. "One of our children has vanished."

CHAPTER 7

I BLINKED. "YOU'VE LOST A *CHILD*?"

"Not me," Robert said. "The widow Jane. Works here, on the farm; her daughter's gone missing. May I bring her to see you?"

"I . . . all right."

I sat there, confused, as Robert left the cob house. How would my being a lord help him find a missing child? And speak for him? About what? To whom?

Never mind my missing memories, all these questions were making me dizzy. I heard shuffling behind me and turned to see the little girl slide her bowl out from under her blanket. She'd set the deerskin on her head, so it hung over her like a shawl.

"I don't suppose you know what's going on?" I said. When she didn't answer, I tried the pigeon. "How about you?"

The bird walked over my fingers and sat in my hand.

"You're pretty friendly for a demon," I said. "Any chance you know my name?"

She cooed.

"I can't call myself 'Coo.' People will think I've gone mad." I paused. "Then again, I've lost all my memories, and I'm talking to a pigeon."

Plus there's a voice in your head, the Voice said.

I couldn't help but laugh. "Maybe I'm mad after all. What do you think, moppet—?"

I stopped. The girl had half risen from behind the palliasse, the blanket fallen to the dirt behind her.

"What is it?" I shifted in my chair and noticed her eyes following, not me, but the bird. "Would you like to see her?"

I stood. The girl hunched back. She looked so small, so scared.

"Don't worry," I said. "She's very sweet. See?"

Slowly, I knelt in front of the palliasse. The girl's eyes flicked to the opposite corner.

"This bird saved my life," I said. I set her down on the palliasse and stepped away.

The girl waited until I was safely back in my chair. Then she reached out a grimy hand, palm up.

The pigeon looked at her curiously. Then, with a grand flapping of wings, she hopped up and landed on the girl's wrist. Gently the girl began to stroke her feathers.

The pigeon cooed. The girl leaned back and held the bird to her chest. She stayed like that, head down, as the pigeon nestled into her arms and closed her eyes.

Well, look at that, I thought. Perhaps the pigeon was the way to get the girl to speak.

I didn't get the chance to try. The door opened, and the girl dove back behind the palliasse as Robert returned. Wise was with him, carrying two more bowls of stew. Behind them came a short, squat woman, long black hair knotted in a braid. She squeezed her fingers together as she shuffled in, not quite daring to meet my gaze.

"This is Jane Lisle," Robert said. "She helps tend our fields. Go on, Jane, ask him."

In her own way, Jane seemed as frightened of me as the girl behind the palliasse was. I tried to put her at ease. "Would you like to sit?"

I offered her the chair. She didn't take it.

"Robert says your daughter's gone missing?" I said.

That broke her shell. "Oh, not missing, my lord. Not missing. She's been taken."

"By whom?"

For a moment, she didn't speak. When she did, her voice was so low, I could barely hear it over the crackling of the fire. "The White Lady," she whispered.

Robert frowned. Wise's expression didn't change, but I noticed he crossed his fingers.

"Who's the White Lady?" I said.

"She steals children, my lord. She steals them to eat their souls."

And despite the warmth of the fire, I shivered.

"She sent the demon child," the woman continued. "I don't want that *thing*. I want my Emma back."

I was confused. Robert nodded toward the palliasse. "She means the moppet."

I turned. The girl had burrowed back under the deerskin.

The blanket twitched as Jane's voice rose. "I want my *Emma* back!" she screamed. "Oh, please, my lord, help me get my little girl back."

I floundered. "What can I do?"

Jane flung herself at my feet and grabbed my hands. "This is all I have. Please, my lord: Offer it to the White Lady. Offer her *my* soul in exchange for Emma's."

She pressed four coins into my palm: two pennies, ha'penny, and a farthing. This had to be everything the woman owned. My purse weighed so heavy on my belt. "I . . . no. Keep these."

She wouldn't take them. "Oh, please, please, please, my lord. Just give those to her. Promise her anything. Please."

Her desperation broke my heart. I couldn't bear to tell her no. "I'll . . . see what I can do."

She sobbed in gratitude. She bent down and kissed my feet. "Thank you, my lord, thank you," she said, until Wise escorted her from the cob house. I stood there, lost, miserable, and ashamed.

"I thank you, too," Robert said quietly after she was gone.

"What is it you think I can do?" I said, face still burning. "Who's the White Lady? A local noblewoman?"

"No," he said. "She's a ghost."

CHAPTER 8

I STARED AT HIM. *"WHAT?"*

"It's a legend," Robert said as Wise returned. "The White Lady was a woman who lived long ago. She committed a terrible crime, and in punishment, God cursed her to walk the River Axe for eternity."

I couldn't believe what I was hearing. "You want me to speak to a *wraith*?"

"Not I. I think you should talk to Old Sybil."

"Who?"

"Sybil O'Malley. She's one of the cunning folk."

Cunning folk were wizards, diviners, practitioners of white magic. "I should go see a conjurer?"

"Actually, my lord, *she* asked to see *you*."

A chill ran down my spine. "Why?"

"We called for her when you were sick." Robert nodded toward the entrance. "She's the one what marked the door. She cut your hair to make the charm at your feet. That's what chased the demon from your body. That's what made you better."

"Why does she want to see me?"

"Don't know. But she sat with you while the demon was raving inside. She channeled the Spirits of the Wood, and through them, she spoke to it."

My chest tightened. "What did it say?"

"Apologies, my lord. Don't know that, either. You were speaking some strange tongue."

Wise touched Robert's shoulder. He pointed to his mouth, then made his hands into a cross.

Speaking . . . with a cross. Holy words? Did he mean . . . "Latin? Was it Latin?"

Wise nodded.

"Did you understand it?"

He shook his head.

Robert explained. "Wise only picked up a bit of language while he was crewing ships."

Even a few words might help me figure out what I'd said. "Could you write down what you heard?"

Wise spread his hands helplessly.

"He can't write," Robert said, apologetic. "None of us can. Don't have much call for the scholarly life round these parts, my lord."

I slumped, disappointed. "And she didn't tell you anything about what we spoke of?"

"Not my place to ask. All she said was that I should send you to see her when you recovered. But if I had to guess, I think she might know who you are."

I practically leaped from my bed. "I'll go now."

Robert stopped me. "Apologies, my lord, but that's not possible. Her home's too far, and it's too late in the day. With this snow, you'd never make it before dark. Tomorrow—"

Wise touched Robert's shoulder again. He gestured, Robert watching him until he understood. "Wise says Sybil's gone to the market at Lyme, for ingredients for her spells. She won't return until Tuesday."

I wanted to scream with frustration. Robert had said today was Sunday. That meant I'd have to wait not one but *two* days to find out who I was—assuming that was, in fact, what the cunning woman wanted to tell me. "What about

Exeter?" I said. "There must be a local lord. He might know my family."

Robert shook his head. "Take days to get to town in this snow. The roads have disappeared. Quicker to just stay until Sybil returns."

I needed to *do* something. "There's no one else?"

"Well . . . you might try down at Seaton. A fair bit of local trade passes through there. The port's fallen on hard times, but if you landed this close, maybe that's where your ship was going. Someone in the village might recognize you."

"How far is that?"

"A half-day's journey, with the snow. You could go there tomorrow. Wise'll show you."

With surprising skill, Wise used the ink and quill from my sash to draw a remarkably detailed map on an old rag. "Here's my farm," Robert said as Wise sketched. "If you follow the brook to the east, it'll meet the River Axe. From there, you go south. Seaton's here, on the coast . . . and the village of Axmouth is farther upstream . . . and Sybil's house is north of that. You'll know you've gone too far if—" He snapped his fingers. "Baronet Darcy."

"Who?" I said.

"Sir Edmund Darcy. He has an estate on the Axe. It's a ways north, but he's been kind to us. He helped replenish my cattle a few years ago, when they fell to the quarter evil. I know a baronet's not a lord, but it's said he knows many of the peerage. Perhaps he might recognize you."

Wise scratched Darcy's estate onto the cloth. As neither of them could write, I inked the names on the map myself, trying to fix the directions in my mind.

Both Seaton and the Darcy estate sounded promising. Robert told me they were too far apart to reach in the same day, so I decided I'd try Seaton first. With Sir Edmund's estate so close to Sybil's, I could go there on Tuesday when I visited the cunning woman.

Robert agreed that made the most sense. "You'll remember to ask Sybil about Emma, won't you?"

I felt guilty. In trying to solve my own problem, I'd forgotten about Jane Lisle's daughter. I looked over to the corner, where the moppet played silently with the pigeon.

"Jane mentioned a trade," I said. "The White Lady took her daughter—and left this girl in exchange?"

"That's what she thinks. Emma vanished four days ago. We found this little one the next morning."

"Do you believe it?"

"No. This girl's no demon child. But you saw the marks on her body, and she refuses to speak. *Something* terrible happened to her out there."

"You think the White Lady had her."

Robert scratched at his beard. "Maybe. Though if she did, I don't know how the moppet escaped. The White Lady doesn't give children back."

I had no way of knowing where this girl had come from. But Jane's daughter . . . "With the weather this bad, isn't it possible Emma just got lost?"

He shook his head. "Would have seen her tracks in the snow."

I bit my lip, thinking. "Maybe you'd better show me where she disappeared."

The creek where Emma vanished was close to the farm. We set off north, through Robert's fields, into the thin line of woods that followed the stream. Robert explained there'd been a heavy snowstorm that night.

"Then what was Emma doing up here?" I said.

"Collecting water," Robert said.

"From the creek?" I frowned. "Why send her out in a storm? Why not just melt the falling snow?"

"*Because* of the storm. Wasn't natural. Jane believed it was tainted with black magic."

The snow thinned slightly as we moved under the branches that hung over the stream. I could see faint tracks, rendered mere depressions in the white by the snow that covered them over. As for the creek itself, it surprised me: Though the water ran shallow, it was wider and faster than I'd expected. And, despite the cold, only a few inches of ice jutted from the banks.

"Too swollen to freeze, my lord," Robert said. "Before the snow, we had heavy rain for weeks."

The storm had left very little to see. I spotted a lump next to the riverbank. When I brushed the snow off, I saw the top of a bucket. "This was Emma's? For gathering the water?"

"Yes, my lord."

"Who first noticed she was missing?"

"Well, her mother was the one who came to me. But Wise was the first to spot it."

I turned to the old man. "You followed her tracks down here?"

He nodded and pointed to the bucket.

"You saw the bucket . . . but no Emma."

He nodded again.

"Was there any blood? Any signs of a struggle?"

He shook his head.

"Anything else? Where did Emma's footprints go?"

He moved his fingers like walking legs, then pointed to the water.

"The tracks went to the creek . . . then stopped?"

He nodded.

"Could she have crossed it?" I asked.

"No," Robert said. "We searched the entire area the next morning. There weren't any tracks to be found."

Maybe that was because she'd stepped onto something that wouldn't leave them. "Does anyone on the farm own a boat? Or a raft, something like that?"

He shook his head. "There are rocks, upstream and down. Water's not deep enough to let one through."

An awful idea occurred to me. I snapped a branch from a nearby tree and stuck it in the water. The current tugged on the wood. By the time I stretched far enough for the creek to deepen, my fingers strained to keep their grip. "How old was Emma?"

"Five, last October. 'Bout the same age as the moppet."

I thought I knew what had happened. "I don't want to dash anyone's hopes," I said, "but isn't it most likely the girl fell in? The water's high, it's fast, and it's cold. If Emma stepped into the edge of the creek to collect it, she could easily have slipped and been carried away. She probably drowned."

"It's possible," Robert admitted. "We looked a fair distance downstream, though, and saw no body."

With such a heavy snowfall, the water could have dumped her into a bank, where her corpse would have been covered. "We should check."

We walked the banks of the river for half a mile. It was hard going in the snow, made even slower by the fact that we didn't want to pass her for lack of care. We didn't see anything. Once we reached the downstream rocks, however, I noticed that while there wasn't enough space for a boat to pass, there *was* enough to let through a body. Especially a five-year-old girl's.

"You said this leads to the River Axe. And from there?"

"Past Axmouth and Seaton, into the Channel."

It was hard to imagine a body floating through two towns and no one noticing it. Then again, it had been night, and the snowstorm would have kept most people inside. It was also possible there was no body to find because something *else* had taken it.

"Are there animals around here?" I asked.

Robert didn't like the thought. "There's a pack of wild dogs that roams the forest. But we would have seen tracks. Blood."

Yet he wasn't convinced of that, and for good reason. If her body was dragged off before the storm ended, the snowfall would have hidden the evidence. I shook my head. The most likely explanation was that Emma had drowned. A fast-flowing stream; the bank slippery with snow; no one around to hear her scream. Emma being snatched by the White Lady was probably just a fantasy. A terrible fantasy, yet still better than the girl drowning: After all, if she was taken, there was still hope her mother might get her back.

I said as much to Robert and Wise. They didn't disagree, though Robert sounded disappointed. "Does this mean you won't ask Sybil about her?"

"I will," I said. "I promise." But I didn't hold out any hope.

My fingers were stinging badly by the time we returned to the farm. Despite the wonderfully warm sheepskin gloves Robert had gifted me, being frostbitten left them sensitive to the cold. I soaked them in water heated over the fire, which soothed them somewhat, and it was then that I remembered the sash around my waist. For all its bulkiness, I'd forgotten it was there. It just felt so natural to wear it.

The sash held two pain relievers, I discovered: willow bark and poppy. As the water had already relieved some of the pain, I decided to save those in case they were needed later for something more severe. I did, however, open the vial of aloe syrup. I slathered it over my fingers; it would help regrow my reddened skin.

It occurred to me then: What other injuries might my body reveal? I checked myself over, and found a terrible scar on my chest: my flesh, melted, as if I'd been burned. I ran my fingers over it, wondering what had happened.

I found more scars to wonder about after that. The biggest was on my left shoulder—it looked like I'd been stabbed—and the most recent was on one of my fingers, which I'd missed under the peeling skin. That scar was still raw and tender. I must have been cut badly.

These scars tell stories, I thought. But those stories, like all the others, remained silent in my head.

I stayed the rest of the night in the cob house. Robert invited me to join his family, but I didn't want to cause trouble with his wife. So he brought me and the moppet our supper, plus some seed for the pigeon, and we three spent the evening in silence.

The girl didn't want to let go of the bird, and though I called for the Voice in my head, that had disappeared, too. So I had little to do after dinner except lie on the bed and test my memory. It was slow, frustrating, and nauseating—literally—because any time I tried to recall something personal, it set my head to spinning and made me feel like throwing up.

Whatever my illness—*or possession*, I thought with a shudder—had done to me, it had left me with an affliction beyond strange. I discovered I could recall facts without trouble: recipes that used the ingredients in my sash; towns and villages of England; languages I could speak; the names of famous people, like our king, Charles II, or his brother James, the Duke of York, or his Warden, Lord Richard Ashcombe. But even the slightest push of my mind toward something personal made me sick. I finally stopped when a drive to remember my family had me retching over the side of the mattress. I just lay there, panting, and waited for the calm of sleep.

But the dream returned.

CHAPTER

9

I'M SO COLD.

A terrible wind whistles across the plain. I feel its chill, not in my skin, but in my bones; I hear its howl, not in my ears, but in my soul. It turns me to ice, far worse than any earthly storm could ever achieve.

Ice. My hands, my legs, are stuck in it, endless, deep, eternal. My friends are all dead. Only the bird, the bird of nothing-feathers, the bird of onyx eyes, remains, perched on its bent and crooked branch. I am alone.

BUT YOU ARE NOT ALONE, *the bird says, and I look down, and I see it is not lying.*

There is someone beneath the ice. I strain, and, as if

delighted to show me, the soul-wind blows away the ash that covers the plain. I see her now. It is a girl of five, with long black hair knotted in a braid. Her mouth moves as she begs for my help, but I cannot hear her; her words are trapped below the ice. Only her fear can be seen.

It is Emma Lisle. I know this, though I do not know how. Her fingers scrabble against the ice that forms her prison, scratching and scraping in terror until her nails crack and bleed. She screams for me, and I can do nothing.

"Let her go," I plead.

The bird replies. I WILL NOT.

The wind whistles and carries my words. "She is innocent! She is blameless!"

THEY ARE ALL INNOCENT. THEY ARE ALL BLAMELESS. MY INNOCENT, BLAMELESS PETS. I WILL KEEP THEM FOREVER.

And now I see: Emma is not alone. The plain stretches without end, and beneath it, children cry, children scream, children beg for release. There are hundreds, thousands, millions of them, all trapped under the ice.

The bird of nothing-feathers and onyx eyes looks down. The jewel-eyes glitter, and in the empty echo of the plain I hear its terrible words.

YOU
BELONG
TO
ME

The screaming woke me. And it was a time before I understood the screams were mine.

In panic, I yanked my hands from the ice—but they were not in ice. As the dream faded, I understood: I was in the bed in the cob house, where I'd always been.

A sob racked my chest. My hands were shaking. I felt the clinging wetness of the sweat that soaked my neck. My face was wet, too, but not from sweat. I'd been crying.

I sat like that for a moment, taking deep slow breaths, listening to the crackling of the fire. Then I noticed I wasn't alone.

The moppet stood beside my bed, holding the pigeon. She looked at me, and in her eyes I saw sympathy. Slowly, she placed the bird on the bed.

The pigeon flapped her wings and hopped onto my lap. I took her, hands trembling, and held her against my cheek.

"Thank you," I said.

The girl turned away.

"Wait."

She hesitated.

"Do you have them?" I said. "The dreams. The . . . bird. Does it come for you, too?"

She didn't answer. She just walked back to her palliasse and curled up in the straw. We lay there, she and I, in the quiet, neither one wishing for sleep.

MONDAY, DECEMBER 21, 1665

p e r

b u q s

CHAPTER 10

WHEN MORNING CAME, I CHANGED
into "my" clothes: the ones they'd found me in on the
beach. Such finery wasn't tailored to withstand the cold,
so, in an offer of kindness gratefully accepted, Robert gave
me an oversize woolen shirt and deerskin breeches to wear
on top. All this, plus the sheepskin coat, gloves, and hat
from yesterday, left me looking faintly ridiculous but feeling pleasantly warm in the snow.

Robert came with the cock's crow to give me provisions
and something to start my journey to Seaton: wedges of
freshly baked flat bread, slathered with clotted cream and
strawberry preserve. The taste was heaven: rich and sweet,

with the nutty flavor of cooked milk and strawberries, and it half made me think I should just stay at the farm until Sybil's return.

But that would have meant another day of questions unanswered—and another night of terrible dreams. I needed to do *something*. Even if Seaton proved fruitless, at least I'd be moving. Beyond the map Wise had drawn, I asked if there were any further directions Robert could give.

"River's the easiest path," he said. "Coast's too dangerous with cliffs, and all the roads are under snow. Be slow going, but stay beside the water. That way there'll be no chance of getting lost."

He pointed to the locations Wise had marked.

"You can't miss Seaton. Baronet Darcy's estate will be easy to find, too, when you go there. Looks like a castle, with a tower in the center."

"And the cunning woman's house?"

"That's a little trickier. It's not far from the Darcy estate, but it's back from the river, in the woods. About half a mile north of the west river branch, you'll see a tree that looks like a squashed giant. Walk a quarter mile east into the trees, and you'll find her. She lives alone."

A strange buzzing filled my head. *A squashed giant,* I thought. Where had I seen that before?

Had I seen it before? Or—

The Voice returned. *The giant,* it said. *Think about the giant.*

I pictured one in my mind. He was tall and strong, and maybe a little bit . . . pudgy? Or he *had* been pudgy? He wasn't anymore.

Where had I seen him—?

It came to me. My dream.

Yes. There'd been a giant

in my

dream

I found myself dangling from Robert's arms.

"My lord," he said, worried. "Here. Sit down."

"I'm all right." I sat at the edge of the bed, catching my breath. "Just a dizzy spell. I'll be fine." Though I wasn't so sure of that. I'd almost passed out.

Robert didn't want me to go. He nearly insisted—but of course he couldn't order me about. "You really should rest. At least another day."

I declined. "Thank you for caring for me. Especially

given . . ." I let the words hang between us. "I have something for you."

I opened my coin purse and pulled out a gold *louis*.

His eyes widened. Then he clasped his hands behind his back and shook his head. "Very thoughtful, my lord. But it's my privilege—my duty—to give aid to those in need."

Reluctantly, I put my coin purse away. I looked over at the moppet, who'd grabbed her own plate of clotted cream and strawberry when the farmer had come in and huddled behind her palliasse to eat it. Her face was sticky with preserve. "What about the girl?"

"If you find anything in your travels that tells you where her parents are," Robert said, "just send word. I'll see she gets home safe. Otherwise, once the snow clears, I'll take her to Exeter and see if I can find to whom she belongs."

"But your wife. And Jane . . ."

"Don't worry about them. The girl has a place here as long as she needs it. As do you."

Our farewells said, I asked for one more thing. "Is Wise around?"

I caught the old man just in time. He was on his way to the woods, longbow slung over his shoulder, quiver full of arrows for the day's hunt. He waited for me to catch up.

Even as short a run as that left me light-headed. I'd have to be careful about not pushing myself while I was out there, or I'd end up facedown in the snow. "You found me on the beach," I said, between breaths.

He nodded.

"Could you show me where?"

We set off the half mile to the coast, clouds covering the sky, boots crunching through the snowy crust. I was pleased to see the pigeon following me; she was one of the few things that had started to feel familiar. Though I did feel a pang of guilt: Holding the bird had been the only time the moppet hadn't seemed so scared. Now I was taking away the one thing that brought her comfort.

At least leaving gave me another chance to repay some of Robert's kindness. "You seem a practical sort," I said to Wise as we walked.

He raised an eyebrow.

I took a *louis* from my purse. "I tried to give this to Robert, but he refused. If I give it to you, will you buy things he and his family need? You'd have to keep it a secret."

He winked.

We grinned at each other as he took the coin. I added

a second *louis* to his palm. "For you. My thanks for saving my life."

He shook his head and tried to hand the coin back. He pointed at the sky, then at me, then made a cross with his hands. *A miracle. Give your thanks to the Lord.*

I certainly would. But I had plenty of gold, and the farm needed it more than I did. "I'll tell you what," I said. "If things go well and I return with Emma, you can give that *louis* back. Otherwise, use it to help the widow Jane. It'll be hard enough for her without her daughter."

That made him pause. Finally, he nodded and pocketed the coin.

"And if you happen to need anything yourself . . ."

He waggled his head at me, and I laughed.

The site where I was found made me shiver.

Wise led me to an inlet on the coast. He stepped carefully along the cliff, the path craggy with rocks, a steep route down to the water. I followed, clinging to the side, certain I would slip and crack my skull.

I didn't relax until my boots touched the pebbled beach. The water lapped at the shore, larger waves crashing on the coast, filling the tiny cove with endless thunder. Wise pointed toward the rocks farthest from the ocean, where snow had collected in a lump.

I had to raise my voice to be heard. "That's where you found me?"

He nodded and brushed away the snow. The lump, I saw, was a long, broad, slightly warped plank, splintered at one end, and half encased in ice.

I knelt beside it. Barnacles crusted in a patch near the splinters, the wood stained by exposure to seawater. This had unquestionably come from the hull of a ship.

I must have clung to it after my shipwreck. I tried to remember. I caught the faint sense of a storm—and terror—before I backed away. Even that slight attempt left me dizzy. I felt pain, too, and it took a moment to realize my fingers were stinging.

"Was there anything else?" I said.

Wise shook his head.

I sighed. I'd hoped to spot something he'd missed, something that would give me an inkling of who I was, where I'd come from. Again I wondered about all those souls who'd been aboard the ship. My family, my friends . . . all dead?

Finding no answers left me sad—and afraid. Because, as I left Robert's farm, I left behind the only people I knew in the whole world.

. . .

Even the pigeon abandoned me.

Wise walked me back to the creek. He saw me off with a clasped hand and a kind smile, then went his own way, upstream. On Robert's instructions, I followed the flow of the river, keeping a decent distance from the bank so I didn't slip in and suffer the same fate as poor Emma Lisle.

Thinking about her left me rattled. I tried to force the terrible image of last night's dream from my mind, but I kept seeing her bloody fingers scratching at the bottom of the ice. It felt almost like she was me, my memories, screaming to get out, to tell me what was happening.

There I was, then, already feeling lost and friendless, when I noticed the pigeon was no longer following me. I looked forlornly at the gray of the clouds above, hoping I'd spot her, but she was gone.

Spirits as low as they could go, I trudged my way downstream, boots sinking deep into the snow. Minutes turned to hours, and woods gave way to rolling hills, and that only made the journey harder. I puffed icy clouds from my lips as I slogged up and down, grateful, at least, for the deerskin breeches that kept me dry.

And it was here that the pigeon returned. She swooped

over the hill and flapped right into my arms. I'd never been so happy to see another living thing in my life.

I pressed her to my cheek. "Where have you been?" I said.

Then I heard a scream. *"Christopher!"*

I looked up. From atop the hill, a girl sprinted toward me, heels kicking up puffs of snow. She was dressed in a fine sheepskin coat—much nicer than the one I was wearing—and a matching hat. Her face was covered by a thick woolen scarf. All I could see was a shock of auburn curls bouncing behind her as she ran.

I stood there, not entirely sure what to do. As she came closer, she tore the scarf from her face. She had intensely green eyes, and her nose was lightly dusted with freckles. Her cheeks were reddened from the cold, and she was huffing, and I couldn't help thinking, *Goodness, she's pretty.*

And she was really barreling toward me. I took a step back, wondering how long it would take her to stop.

She didn't stop. She didn't even try. Instead, when she got close enough, she launched herself at my chest, wrapped her arms around me, and tackled me into the snow.

CHAPTER
11

WE SLID ALL THE WAY DOWN THE
hill. The girl squealed in delight as she clung to me, riding
on top like I was a sled. She held me as we skidded to a
stop, arms wrapped around my neck, fiercely, then ten-
derly, then fiercely once more.

I lay there, dazed, until she stood and pulled me up. She
placed her hands on my chest, my face, cupped my cheeks.
All the while, she stared at me in wonder.

"I thought you were dead," she said. "I *saw* you die. I
thought you were *dead*."

She flung herself at me once more, head buried in my

neck, pressing me close. I could smell her hair, lavender and rose water.

The girl stepped back, gazing into my eyes. The pigeon flapped at my feet. My mind whirled, and not just because her tackle had rattled my brain.

"Who are you?" I said.

She flinched, as if I'd struck her. Then she looked embarrassed.

And then she got angry.

She balled her mittens and began thumping my chest. "You—rotten—little—!"

"Ow! Stop hitting me!"

"We've been searching for you for *weeks*!" she said. "I just ran"—whap—"three"—whap—"*miles*"—whap—"to find you! And all you have for me is bad"—whap—"*jokes*?"

WHOMP

I flopped back into the snow. "It's not a joke!"

She stood over me, hands on her hips. "What do you mean, it's not a joke?"

"Something happened to me. Something took my—" I stopped.

"Your what?"

I was afraid to tell this girl what Robert thought. So instead I said, "My memories. They're gone."

The effect was startling. The anger in her eyes vanished, replaced by a flicker of fear. "Your memories?"

"Yes."

Her breathing quickened. "Did you get hit on the head?"

"No," I said, taken aback. "At least, I don't think so. I was . . . sick. For a long time. And when I woke up . . ." I waved my hands at the hills. "I don't know where I am. I don't know *who* I am. I'm lost."

She stared at me. "You're *not* joking."

"I wish I was."

"Oh . . . oh *no*." She knelt and hugged me again. I didn't mind, exactly, but it left me even more confused. She sat back, studying my face. "You don't remember me at all?"

I shook my head.

"What about Tom?" she said. "Master Benedict? Surely you remember them?"

"No. Who are they?"

"Do you remember *anything*?"

"Nothing personal," I said. "Just facts."

"Facts?" she said. "What's the recipe for gunpowder?"

It came without thinking. "One part sulfur, one part charcoal, five parts saltpeter. Grind separately. Mix."

I blinked. I hadn't even been aware that I'd known that.

The girl, however, looked delighted. "Well, you're still in there somewhere."

"If I ask you who you are again," I said, "will you go back to hitting me?"

She put a mitten to her cheek. "Oh! I'm sorry about that. I just . . . I mean, I'd just . . ."

She flushed a little. Then she stood and held out a very formal hand. I took it.

"I'm Sally," the girl said. "Sally Deschamps. We're . . . friends."

"And who . . ." My guts churned. "Who am I?"

"You're Christopher," she said. "Christopher Rowe."

Christopher Rowe.

I rolled the name around in my head, waiting for it to lock into place. To remember, not just the name, but something greater: to remember *me*. I wished for it. I prayed for it.

But I felt nothing.

I hadn't thought anything would be more frightening

than waking and not knowing who I was. I was wrong. Knowing my name, yet not really *knowing* it . . . I'd never felt so terribly empty.

I returned to my questions. Anything to fill the void. "Who's my father?"

She looked surprised. "Your father?"

"Yes. Why? Is something wrong?"

"He died. When you were a baby. You never knew him. You grew up in Cripplegate. That's where we met."

That name brought no more meaning than my own. "Is that my family estate?"

"Estate? It's an orphanage."

"An orphanage?" That didn't make any sense. "Aren't I a lord?"

"No. Why would you think that?"

"My clothes. And I have money. A *lot* of money."

It occurred to me then that I probably shouldn't be wandering around the countryside telling strangers I had a lot of money. But Sally only nodded in understanding. "Oh. Right. I hadn't thought of that. That's your disguise."

"I'm disguised as a *lord*? But . . . that's a crime!"

"Well, yes. It's all right, though, because you were on a mission for the king."

"What king?"

"Of England."

I blinked. "King *Charles*?"

"That's right!" she said, pleased that I remembered.

Except not only did I not remember it, I didn't even believe it. "*I* work for King Charles?"

"Not exactly. You did. I mean, *we* did. But you're really an apothecary's apprentice."

Like my name, that stirred no feelings inside. But something did finally make sense. "I have this sash," I began.

Sally was already nodding. "You wear it around your waist. Under your shirt."

Any doubts I'd had about the girl vanished. I threw questions at her, not even waiting for the answers. "Where do I come from? Where do I live? How did I get here?"

She chewed her thumbnail, thinking. "Maybe I'd better start at the beginning," she said. And she told me the life story of a stranger.

I'd grown up in London, in the Cripplegate orphanage. I'd been rescued from that terrible place by a stern but kindly apothecary, Master Benedict Blackthorn.

"B. B.," I said.

"What?"

"The initials: B. B. They're on my sash."

She nodded. "It was his. He gave it to you, after he died."

"My master's dead?"

She looked at me sadly before continuing, and though I *felt* nothing, that look made me understand how much I'd lost when my memories had been stolen. My master had been murdered, Sally told me, and I'd nearly been killed myself. After stopping that conspiracy, I'd found myself in other adventures, the last of which had seen me off to Paris on behalf of Charles II, disguised as Christopher Ashcombe, Baron of Chillingham, grandson to the Marquess Richard Ashcombe.

"Ashcombe?" I said. "The King's Warden?"

"Do you remember him?" Sally said.

I shook my head. "I just know the name. It's . . . a fact. Like the recipe for gunpowder. Richard Ashcombe is the King's Warden. He's supposed to be scary."

"Terrifying. He has only one eye, and three fingers on his right hand, and this terrible scar across his face. He got it fighting the monsters who killed your master."

I thought of the scars I'd found on my own body and wondered: Had I got them in those same battles? Had I fought alongside the King's Warden?

"But Lord Ashcombe is a good man," Sally said. "He looks mean, but he's fiercely loyal to the king—and to you, too."

"Me?"

"He likes you. And he trusts you, or he would never have allowed us to go to Paris on the king's behalf. Especially using his family name."

"So are you in disguise, too?"

She gave an impish smile and twirled. "I'm the Lady Grace. Can't you tell?"

"I . . . All right."

She laughed. "Tom and I decided we should keep our disguises while looking for you. People are a lot more helpful to a lady than an orphan girl."

I couldn't argue with that. Sally continued her story, telling me we'd been sent to Paris to stop an assassin. To do that, we'd hunted for the secret treasure of the Knights Templar. And all of this had gained me a terrible enemy.

"He calls himself the Raven," she said. And, for the first time, her words evoked a feeling.

It was terror.

CHAPTER
12

THE DREAM.
The bird. The
black bird
    of nothing-feathers and onyx eyes
    stood atop that twisting
branch.
  YOU
  BELONG
    TO
   ME
it said.

"Christopher?"

The girl—Sally—was holding my arm, looking worried. "Are you all right?"

The pigeon walked over my boots. "What—" My voice cracked. I tried again. "What do you know about the Raven?"

"Not much." She explained how we'd foiled his plans in Paris, and how he'd left me a letter, a promise to return. A promise of revenge.

The black bird. "Do you have the letter?"

"It's at the inn, in Seaton, with the rest of your things. What's wrong?"

I was scared to tell her about my dream—about what it meant. "If I was in Paris, how did I get here?"

Sally confirmed what Robert had suspected: I'd been in a shipwreck. "We were on our way back to England. We'd got halfway to Dover when the storm broke." She trailed off for a moment, lost in memories I no longer had. "It came out of nowhere. Like it had been conjured. The crew managed to take the sails down before the wind ripped the masts from the deck, but after that, we were helpless. We rocked in that ship for hours, blowing west. I swear, Christopher, I didn't think it was ever going to end. And then the ship came apart."

She shuddered. "It was the hull. A beam snapped, and suddenly we were taking on water. Sailors began throwing things overboard: crates, barrels, anything that might float. The captain told us to get in the yawl—that's the little rowboat they use for taking people ashore. But before you could climb down, a wave hit.

"It was like . . . I know this sounds mad, but it was like the wave was *alive*. I'd swear it came just for you. You went overboard, and . . . and . . ." She was shaking. "You were gone. We called for you, but you were gone."

She blinked away tears, remembering. "Tom tried to jump in after you. The captain had to knock him out to stop him."

That was the third time she'd mentioned that name. "Who's Tom?"

"Tom Bailey," she said. "He's your best friend. You're like brothers. Anyway, we rode out the storm in the yawl. By the time we found land, we'd already passed Southampton."

Southampton was one of England's most important ports on the Channel. I wasn't certain how far it was—a hundred miles, maybe?—but I knew it was well to the east of Devonshire.

"When Tom came to," Sally said softly, "he was furious. I was sure you were dead, but Tom just refused to believe it.

He made us start searching. Since then, we've been walking the coast, stopping in every town, every hamlet, every farm, to see if anyone had word of you."

"You walked all the way here from Southampton?" I said, amazed.

She nodded. "We got to Seaton Saturday night. As for Tom . . . I don't think he sleeps anymore. He doesn't even eat. He just sits in the parlor all night, looking at the door every time it opens, in case it's you."

She flung her arms around me again. "Oh, he'll be so happy when he sees you. I doubted it for so long. But then, this morning, I saw Bridget."

"Who?"

She laughed and pointed at my feet. And there, sitting contentedly on the tip of my boot, was the pigeon.

I picked her up. "Bridget?"

She cooed and flapped her wings.

"Tom left the inn early to look for you," Sally said. "I'd just gone out to find him when Bridget showed up. And I knew. When she wouldn't stay with me, when she kept flying away, I knew. She led me right to you."

I stared at the bird. Could it be possible she'd gone looking for help?

Sally thought so. "She's incredibly clever. She has a brilliant sense of direction, and she follows you everywhere." She stroked the pigeon's feathers—*Bridget,* I thought, *her name is Bridget*—and the bird hopped happily into her hands. "In Paris, she even saved my life."

She'd saved mine, too. I found myself barely able to believe it. Then again, a clever pigeon was hardly the strangest thing I'd encountered recently.

"So where's this Tom Bailey, then?" I asked.

She waved her hand at the hills. "Out here, somewhere. But you . . . what happened?" she said. "How on earth did you survive?"

I told her what Robert had said, and about the ship's plank I'd found in the cove. I explained how Bridget had led Wise to find me, and how I fell ill, and finally, how I'd woken in the cob house without my memory, in the care of Robert and his family.

"Oh," she said. "Is that where you got the girl?"

"What girl?"

She pointed back at my tracks. "There's a little girl hiding behind that hill. She keeps peeking at you over the ridge."

Little girl? "It can't be," I said.

I walked back toward the hill. As I did, a tiny sheepskin hat poked above the crest of the snow, then ducked down immediately.

"It's the moppet," I said, amazed.

"Who?"

I hurried to the top. The girl had already floundered halfway down the hill. She stopped, watching me.

"She was at Robert's farm," I said to Sally. "She showed up a few days ago, lost in the snow."

"Why is she following you?"

"I think maybe it's because of Bridget."

I took the bird from Sally and placed her on the snow. The girl looked between the two of us, but she didn't move.

Sally stepped toward her. "Hello."

The girl took a step back.

"She won't let anyone touch her," I said.

Sally took another step closer; the girl matched her, keeping her distance. "What's her name?"

"We don't know. She hasn't said a word since Wise found her, and Robert didn't think she was a local girl. We've just been calling her the moppet."

"Moppet." Sally mulled it over. "Shall we call you Moppet? Unless you'd like to tell us your real name."

The girl just watched, silent.

"All right. Moppet it is," Sally said. "She just showed up at the farm?"

I nodded. "Robert thought she might have been in a shipwreck, too."

"If she was, it wasn't ours." Sally thought about it. "We should take her to Seaton. There's a boat in the harbor; if she's not local, maybe that's where she came from."

"Shouldn't we take her back to the farm?"

"Why? She'll just run away again. She clearly means to follow you."

I was pretty sure it was the pigeon she was after, but Sally had a point. The girl was undeniably willful. And while my tracks were fresh enough to follow today, if she tried to come after me later, she could easily find herself lost again.

I didn't really want to bring her along. I didn't mind caring for her in principle, but I still didn't know who *I* was. "Where would we keep her?"

"If we find her parents," Sally said, "we won't need to keep her. Until then, she can stay in my room, at the inn. At least she'll be safe."

I supposed she was right. We could always return her to

Robert after seeing Sybil. Besides, I didn't want to waste the whole day going back and forth through the snow. What I really wanted was to meet this Tom. It would be nice to see my best friend. Even if I didn't remember him.

We made our way eastward, following the river. Despite Sally's cajoling, Moppet wouldn't come any closer. She just followed us, carrying Bridget in her arms.

The hills we traveled turned back into woods. As we walked, Sally told me more about my forgotten adventures. She seemed rather keen to hear about my missing memories—almost too keen—until she explained that she'd lost memories, too, after someone had hit her in Paris. I asked her what that was like. She just shrugged.

"Is everything all right?" I said.

"Why wouldn't it be?"

"I don't know. You sort of gave me a look when I first told you what happened to me."

"I was worried about you."

I didn't think that was it. "Did you not get your memories back?"

"I did." She hesitated. "Some of them. I'm fine."

She didn't seem fine. I glanced over at her as we walked.

She noticed. "What?"

"Nothing," I said.

"Good," she said, somewhat tightly.

I was confused. Something I'd said had angered her, and I had no idea what. I wanted to ask her about it, but I had the sense that would make her even more cross. So we walked along in silence, with me wondering what I should do.

And then we heard the scream.

CHAPTER

13

IT CAME FROM BEHIND. I TURNED, confused—*who was that?*—but there was only one person it could have been. I'd just never heard her make a sound before.

"Moppet!"

We sprinted through the woods, following her screams. Thirty yards away, her coat dropped out of sight. A furrow the width of her body cut through the snow, a path leading deeper into the trees. Something was dragging her.

We ran faster now. Mixed in with her shrieks, I heard a snarl. And then we saw the monster that had her.

It was a dog. The beast was tall—almost impossibly

so—with jaws big enough to swallow my head. It had Moppet by the leg, and it dragged the girl as she grasped at the ground, catching nothing but fistfuls of snow.

Robert had warned me there was a pack of wild dogs in the forest. It appeared we'd stumbled upon one of them—and one that had seen better days. I could see its ribs through its mangy black coat. This dog was starving.

It froze when it saw us. Sally and I skidded to a stop as the beast crouched, ears flat, eyes dark brown pools of hatred. It snarled. Then it began dragging the screaming girl away.

I didn't know what to do. I looked to the trees for a branch to use as a staff, but anything strong enough, stout enough, was too high overhead.

I shouted, waved my arms, stamped my feet—anything to make the dog think twice. Sally did the same, as Bridget fluttered overhead, grunting in alarm. The dog's snarl grew, a rising howl of fear and rage. It snapped its head, trying to keep its eyes on me and Sally at the same time. Still it held on to the girl, its fury—and its teeth—a promise: Whoever tried to steal its prey would be the next in its jaws.

What do I do? I thought, panic rising. *I need a weapon.*

The Voice spoke. *You* have *a weapon.*

For a moment, I didn't understand what it meant. Then it came to me.

My sash.

I dropped my gloves in the snow, pulled open my coat. The dog growled. It lowered its body, flattened its ears.

Slowly, slowly, I lifted my shirt, fingers searching the vials beneath. *What do I use?* The first thing that came to mind was oil of vitriol. It would burn the dog terribly if sprayed in its face. Though I hated to use a weapon so cruel.

You have something better, the Voice said. *Something that would drive away a dog for good.*

I racked my brain. Other than the vitriol—or something like it—what could I possibly use that might—

My hand fell upon one vial. *Yes,* I thought. *That's it.*

The dog stopped retreating. Now it turned all its focus to me. Its lips drew back, and I could see its teeth pressed into Moppet's boot. If the sheepskin hadn't been so thick, the animal's fangs would have already shredded her skin.

The girl reached out for me, eyes begging me not to abandon her. The dog, I think, was beginning to understand I wouldn't. Beyond its rage, I saw desperation—and that frightened me more than anything else.

I snatched the vial from my side.

The dog released the girl's boot.

I pulled the stopper out.

Now the dog moved to the side, snarling at me. It stepped closer as I dumped the red powder into my palm.

Sally inched inward, toward Moppet's outstretched arms. The dog readied itself to leap—

—But I did first. And I threw the powder right in its face.

Sally darted forward. She grabbed hold of Moppet's wrist, hauled the girl away, heels digging in the snow. The dog ignored her, springing at my neck instead.

It crashed into me. I brought my arms up as we toppled. I jammed my forearm under the beast's snapping jaws, trying to keep its teeth from my throat.

Then the dog rolled off me, wheezing. It snapped its jaws on empty air, then suddenly gave a hacking cough, a vicious sneeze. It shook its head, blinking and whimpering, as it began pawing at its face.

Its whimper turned into a howl. I backed away, and the dog did, too, driving its face over and over into the snow. I saw streaks of red—the powder I'd thrown—as the beast tried to rub the source of its torment away. It gave one final cry of despair, then turned, yelping, and bounded through the white.

I moved, still trembling, to check on the girls. Moppet had wriggled free of Sally's grasp and climbed a tree. In the struggle, she'd lost her boot; she stood on a branch with one sole and one snowy stocking. Sally leaned against the trunk, hand to her chest, trying to control her breath.

"Are you all right?" she said.

I wasn't sure. I checked myself over, and, blessedly, the dog's teeth had missed me. Sally plucked Moppet's boot from the ground and held it up to her. She took it, shaking the snow from her foot.

"What was that powder?" Sally said.

"Capsicum," I said. "Dried ground guinea pepper. It's good for stimulating the stomach." And fighting off dogs, too. "It'll hurt for a while, but the dog will be all right in a few hours."

I wondered if I'd made the right choice. I hadn't thrown vitriol because I didn't want to be cruel; the dog had only attacked Moppet because it was starving. Still, leaving it out there meant it would be free now to attack someone else. I thought about Emma Lisle, and I couldn't get the image of Moppet being dragged away out of my head.

That must have been Emma's fate, I told myself.

Then where were the dog tracks? the Voice asked.

It was snowing, I said. *The tracks got covered. That's why we didn't see them.*

Is that what you believe? Or what you want to believe?

I tried not to think of the dream. All those children . . .

"Christopher," Sally said.

I flushed. I'd been having a conversation in my head, right in front of her. But she looked as if she had something else on her mind.

"You knew," she said.

"Knew what?"

"That powder. You—" She stopped, held a hand up. "Did you hear that?"

Her fingers whitened as she hugged the tree trunk. Moppet stood frozen on the branch overhead, one boot still off.

I stopped. I listened.

And then I heard the baying, too.

My guts twisted. Dogs don't live alone. I'd forgotten about the rest of the pack.

Every inch of my body shrieked at me to run. I looked at the vial in my hands. I'd already used half the powder to drive away the first animal. If the rest came . . .

Moppet had the right idea; we'd be safe in the trees. But

if they cornered us there . . . starving dogs would wait a long time for an easy meal. We'd freeze to death before they left to find other prey.

The baying grew louder. "What do we do?" Sally said.

Suddenly I heard a different sound. A bellow. A man?

"Tom!" Sally gasped. "That was Tom! Christopher—the dogs are after him!"

Tom. My best friend, whom I couldn't remember. I thought of what Sally had said. *I don't think he sleeps anymore. He doesn't even eat. He just sits in the parlor all night, looking at the door every time it opens, in case it's you.*

"Keep Moppet safe," I said to Sally.

Then I rushed toward the howling of the dogs.

CHAPTER

14

I RAN, DUCKING UNDER BARE branches, boots crunching in the snow.

My stomach fluttered. From the barking, the whole pack was out there. I had enough capsicum for only one more dog. The rest of them? What was I supposed I do?

I heard them more clearly as I got closer. The dogs barked and yapped and snarled, half toying with their prey, half desperate. A voice boomed out low. "Get away from me! Go!"

I followed it, rushing through the trees.

"Don't make me hurt you!" the boy shouted. I could tell he was trying to sound brave, but the quaver betrayed his fear. When I finally saw him, I didn't blame him one bit.

He stood in a clearing among the trees. Eight dogs surrounded him, howling as they danced in and out of the circle. Their jaws snapped at his face, their teeth nipped at his heels. It would only take one bold beast to drag the boy to the ground.

I said "boy" because Sally had already told me he was fourteen, same as me. But except for the innocence in his face, he looked like no boy. He was a giant,

and I remembered my dream, the giant felled with a thousand arrows

a Viking come to life from tales of old. Well over six feet, he towered over even these brutish dogs. And in his hands he held a sword.

The blade was stunning. Three feet long, it gleamed with a golden inscription inlaid on both sides of the steel. The crosspiece was gold, too, and the leather of the hilt, large enough for two hands, was wrapped in fine gold wire. Its pommel was a moonstone, pale and perfect, glowing with its own inner bluish-white light.

He held the weapon high. The dogs snapped and snarled, darting in wherever he turned his back. Tom spun around, trying not to give them a chance to seize an ankle. If they brought him down, he was finished.

"Go!" he shouted. He swung at one of them. The dog leaped back to avoid the blade, but hunger drove the rest of them forward still.

Closer they edged now, the circle tightening. They were so focused on him, they hadn't yet noticed me hiding among the trees. *What would they do if I ran in?* I wondered. *Would I scare them off when they realized their prey wasn't alone? Or would I just be an addition to their meal?*

I needed a distraction. But what? I tried to think of what my sash could do, but I'd already begun to panic. I didn't see any way to save him.

And then the most amazing thing happened. The boy in the center stopped trying to slice at the dogs. Instead, he raised the blade high overhead. He began to whirl it around.

And the sword—I swear it—the sword began to *sing.*

It was a single, clear note. The steel rang out a call, a challenge, and it filled the forest with holy song. *Come then,* it seemed to say. *Come find eternity.*

The sound made the dogs cringe. Two of them backed away, heads low, ears flat. Faster the boy whirled the sword, and the blade sang louder still.

Now all the dogs were afraid. Three of them left the

circle entirely, rushed all the way to the tree line. The rest of the pack looked around, nervous. One of them whimpered, ready to bolt, and I think if they hadn't been starving, they might have.

But here was meat, enough to fill their bellies, and a singing blade couldn't overcome their gnawing hunger. Four of the dogs pressed on, desperate to end the fight.

I had to act now. I sprinted toward the dog closest to me. Backing away from the singing blade, it noticed me coming too late. It spun to meet my charge, flecks of foam spitting from between its teeth.

I threw the rest of the capsicum in its face. It sneezed and sputtered. But my intervention was too little, it had come too late. One of the other dogs leaped for the boy's calf.

"Behind you!" I shouted.

The boy spun automatically. He recoiled as he saw the oncoming dog. Then he dropped to his knees, the blade swinging down in a great swooping arc. The gold shone as it sliced, and the dog ducked just in time to keep its head.

The edge grazed its skull, drawing a long, thin line that sprayed blood in the snow. The dog yelped in pain and alarm. The animal I'd hit with the capsicum added its own cries to the mix, yowling in anguish as it shook its head to try to rid itself of the burning powder.

The rest of the dogs backed away now, confused and frightened. I was out of powder, but the boy in the center still had his sword. He raised it again, swung it about once more. And once more, it began to sing.

The dogs fled.

The sword slowed as the boy watched the pack bound away. He stopped; the song faded into the wind. The boy shook, exhausted, panting from fear.

"Tom?" I said.

The boy whirled to face me. He stared, as if not quite sure what he was seeing.

Then he charged toward me, screaming.

"AAAAAAAAAAAAHHHHHHHHHHHHHH—"

He still held his giant sword. "Wait," I said. "Wait!"

He didn't wait. Just before he reached me, he let the sword go. It fell, disappearing below the crust with a little puff. Then he slammed into me with a bone-jarring *whump*.

We flew back together, the empty vial spinning from my hand. A spray of flakes made a minor blizzard as Tom landed on top of me, driving the wind from my lungs.

"Oof," I said.

He grabbed my collar and shook me, rattling my brain with every joyful word. "I KNEW YOU WEREN'T DEAD!" he said. "I. KNEW. IT!"

My voice swam with my head. "I will be—if you don't—stop doing that—"

"Sorry. Sorry." He yanked me from the snowbank like I was a doll. He stood me on my feet; I had to steady myself against a tree as the world spun. It had barely righted itself before he hugged me again, hoisting me in his arms.

"But I KNEW IT!" he shouted.

"Air," I croaked.

"What?"

"Air. I need it. To breathe."

"Right. Sorry. Sorry." He put me down, but his grin wouldn't fade. And even though I couldn't remember him, I found myself grinning back. After waking up so alone, it was heart-warming to meet people happy to see me. Though all things considered, I preferred getting tackled by the red-haired girl.

The boy slapped me on the shoulder, nearly knocking me off my feet again. Still grinning, he fished his sword from the snow, shaking away the clumps that stuck to the blade.

"I guess this means you *are* Tom," I said.

He paused as he brushed off the moonstone pommel. "I don't get it. Who else would I be?"

Before I could answer, I heard boots behind us, snow squeaking underneath. Tom's grin widened. "Look who I found!" he said.

Sally puffed as she clambered over the snowbank. "We've met. Are you two all right?"

Her words reminded him that he'd been *this* close to becoming dog food. He held his sword up, amazed. "Eternity saved us," he said. "You should have heard her. She was singing, and she scared away the dogs. And Christopher threw some kind of powder in one of their faces and—"

My breath caught in my throat. "What did you say?"

"Your powder?"

"No. About saving us. *Who* saved us?"

"Eternity. My sword. You know."

Its song. The sword's song, when Tom had been swinging it overhead. *Come find eternity,* I'd thought it said. Had I heard that?

Or . . . had I *remembered* it?

Tom was puzzled. "What's going on— Why, who's this?"

Curious, he looked past Sally. Behind her came Moppet, struggling through the snow. The little girl looked up, panting, and saw Tom staring back at her.

She froze.

Smiling, Tom took a step forward. I put a hand on his arm.

"Careful," I said. "She'll run if you try to—"

And then, to my utter amazement, Moppet finally spoke.

CHAPTER
15

"MONMON," SHE WHISPERED.

Then she ran—*toward* him.

Tom watched, eyebrows raised, as the little girl sprinted clumsily through the snow. She flung herself at him, landing with a *thump* against his leg. Less than half his height, she hugged his thigh, eyes closed, holding him like she'd just found her missing father.

Tom didn't know whether to be surprised or amused. He planted his blade in the snow and picked the girl up. When he hoisted her to his hip, she wrapped her legs around his waist.

"What's your name, then?" Tom said.

She stared at him in wonder. Slowly, she reached out a little finger and touched the tip of his nose.

He laughed and poked her right back. "Well, hello to you, too."

She giggled.

I couldn't believe it. "Do you know this girl?" I said to Tom.

"No. Why?"

"Because she's afraid—terrified, really—of everyone. Except you. And, no offense, but you're kind of scary."

Tom frowned. "What's that supposed to mean?"

"And she *spoke* to you. Until now, she hasn't said a single word."

Not that it was much of a word. *Monmon.* It sounded like a name—a pet name, maybe? For someone Moppet loved? Whom Tom reminded her of?

Whatever "monmon" was, there sat Moppet, perched on Tom's hip like he was her big brother. He made a funny face at her, and she giggled again. "Where'd she come from?"

"I don't know. I told you, she wouldn't say."

"Well, why don't we ask her?" He swayed, rocking her on his hip. "I'm Tom," he said. "And you, Your Highness? What's your name?"

He waited. She bit her lip but didn't speak.

"Don't want to tell me?" Tom said. "But then what shall I call you?"

"We've been calling her Moppet," Sally said.

"Well, she *is* a moppet." He rubbed her nose with his own, and her smile returned. "All right, Moppet it is. But when you want to tell me, I'd really like to know your real name."

She seemed content not to answer. She just leaned in and held him gently, her head resting in the crook of his neck.

Tom appeared just as happy to hold her. "If you don't know who she is, then why is she with you?"

"Maybe I'd better tell him," Sally said, and she explained, not only about the girl, but what had happened to me.

At first, he was confused. Then he turned skeptical. Finally, he ended up unsettled. "You don't remember me?" he said.

I shook my head.

He looked hurt. "Not even a little?"

"I'm sorry. I wish I did. I can't remember anyone."

"Master Benedict, too?"

I shrugged.

He thought about it. "What's the recipe for gun-powder?"

"Is that really all I do?" I said. "Blow things up?"

"I wouldn't say 'all.'" He paused. "I *would* say 'a lot.'"

"Christopher *is* in there," Sally said. "I'm sure of it."

She said it with such conviction, I almost felt hope. "How can you know?"

"That pepper you threw at the dog. You went right for it. You didn't even have to think about what you were doing."

"I told you," I said. "I remember facts. I know what capsicum does."

"*What* it does, yes. But how would you know *where* it was?"

That made me pause.

"Any apothecary's apprentice might know what capsi-cum is," she said. "But that sash, that's *yours*. There's noth-ing else like it in the world. Yet you went straight to the right vial. Only *you* could have known where to find it."

I shook my head. "I looked through the vials at Robert's farm. I saw the capsicum. That's how I knew it was there."

"And remembered exactly where it was on the sash? In the middle of a fight? There have to be a hundred vials in there."

"Where's the oil of vitriol?" Tom said suddenly.

I'd barely begun to answer when Sally pointed in triumph. "There! You see?"

I looked down. My hand was hovering over my right side, just above my liver. I checked the sash, just to be certain, but I didn't need to. I already knew what I'd find: The vial of vitriol, sealed with red wax, wrapped in twine.

Could this mean my soul wasn't actually stolen? Had it been . . . I don't know . . . hidden? Was Christopher Rowe really still somewhere inside my head?

"There's a woman," I told them. "Robert said she asked to see me. He thinks she knows what's happened."

"Who's this?" Sally said.

"Her name's Sybil O'Malley. She's a cunning woman."

Tom gasped. "Christopher! No. That's black magic."

"I thought cunning folk used white magic."

"It's *all* wicked."

"How else can I get my memories back?" I said.

"We can tell you about them."

"Sally's already told me my life story, and I don't remember a single bit of it. If Sybil can help, I have to find her. Besides, she asked for me."

Tom looked troubled.

"Where is she?" Sally asked.

"Up north, but she won't be home until tomorrow. I was heading to Seaton, to see if anyone there knew me."

"There's nothing for you in the village." Sally looked at the little girl. "Except finding Moppet's family, I suppose."

"I thought you didn't know where she came from," Tom said. "Or do you think she's one of the missing children?"

I paused. "What missing children?"

"Isn't that what she's talking about? The man at the inn?"

"What man?" Sally said.

"What inn?" I said.

"Where we're staying," Tom said. "At the Blue Boar. A man said children have been disappearing."

I shivered. *My dream.* "When did you hear this?"

"Last night. It was in the parlor, by the fire. Some man was telling a story about missing children."

I grabbed his arm. "How many children? How many are gone?"

Tom looked taken aback. "I don't know. A few. He said they'd gone with some lady."

"The *White* Lady?"

"Maybe," Tom said, flustered. "I wasn't really listening."

I couldn't stop trembling.

No, I tried to tell myself. *It's the dogs. The dogs are taking them.*

You know that isn't true, the Voice said.

The snow, I protested, but the Voice was right. After the storm, one set of dog tracks might have been missed. But it hadn't been snowing every day.

More than one child disappeared? No tracks? No hint of blood? It couldn't have been the dogs.

And now I couldn't keep the dream from my head.

The bird. The

(raven)

black bird, holding the children beneath the ice.

MY INNOCENT, BLAMELESS PETS. I WILL KEEP THEM FOREVER.

"Christopher!"

I returned to the real world, head spinning. Tom held my shoulder. Sally looked worried. Moppet, still on Tom's hip, looked scared.

"What's the matter?" Tom said.

"We have to go back to your inn," I said. "I have to read that letter from the Raven. And then we need to find the man who told you about the children. I need to hear exactly what he knows."

CHAPTER
16

IT WAS STILL LIGHT WHEN WE
arrived at Seaton.

Tom led the way, Moppet riding on his shoulders, his
legs plowing a path for us through the snow. Every so often,
he'd look back at me as we walked. Sometimes he grinned,
overjoyed he'd found me alive. Sometimes he looked worried, troubled by the lack of recognition in my eyes. Sally
glanced at me the same way.

Traveling with them was strange. On the one hand, I
felt heartened. After a day of being terrifyingly alone, to
walk with friends—even friends I couldn't remember—
helped quiet some of my darker thoughts. But Tom's grin

also filled me with a sense of loss, even guilt. I should *know* these people who cared for me so much.

And underneath it all, fear gnawed at my gut. I tried to shake the images of my dream

children trapped in the ice fingers clawing broken and bloody

but they played over and over in my head, a vision I couldn't release. Emma's disappearance, Moppet's arrival, my missing memories—and the black bird that hovered over us all—they couldn't just be coincidences.

I hoped Seaton might provide some answers. The village lay nestled on the coast of the Channel, at the foot of rolling hills some few hundred yards west of the mouth of the river. Cliffs rose from the beach, stretching in both directions as far as I could see. The houses, stone and cob, thatched roofs laden with snow, made me think of Robert's farm, though here they were dwarfed by a sizeable fort on the seafront and a lighthouse raised on a mound of earth.

Smoke rose from every chimney, the smell of burning wood and peat mixing with the salt-and-fish scent of the ocean. Seaton was by no means a large village—a few hundred souls, maybe—yet I was surprised to see so few people traveling its roads. Those who did were utterly quiet, the soft blanket of white muffling their footsteps, the only sounds the waves lapping at the beach and the constant cry of seagulls.

The birds hovered, squabbling with each other over what I thought was a mound of bloody rags. It wasn't until I got closer that I saw they weren't rags but lumps of filthy, matted fur. Someone had killed a score of cats and dumped their broken bodies in a heap outside the village.

I stopped. Mass culling of animals was often a marker of disease.

Plague? I thought.

It's not plague, the Voice said, and I agreed almost immediately. Robert would have warned me. But then what purpose would such brutality serve?

You already know the answer, the Voice said.

If I did, it was locked away with everything else. We just shuddered at the sight and moved on.

The harbor held fewer boats than I'd expected. Most of what bobbed in the shallows were simple fishing vessels. The only ship of significant size was a sea-stained three-masted galleon with a double-deck of cannon and a figurehead of a manticore, a fabulous beast with the head of a man, the body of a lion, and the tail of a scorpion. Except for its pennant—a red flag on the jack staff, the cross of Saint George in the upper corner—its pitch-streaked masts were bare, the sails stripped from the rigging.

With my memories gone, my only knowledge of being tossed overboard came from what Sally had told me. Yet the sight of the galleon left me distinctly uneasy. "Is that the ship you were thinking of?" I asked her.

Sally nodded, looking somewhat uneasy herself. "Moppet?" she said. "Do you recognize that boat? Have you been in Seaton before?"

The little girl ignored her. Tom tried the same question, but Moppet just turned away, staring off into the hills. My spirits sank. I'd hoped to solve at least one of our mysteries here. Now we didn't even have a theory as to where she'd come from.

That left us heading toward the Blue Boar Inn—and me getting more and more nervous. Before we'd entered the village, Sally had insisted we keep the same disguises we'd worn in Paris. I would be Baron Christopher Ashcombe, grandson of the King's Warden; she would be the Lady Grace; and Tom would be our guard. By order of rank, that put me squarely in charge of our traveling band.

With my memories gone, I'd be completely unprepared to answer questions about my life, disguised or otherwise. "Can't I just be Christopher Rowe?" I said. Whoever he was.

Sally shook her head. "We've already been telling people we're looking for Baron Ashcombe."

I sighed. Sally promised she'd step in any time I became flustered, and both she and Tom worked along the way to fill me with facts I should know. I spent half the time trying to memorize them, and the other half wishing I could throw the whole plan into the harbor. Besides, it seemed more like Moppet was in charge. Sitting on Tom's shoulders, the girl steered her valiant steed away from the shore and into the streets by treating Tom's ears as reins.

When we entered the Blue Boar, the innkeeper, a friendly sort by the name of Willoughby, smiled and bowed his head. "Welcome back, my lady."

Sally introduced me. Willoughby was delighted she'd succeeded in her quest. "Come in, my lord, come in," he said. "You must be freezing. Come sit by the fire—out of there, Smalls, you're not even paying."

He kicked a somewhat resentful older gentleman from the cushions by the hearth and gave us his most comfortable seats. Unprompted, he brought mugs of warm spiced ale for the three of us and heated sheep's milk for Moppet. She looked at the cup distrustfully until Tom handed it to her himself, whereupon she drank from it greedily.

Willoughby chuckled at the sound of her gulps. "Seems you found more than you bargained for," he said to Sally.

Sally nudged me under the table with her foot. Right—I was supposed to be in charge.

"I found her," I said. "She appeared at Robert Dryden's farm, lost and hungry. I don't suppose you recognize her?"

The innkeeper looked at her more closely. "'Fraid not, my lord. She's not from the village, that's for certain."

"My fr—uh . . . my man here says a fellow came in last night, talking of missing children."

Willoughby nodded. "That'll be Rawlin. Always on about some gossip or other."

"Could we speak to him?"

"Certainly. He'll be here tonight, without fail; he does enjoy his spiced ale. Perhaps you'd like to relax until then? I have a room set aside which I think you'll find to your liking. Very comfortable, I promise, with its own fire."

Willoughby led us up to the rooms farthest from the common entrance. Sally had already taken one of them; the innkeeper installed me in the other, across the hall. It was clean, and the fire warmed it nicely, and all in all I was the most comfortable I'd been since I'd woken.

"Perhaps we could arrange for a hot bath, too, my lord," Tom said, nose crinkling. "Moppet could use one."

"*All* of you could use one," Sally muttered.

Willoughby hurried downstairs to get a tub. Tom lifted Moppet from his shoulders and nudged her toward Sally. "Go with her," he said. "She'll clean you up."

Sally held out her hand, waiting. Moppet just stood there.

"Don't be afraid," Tom said. "She won't hurt you. She's my friend."

Moppet wrapped her arms around Tom's leg, hugging him close.

"Well," Tom said, half-amused, half-resigned. "Looks like that's settled."

So Moppet stayed in our room after all. I soaked in the tub first, the water warmed with heated stones and scented with rose water, and it was like every aching muscle in my body melted away. I stayed there until my skin wrinkled. Pretending to be a lord did have its advantages.

Tom let Moppet have the tub next, though she seemed less interested in bathing than in splashing Tom and giggling. Tom bore his soaking with great patience, but when she turned her back, he looked haunted. As the dirt rubbed away, her bruises stood in stark and ugly contrast to the paleness of her skin, and her protruding ribs showed how terribly she'd been underfed. I began to understand her silence. Whatever horrible thing had happened to her must have marked her just as badly on the inside.

As she still wouldn't speak to us, I worked on a different mystery: me. Sally left a waxed leather sack in our room. In it were the things they'd rescued from the boat before we were shipwrecked—*my* things. I laid what was inside on the bureau: a half dozen books, five of them handwritten in an angular scrawl, and a cherrywood box, sealed with a pair of heavy locks.

I flipped through the books first. Two of them contained journal entries from 1652. Tom told me these were my master's, written in Paris when he traveled there to help with an outbreak of plague. The other four were about poisons: signs, symptoms, and possible remedies.

I studied the illustrations, traced my fingers over the words, trying to recall something, anything, about the man who'd loved me like he was my father.

Nothing. All I felt was empty. I closed the books and moved on to the box.

"How do I open this?" I asked Tom.

"Don't you have the keys?" he said.

"Why would I have—"

Then I remembered. My sash. At Robert's farm, I'd found a pair of iron keys. I pulled them out, slipped them in, turned them.

Click.

The box opened, and I stared at the collection inside. It was full of death: poisons of every kind in vials and ampoules, held fast to the velvet lining by leather straps. I was shocked to realize I knew what each one of them was and what misery they could cause.

The poisons weren't all I found. Inside was also a small leather bag, its straps knotted tight. I was just about to open it when I spotted the letter, folded and tucked into the lining. My name was written on the back.

Christopher Rowe
Maison Chastellain
Île Notre-Dame, Paris

This was what I'd come here for. I unfolded it with trembling fingers, and read the words of the Raven.

My dear Christopher,

I congratulate you on your victory. You have done the impossible: You found the Templar treasure, where others—including me—could not. Don't worry, I'll tell no one the truth of what happened; I like that you and I now share a secret. And, as vexed as I am, I must admit: It was fascinating to watch your mind at work. I see now why Master Benedict chose you as an apprentice.

Does the mention of your master surprise you? No doubt Benedict never told you about me, so I will: He was a thorn in my side for many years. Now, though he has departed, you come to take his place. And while I try not to begrudge you your success, your discovery has cost me dearly. You owe me, Christopher. And I always collect what I am owed.

Your first payment is the life of Marin Chastellain. No, he did not die from his illness. I poisoned him—and in doing so, I left you a clue. Before you go searching for it, I want you to know that I did not kill him because he was any threat to me. I did it because I knew it would hurt Blackthorn, and, in turn, hurt you. It is, after all, much more sporting to face an opponent who understands the stakes of the game.

I am going to do to you what I should have done to Blackthorn years ago: I am going to make you suffer. I will do this by taking away the things you love, one by one, until there is only you and me. And then, once I have stripped your life bare, you will understand.

Find the clue I've left for you. Ponder it. Then reflect on what it might mean. There's no need to rush; I have several plans in motion that must be completed before our game can truly begin. So, until then, be well, Christopher. Savor your life, while you still have some of it left. For when I am ready, I will come for you.

The Raven

And I could hear the bird from my dreams.

YOU

BELONG

TO

ME

"Are you all right?"

I looked over at Tom. Moppet, wrapped in a blanket and dripping wet, sat in his lap as he brushed her hair with a silver comb borrowed from Sally. Both were watching me.

I had to clasp my hands together to keep them steady. A coppery taste stained my mouth.

"What do we know about this man?" I said. "The Raven?"

"Almost nothing. We met him in Paris, but he was using a false name. He's fairly old, probably somewhere in his fifties. Other than that . . ."

Tom told me about the murder of Marin Chastellain, an old friend of my master's, and how the death had left all of us—including Marin's nephew, Simon—devastated. "Does Simon know anything about the Raven?" I asked.

Tom shook his head. "He doesn't even know the Raven exists. You didn't tell him what that letter said."

"Why not?"

"Simon's kind of hotheaded. You were afraid he'd go hunting after the man and get himself killed. Which is probably true." Tom paused. "But I think you mostly didn't tell him because you were ashamed. You blamed yourself for Marin's death."

It was hard to read that letter and not think the same. The Raven had murdered Marin to hurt me. Which meant the more people I called my friends . . . the more people the Raven would take. And I *would* be to blame. Like I had been in my dream.

I betrayed no one! I'd cried.

BUT YOU DID, the bird had said.

"Why do you keep asking about the Raven?" Tom said.

"Because I think he did this to me," I said. "I think the Raven stole my memories."

Tom's eyes widened. "How?"

That was the question. Did he send a demon to steal them, like Robert thought? Or was it something else?

I ran my fingers over my master's books. *Poisons,* I thought.

Had I been poisoned?

And if so, by which one? I knew of poisons that could kill, or ones that could weaken, or drive the victim mad—

I stopped.

Is *that* what had happened to me? Was I going mad?

The Voice. Was I really hearing it? Or was I just imagining things?

You're not going mad, it said.

A voice in my head, telling me I hadn't gone crazy.

Talk to Tom, it insisted. *You can trust him.*

"Christopher?"

Look at him, the Voice said.

I did. He seemed scared.

Look closer.

I did that, too. And I saw: He *was* scared. But as he held Moppet in his arms, I saw deeper, I saw the truth. He was scared, but not *of* me. He was scared *for* me. What would it take, I wondered, to scour the coast of England—in a snowstorm—searching for someone who almost certainly had to be dead?

I took a deep breath. "Robert, at the farm," I began, and those first words broke the dam that held them all back. "He told me I was taken by a demon. He said the demon stole my soul, and that's why I don't have any memories of my life."

Tom's lips went white.

The words rushed out now, so fast my tongue stumbled. "I've . . . I've been having nightmares. I see myself, trapped . . . I'm trapped in hell. I'm frozen in Cocytus, the ninth circle, where betrayers go. It's my punishment. My punishment for

Marin Chastellain. And there's a bird there. It's a demon, but it's in the shape of a raven. And it has the children. They're trapped with me, buried under the ice.

"And then, when I'm awake, I hear . . . something talks to me. In my head. It tells me things."

Tom's voice was strangled. "Bad things?"

"No," I said. "It pushes me to . . . to think, I guess. To think harder about what's happening to me. To the children. I know it sounds mad, but I think . . . I think it's trying to help."

"This voice. What does it sound like?"

"Like a man, I guess. An older man. It's a deep voice, and—"

"That's Master Benedict!"

My old master? "Really?"

"Yes." Tom slumped in relief. "He loves you. He watches over you. He wouldn't leave you for anything."

Is that true? I said in my head. *Are you Master Benedict?*

Yes, the Voice said.

Why didn't you tell me who you were? I asked. *Why didn't you tell me who* I *was?*

But no answer came.

. . .

Telling Tom the truth made me feel worlds better. But he didn't have any ideas what to do about it, and it didn't do a thing to help me remember. I skimmed Master Benedict's books about poisons, but other than madness, I couldn't find anything the Raven might have used that would explain my condition. I read his letter again, and one passage stood out like a beacon.

I called Sally into our room to join us. "Look at this," I said.

I am going to do to you what I should have done to Blackthorn years ago: I am going to make you suffer. I will do this by taking away the things you love, one by one, until there is only you and me. And then, once I have stripped your life bare, you will understand.

"This is what he's done," I said. "He took my memories—and with them, all the things I love."

Tom shivered at the thought. Sally wasn't so sure. "The letter said he wouldn't come for you right away. It's been barely three weeks since we left Paris."

"So he lied," Tom said. He was scrubbing Moppet's

clothes in the tub, trying to get some of the dirt out, while the girl lounged against him, still wrapped in her blanket, playing with Bridget. "He *is* a deceiver."

Sally shook her head. "He didn't lie once in this letter. He even told you things you weren't aware of. When he comes for you, I think you'll know it. He *wants* you to know."

"Maybe he already has told me," I said. "In my dreams."

"*That's* black magic," Tom said, and Sally didn't have an answer for that.

"The Raven said he'd left me a clue. Did I find it?"

"You thought so." Sally untied the knots on the leather bag I'd found in the cherrywood box and tipped out the two things inside. One was a gold coin. The other, the one Sally handed me, was a salt-and-pepper-speckled feather.

I looked over at Bridget, in Moppet's arms. "A pigeon feather? This was the Raven's clue?"

"You found it under Marin Chastellain's bed," Sally said. "After his body was taken away. That feather was tucked between the mattresses."

"What does it mean?"

She shrugged. "You didn't know. You couldn't figure it out."

I turned the feather over, examining it. It might have

been Bridget's, but it could also have come from any pigeon with similar coloring. Beyond that, I couldn't see anything special about it; it seemed like an ordinary feather.

As for the coin, that *was* something special. It was over five hundred years old. *Baldvinus Rex de Ierusalem,* it said: King Baldwin of Jerusalem, whose royal decree founded the Knights Templar. Its center was stamped with an equal-armed, flared cross—the Templar cross.

"Is this what I think it is?" I said.

Tom nodded. "That was the Templars' gift to you. A blessing for someone who'd served them well."

"Does it do anything?"

"I think it marks you as an ally. You'd probably be able to use it to call for help."

If there was one thing I needed, it was help. "How do I get in touch with them?"

"I have no idea. Everything they do is secret."

"Then what's the point of the coin?"

Tom shrugged.

Sally looked pensive. "If you want help," she said, "what about Lord Ashcombe? You might write to him, let him know what's happened to you."

Tom was shocked. "We can't call on *him.*"

"Why not?"

"He's the King's Warden. We don't have the right."

"Of course we do," Sally said. "He sent us to Paris. He gave Christopher his own name as an identity. And he cares about him. If anyone has the right, it's us."

I wasn't so sure about that. I didn't know what Lord Ashcombe could do, anyway. "He can't give me back my missing memories," I said.

"No, but he can send a carriage to take us to London once we're finished here. Besides, he probably thinks we're dead. You might at least let him know we're not."

"Why didn't *you* send for a carriage, then?"

"We didn't want to go to London. We were looking for you, remember? Write him a letter."

"How would we send it?" Tom said.

"I'm sure we could hire someone in the village to carry it."

"What about the fort on the coast?" I said. "We could give a letter to the soldiers."

"The fort's empty. Willoughby told us when we came. The new garrison was supposed to arrive, but with the weather . . ."

I still didn't see the point. Sally insisted. "Even if Lord Ashcombe only sends a letter back, it'll be a wonderful support for your disguise. Just do it, Christopher. The worst he can do is say no."

"That's hardly the worst he can do," Tom grumbled, but I gave in. I used the ink and quill from my sash and paper from the innkeeper for the message. Sally read over my shoulder as I wrote.

To my lord, the Marquess of Chillingham

"No, no, no," Sally said. "That's too formal. You're supposed to be his grandson."

I frowned. "I'm pretty sure he remembers I'm not."

"And what if someone else reads the letter? You have to stay in disguise all the time."

This was absurd. I tried again.

Dearest Grandfather,
I need your help. The Lady Grace and I were in
a shipwreck, and now we're stranded in the village of
Seaton. Strange things are happening, Grandfather:
Children are disappearing from the local villages,
and

Sally stopped me. "Don't say you lost your memory. You don't know who might read this."

and I'm very sick. I'm staying at the Blue Boar Inn. We need a carriage to take us home. Please, please send help.

    Your devoted Christopher

"Perfect," Sally said.

"Ridiculous," Tom said.

I agreed with him, but it was done now. I checked with Willoughby for a courier.

"It'll be hard to find someone to carry this to Oxford with all the snow," he said, "but I think I might know a boy. Let me see what I can do. In the meantime, you must be hungry?"

Tom looked so happy that we were finally getting a meal. I had Willoughby send up a supper of spiced mutton wrapped in mint leaves. Sally dined with us, then returned to her room. I lay on my bed, pleasantly stuffed, the warmth of the fire leaving me drowsy.

I wasn't the only one. Moppet had begun to doze on Tom's shoulder. He held her, still wrapped in the blanket. He rocked her back and forth and began to sing.

Lully, lullay, thou little tiny child
Bye bye, lully, lullay
Thou little tiny child
Bye bye, lully, lullay

His voice was warm and soft, and though he wasn't a good singer—at all—the lullaby was soothing.

O sisters, too, how may we do
For to preserve this day
This poor youngling for whom we sing
Bye bye, lully, lullay

The girl nestled into him. His song was having the same effect on me now. I could barely keep my eyes open.

It's all right, the Voice—Master Benedict—said.

I didn't want to sleep. I was scared. I was scared of the dreams.

Herod the king, in his raging
Chargèd he hath this day
His men of might in his own sight
All young children to slay

I was floating. I fell into blackness, and inside, a part of me screamed. *Please. I don't want to go.*

It's all right, Master Benedict said again. *Tom is here. I am here, too.*

And, for the first time since I'd awoken, I found peace. I drifted away, but this time, there was no ice, no slate-gray sky, and no Raven. Just the words of the song, fading away.

That woe is me, poor child, for thee
And ever mourn and may
For thy parting nor say nor sing
Bye bye, lully, lullay

CHAPTER 17

A HAND SHOOK ME AWAKE.

"The courier's here, my lord," Tom said.

I sat up, rubbing sleep from my eyes. The courier—a skinny boy of seventeen, face covered in pimples—was already standing in the doorway, with Willoughby behind him. The boy's boots were wet from the snow.

I handed him the letter. "You can take this to Oxford?"

"Certainly, my lord," he said.

"Hand it directly to the Marquess of Chillingham. Then return here immediately." I gave him several *écu* as payment. "Any chance you'll be back by the end of the week?"

The courier looked at Willoughby, confused. The inn-keeper shifted, uncomfortable.

"What's wrong?" I said.

"It won't be a week, my lord," the boy said.

"How long, then?"

"More like four."

"Four days?"

Now the courier looked nervous, too. "Four weeks."

My jaw dropped. "Four *weeks*? To *Oxford*? Why?"

"The snow, my lord," he said apologetically. "The roads are impassable. I'll not be able to sleep outside; I'll need to find shelter every night. And if any more snow falls, I'll have to wait it out. I'll be lucky to get ten miles a day."

Willoughby had told us the safest route to Oxford covered 150 miles. So, a fortnight to get there, and a fortnight to return. Nearly a month before we'd get a carriage home—and how would a carriage even get through the snow?

My spirits sank. We were going to be stuck here all winter. "Is there nothing you can do to go faster?"

The courier thought about it. "The quickest route would be by boat. Sail up the coast to Southampton, then travel north to Oxford from there. The roads'll be better, too. Probably take a week to get there, and another week back."

Two weeks, then. Still longer than I'd hoped, but better than the alternative. "That's fine. Go by boat."

He hesitated again. "Uh . . ."

"What is it now?"

"Well, I'll need a boat for that."

"The harbor's full of them."

"Yes, but . . ." He ducked his head in apology. "I'm sorry, my lord, but I doubt I could convince anyone to sail now. The storms, you see. Everyone's afraid. Even the fishermen are staying ashore."

This was getting worse by the second. "Is there no one who could be convinced to go? I have money."

Willoughby exchanged a glance with the courier. "There may be one man who'd dare the passage."

"That's perfect," I said. "I'll use him."

"Well . . . ," Willoughby said.

"What's the problem? I said I'd pay him."

"Oh, you'll definitely need to pay him, my lord. It's more . . . well . . . the man himself. The captain, I mean. Roger Haddock. I'm not sure he's all that trustworthy."

"Why not? Is he a drunk or something?"

"They're all drunks in the winter, my lord."

"Is he not a worthy seaman?"

"No, he's one of the best."

The innkeeper's caginess was making me lose my temper. I wanted *out* of here. "So then what's the problem with Captain Haddock?"

The courier cleared his throat. "He's a pirate."

CHAPTER

18

I WASN'T SURE I'D HEARD HIM right.

"A *pirate*?" I said. "You have a *pirate* in port?"

"He's not a pirate," Willoughby said quickly. "I mean, he is. But he's *our* pirate."

Now I understood. "You mean he's a privateer."

A privateer was . . . well, a pirate. But a privateer had a letter of marque from the Lord High Admiral that permitted him to attack enemies of England. So, like Willoughby had said, he worked for our side. "Who are we fighting now?"

They looked at me strangely. Sally laughed. "The Dutch, silly. Or have you forgotten the war already?"

I flushed. This was why I didn't want to do the talking.

"His ship's laid up for the winter," Willoughby said, "so I doubt you'll get him out of port. But he'd be the one to ask."

"Which vessel is his?"

"The *Manticore*. It's the galleon in the harbor."

I remembered it. So it was either send the courier by land and wait a month for help from Lord Ashcombe, or shorten that to a fortnight by talking to Captain Haddock.

It appeared we were off to see a pirate.

Willoughby warned us about Haddock's preferred choice of lodging. "It's the Blood and Barrel, down at the docks." He turned to Sally. "Apologies, but it's no place for a lady, and certainly not fit for a child."

Leaving them behind wasn't an option. I needed Sally along to prompt my memory. As for Moppet, she refused to leave Tom's side, and there was no way I was going to the docks without him. If things turned ugly, we'd need his sword.

So we all went together, our way lit by the glow from the lighthouse. Tom wore Eternity strapped to his back as usual, though he covered the hilt and crosspiece with a sheath of cloth.

"Is that to protect the moonstone?" I said.

"Partly," he said. "Mostly it's so no one will notice how nice the sword is. It was your suggestion, actually."

I didn't remember making it, but I understood why I had. The sword was magnificent, craftsmanship fit for a king. Its name—Eternity—came from the inscription, a gold inlay on both sides of the blade: *Ego autem non exspecto aeternitatem / Sempiternus sum.* That was Latin, meaning "I do not await eternity. I am eternity." Keeping the sword hidden made sense: It would be hard to explain what such a weapon was doing in the hands of a guard of a minor noble.

I found it endlessly fascinating—as did Moppet. Though she kept well shy of the blade, she was utterly mesmerized by the moonstone. Tom explained that Eternity was a gift from the Templars back in Paris. I remembered its holy song, and just thinking about it made me feel safer.

That feeling didn't last long. The Blood and Barrel was everything Willoughby had suggested. The roads around it seemed to sour under the crudity of the songs that spilled through the crack in its door. Moppet covered her ears as we came down the path, trying to shut out the curses. By the time we'd reached the entrance, she'd buried her face in Tom's neck.

Tom was wishing he could do the same. "Maybe we

should think up something else," he said. Sally had gone a little pale; I think she'd begun to regret suggesting the letter. As for me, I'd have been happy to turn around and go. But we needed a boat. So I opened the creaking door and went inside.

The parlor was packed, smelling of fish, stale beer, and even staler sweat. It was hot, almost sweltering, heat bleeding as much from the press of bodies as the fire in the hearth. The tables seemed ancient, etched with rude words—and even ruder drawings—carved into them by countless patrons over the years. The men were a fitting match: worn and scarred, with rough voices that cursed as easily as they cheered. Tom stroked Moppet's hair, whispering soothing words into her ear. I wasn't sure if that was to keep the girl calm, or himself.

The moment we entered, all eyes swung toward us, strangers in their midst. The singers faded and stilled—except for one. A red-faced, bushily bearded man drawled on, sitting alone at a table by the fire.

The innkeeper looked us up and down. "I think you're in the wrong place, boy."

"We're—" My voice cracked. I had to clear my throat and start again. "We're looking for Captain Haddock."

The innkeeper hesitated. He looked us up and down again. Finally, he shrugged, as if to say, *It's your funeral*, and pointed to the red-faced man in the corner.

Tom pushed our way through the tables. The few men who shifted their chairs to let him pass did so resentfully, and I wondered what was forestalling violence: Tom's size, or his sword.

Captain Roger Haddock slouched in his chair, feet on the table. He was younger than I thought he'd be, thirty at the most, and possibly not even that. His hair was long and greasy, and his bushy black beard had something stuck in it—it looked like a piece of kippered herring.

He stared into the fire as he sang, oblivious to the fact that everyone else had stopped. He waved his half-empty mug in badly kept time with the beat.

In Amsterdam, there lived a maid
Mark well what do I say!

"Captain Haddock?" I said.

In Amsterdam, there lived a maid
And this fair maid my trust betrayed!

"Captain Haddock? I'd like to speak to you about hiring your boat—"

I'll go no more a-rovin' with you, fair maid!

I felt a hundred eyes on my back, a mouse in a den of cats. Sweat trickled from my brow, but I didn't dare wipe it away. Every moment I stood ignored was further encouragement for the captain's men to turn on us. I wondered if Tom, hands full with the frightened Moppet, would even have time to draw his blade.

But then a second voice joined Captain Haddock's song. It was high and sweet and in perfect harmony.

A-rovin', a-rovin', since rovin's been my ru-i-in
I'll go no more a-rovin' with you, fair maid!

The pirate captain looked up, startled. Tom and I were equally astonished. It was Sally, singing along with him.

Haddock's eyes lit up. He launched into the second verse, the song turning slightly bawdy. Sally continued, hitting every beat. When he moved into the third verse—where the words became *considerably* more vulgar—Sally flushed. The pirate grinned and pressed on.

And then the rest of the tavern joined them. Captain Haddock kept his eyes on Sally the whole time, as if daring her to stop. But though she'd turned as red as a tomato, she didn't miss a note, right up until the end.

> *I'll go no more a-roooovinnn' . . .*
> *With youuuu, faaair maaaaid!*

The room burst into a cheer. Curses and calls for more ale were followed by a half dozen songs from the different tables, filling the already sour air with a racket that made Moppet burrow further into Tom's chest. Captain Haddock didn't join them. Still grinning, he drained his mug and patted his thigh.

"Come sit with me, little lass," he said, "and we'll sing the chill away."

I took the empty chair next to him, and he shifted his bleary-eyed gaze to me. "You, sir," he said, "are not what I had in mind."

"Are you Captain Haddock?" I said.

"I was when I came in here." He belched. "Course, that was three weeks ago. I could be anybody by now."

"I'm Christopher, Baron Ashcombe of Chillingham."

"Good for you."

"We need a ship."

"Who doesn't?" He stared sorrowfully into his mug. "This is empty."

"Why don't I take care of that?" I said, and I pulled a half penny from my coin purse to call the barmaid.

"You're a good boy." Haddock gazed at the server as she left. "Could you get me one of those, too?"

"She's not a mule, Captain," Sally said tartly. "You can't buy and sell her."

Haddock punched me in the arm. "This one's got spirit, eh? If only I was thirty years younger. No, wait . . . then I wouldn't be born yet." He started counting on his fingers. "Twenty-seven . . . twenty-six . . . twenty-five . . ."

Getting him to focus was going to be harder than I thought. When the barmaid brought his mug, I dragged it away from him.

"Awww," he said.

"I told you," I said. "We need a ship."

"What do you want me to do about it?"

"Don't you have one?"

"The *Manticore*!" he shouted.

"THE *MANTICORE*!" came the reply from every man in the room.

"England's pride," Captain Haddock said. "Finest ship on the waves."

"We'd like to hire it," I said. "We need a courier taken down the coast, to Southampton."

"Come back in two months." He snatched the mug from my hands and drank deeply.

"We need it now."

He shrugged. "Life is full of disappointments. When you're older, you'll understand."

"What's the problem?" Sally said.

"The problem, my darling, is the weather. It's cursed." He leaned in. "The storms of late are unnatural. Like they're called from dark places."

Tom shuddered. My own stomach tightened, as if I were riding those terrible waves in my chair.

"Oh, I see," Sally said. "You're afraid."

Haddock scowled. "Afraid? Me? I fear nothing on the sea."

"Then why not go?"

"Because I'm happy here. It's warm, it's dry, the ale flows, and, once in a while, a pretty girl like you brings in the sunshine."

"There's ale and pretty girls in Southampton," I pointed out.

"No doubt. But they are *there*"—he pointed eastward—"and I am *here*. And to get there from here would require getting cold and wet. No thank you. We took enough spoils from the Dutch to last two months. So come back in two months."

I thought about it. "How about three?"

"If you come back in three, we'll be gone."

"No, I mean: How about enough money to stay in Southampton for *three* months. I'll give you another month's worth of ale if you go."

He looked at me, and I caught a glimpse of something shrewd behind the dullness of the drink. "It'll take a peck more than ha'penny to pry my posterior from this . . . I need a word that begins with *p*."

"Perch," Sally said.

"Ooo, that's a good one."

I placed four gold *louis* on the table. "How about these?"

He stared at them. "Those are French."

"They're still gold. Each worth more than a pound."

"This is England," he growled. "Nothing's worth more than a pound."

"Either way, they'll keep you and your men in cups for a month."

His eyes narrowed. "Double it, and you have a deal."

"I'll give you six," I countered.

"You'll give me eight, or you'll find another boat."

"Fine," I grumbled, and I threw the coins on the table. "You *are* a pirate."

He stood in mock indignation. "I, sir, am a privateer." He snatched the coins, drained his mug in three great gulps, then kicked his chair aside. "Scroff! Where are you, you degenerate?"

A bulky sailor answered from the next table. "No need to shout. I'm right here."

"Grease the old girl," Haddock said. "We sail this evening."

"Sail? Tonight?"

"What's wrong with that?"

"The men are drunk."

"So am I."

"Well . . . what about the storms?"

"Which would you rather face?" Haddock said. "Winter's storms, or my boots?"

Scroff sprang from the table. "Everyone up! The *Manticore* sails!"

There was a great deal of grumbling, but Scroff hustled the men from the tavern. Captain Haddock watched them go proudly.

"God love an Englishman," he said.

The sailors scurried in the torchlight, setting the rigging, hoisting the sails. We watched from the shore until Haddock shouted from the deck. "We leave within the hour, Ashcombe. So if you want your courier to come, you'd best send him along."

That took us back to the Blue Boar, where I hustled the boy off to the *Manticore* with the letter for Lord Ashcombe. Rawlin, the man who Willoughby said knew about missing children, still hadn't come in, and though we'd only eaten a few hours ago, I found myself starving again. Tom, I learned, was always hungry, so I bought us all a bowl of mutton stew, flavored with mint and barley.

We decided to stay in the parlor, waiting for Rawlin to return, and as we ate, I noticed something odd with Sally. When breaking the bread to dip in the stew, she kept putting her spoon down to tear the loaf one handed.

"Is something wrong?" I said.

"What do you mean?" she said.

"You're not using your left hand."

"It's fine." She hid her hand in her lap. "I broke a finger-nail. It hurts."

"Are you bleeding? I have lots of—"

"I told you—it's fine."

I looked over at Tom, puzzled. He glanced up from Moppet, who clung to him like she was afraid he'd disappear if she let go. He shook his head, a caution. *Leave it alone.*

I didn't understand, but I let the matter drop. As for Tom, he was having troubles of his own. Moppet wouldn't eat. Every time he brought the spoon close, she turned away and buried her head in his chest.

"You have to have something," he said. "How about some bread?"

She wouldn't take that, either. "I think the day's been too much for her," Tom said. "Can we go upstairs?"

"Might as well," I said, and I asked Willoughby to send the rest of our food up to my quarters.

Even in the quiet, Moppet wouldn't calm down. She clung to Tom more fiercely than ever. When he pulled her head from his chest, she was crying.

"What's wrong?" Tom said. "What is it?"

Tom sat on the bed, Moppet so small and fragile on his

knee. Sally crouched in front of her. I gathered Bridget from where she sat on the windowsill and handed the pigeon to the little girl. She took the bird almost desperately, hugging it to her chest.

"You're safe here," Sally said soothingly. "No one's going to hurt you. Will you tell us what's wrong?"

She reached out, but the girl recoiled from her touch. Tom rocked her gently. "It's all right. These are my friends. You can tell them anything."

She looked up at Tom. Then she spoke, her voice barely a whisper.

"Puritan," she said.

CHAPTER
19

TOM GASPED.

"Puritan?" I said, confused. "What Puritan? Did someone hurt you?"

She buried her head back in Tom's chest.

"Gently," Sally chided.

"But I don't know what she's saying."

"Maybe it's another conspiracy," Tom said.

"Another conspiracy? What was the first one?"

"I told you about it," Sally said. "Last spring, with the
Cult of the Archangel. When Master Benedict was killed."

I knew about the conflict between the Puritans and
our king. Sixteen years ago, the Puritans had seized power,

executed Charles's father, and exiled the young king, ruling the country as the Commonwealth. Charles had only returned five years ago, when the Puritans themselves had been ousted. Since then, there had been several plots against the Crown—one of which, Sally told me, had murdered my master. "I thought we stopped the Cult of the Archangel."

"Some of them got away," Tom said, nervous.

"And you think they came here?" That would be an extraordinary coincidence. Besides: "What does this have to do with Moppet?"

"I don't know. But she got scared when we went to the Blood and Barrel."

"*I* got scared when we went to the Blood and Barrel. And if there's one thing we can guarantee, there weren't any Puritans in *that* tavern."

"You know," Sally said thoughtfully, "the south of England had a lot of Puritan support during the Interregnum. What if she saw somebody in town who frightened her?"

"None of the pirates could be Puritans," I insisted.

"It doesn't have to be the pirates. It could be anyone we've seen. Someone in the parlor, downstairs."

Right. That was where she'd first refused to eat. "We should take her down again."

"No," Tom said.

"We need to find out what's got her so upset. If she points to someone—"

"You can't ask her to do that," Sally said.

I frowned. "How are we supposed to figure out what's happened if we can't ask her to do anything?"

"I don't know. But she's a child, Christopher. She's lost, and she's scared, and she's not made for this sort of thing."

I wanted to laugh at that. *I* was lost, and *I* was scared, and, despite the stories Sally had told me, I didn't feel made for this sort of thing, either. Nevertheless, I threw up my hands.

"Fine. I'll go. Though I don't know what I'm looking for." I leaned in and spoke gently to Moppet. "I don't suppose you'll tell me anything else?"

She just nestled into Tom.

I sighed. "All right. Puritans it is."

I clomped back downstairs, frustrated.

The girl told you something important, Master Benedict said. *You need to listen.*

"I *am* listening," I grumbled. "My problem is that I'm not understanding."

Silence.

"Well?"

"Pardon, my lord?" a high voice said.

I turned to see a girl of around twelve, carrying a bucket. Willoughby's daughter, judging from her round face and wide eyes. She'd been scrubbing behind the steps as I'd been talking to Master Benedict.

I flushed. "Nothing. No, wait."

She stopped.

"Are there any Puritans in town?" I said.

The girl reddened and began to stammer. "W-we're all faithful subjects of His Majesty, my lord."

Her sudden fear surprised me—and made me think of Moppet, terrified, upstairs. Willoughby came over from the bar, nervous at the sight of his frightened daughter. "Is there some trouble?"

"I was just asking about Puritans," I said.

The innkeeper paled slightly. "You'll find none of that here, my lord. We're all faithful subjects of His Majesty."

I blinked. His daughter had just said the same thing— the *exact* same thing. I glanced into the parlor. There were fourteen people at the tables, mostly men, mostly in groups. Only one sat alone: an older man, sipping wine carefully from a glass.

"Do you know everyone here?" I said.

"Certainly. I promise you, none of them are Puritans. You can ask our Reverend Chatwick, he'll tell you. Church of England, all of us."

"Have you seen anyone today who was a stranger?"

"Just yourself, my lord. And the little girl."

"And there are no Puritans in town."

"I swear it."

"How about in the hamlets nearby?"

"I really wouldn't know, my lord. That Cromwell business was a long time ago."

The door opened, blowing cold air into the room. A man entered, shaking snow from his cap, running his fingers through his graying hair.

Willoughby looked relieved at the distraction. "Oh! He's here. Rawlin!"

The man at the door looked over. He studied me with sharp, appraising eyes before ambling over, cap in hand.

"Joseph Rawlin," Willoughby said. "This is his lordship, the Baron of Chillingham."

Rawlin bowed a little. "An honor, my lord."

I nodded coolly, like I imagined the Baron of Chillingham would. "I have some questions for you, if you have the time."

"Certainly. I was just about to take my dinner . . . ?"

He motioned to the tables, but I didn't want to talk here. "Why not join me in my room?" I said. "I'll have your meal brought up." I remembered what Willoughby had told me about the man. "And some warm spiced ale, if that suits you."

He gave me an oily sort of smile. "Well, now, my lord. That suits me just fine."

He looked about my room curiously as he entered. "Lived in Seaton nigh on sixty years," he said. "Don't think I've ever been in here."

I motioned for him to join us at the table near the fire.

"My lady," he said to Sally. He nodded to Tom, then smiled at Moppet, all teeth. "Here's a little darling—"

She flinched as he reached out to ruffle her hair.

He pulled back. "Apologies. Meant no offense. Should keep my hands to myself, that's what I should do."

"It's all right," I said. "You don't recognize the girl, do you?"

He peered at her. "Can't say as I do. Should I?"

"She was found wandering around Robert Dryden's farm."

"Know it well. Good man, our Robert." He studied Moppet more closely now. The girl shifted in Tom's arms, uncomfortable under his scrutiny. "She's not from around here," he said finally.

"You're sure?" Sally said.

"I've seen every soul that's drank from the River Axe. Never laid eyes on that one." He leaned back in his chair, troubled. "She's not where she's supposed to be."

"Where should she be?" Tom said.

"Somewhere else, boy. Somewhere else."

"What does that mean?" I said.

There was a knock on the door. Tom opened it, and Willoughby entered with Rawlin's meal. The innkeeper's daughter brought more spiced ale, a mug for each of us, and milk for Moppet.

Rawlin stayed silent until they were gone. Then he asked, "Might I ask the whereabouts of Chillingham?"

Sally answered him. "Not far from London."

"Ever been round these parts before? Any of you?" When we shook our heads, he said, "This isn't the east, my lord. Strange things happen here. Very strange things."

"You're talking about the White Lady," I said.

He looked at me with interest. "So you know of her."

"Have you seen her?"

"No. And I pray I never do. She's evil, my lord. Unrelenting evil. And she's returned to feed on children's souls."

CHAPTER

20

TOM HELD MOPPET CLOSE. I SHIV-
ered as I thought of what Robert had told me. *The demon.
He's stolen your soul.*

"Who *is* the White Lady?" I said.

"A spirit from long ago," Rawlin said, as he stirred his
stew. "She returns, from time to time, and takes children to
keep her warm in the cold."

Tom looked at me, eyes wide.

"I know of one child who's gone missing," I said. "Emma
Lisle. My man said you claim there are more."

"Five," Rawlin said. "There are five who've disappeared."

"Five?" Sally said.

"Five of twelve."

"What do you mean, twelve?" I said.

"That's what she takes. That's the White Lady's payment. Twelve pure souls, to light her way back to hell."

My blood was ice. Five missing children. Five souls gone.

Or did mine make it six?

I cleared my throat. "You said you've never seen the White Lady. How do you know she's the one taking the children?"

"Because she's left her mark."

We stared at him, uncomprehending.

"At Crook's Hollow," he said, "on the river, a half mile north of the Dryden farm. They found the mark on a stone."

"What mark?"

"A symbol, written in blood."

"What did it look like?"

He shrugged. "Don't know. Don't want to know. Marks of wickedness are evil in themselves. Just looking upon them blackens your soul."

"If you've never seen it, how do you know it's the mark of the White Lady?"

"Whose else could it be? There's no doubting it's dark

magic. If it's not the White Lady's, then it came from the witch."

"There's a *witch* nearby?" Tom said.

Rawlin nodded. "Lives in the woods, just south of the Darcy place."

I recalled the directions Robert had given me. "You're talking about Sybil O'Malley."

"You know her?"

"Robert said she's a cunning woman, not a witch."

Rawlin shook his head. "Robert Dryden's a good man—maybe too good. He always thinks the best of people, even when they don't deserve it."

"But she helped me."

The old man looked at me curiously. "Did she now? And how did she do that?"

"She brought me out of an illness."

"Ah. And you're all right now, then, are you, my lord?"

My skin prickled. "Why wouldn't I be?"

"Because you might think she helped you, but she didn't. She does nothing for the sake of goodness. She took something from you, I guarantee it."

I couldn't answer. It was like my tongue was frozen.

Rawlin looked vindicated. "Aha, you see? I *am* right."

Suddenly he remembered whom he was talking to. He fidgeted in his chair. "Meant no offense, my lord. You'll be in my prayers tonight, I swear."

"Never mind me," I said sharply. "How do you know Sybil's a witch?"

"Everyone knows."

"Robert Dryden doesn't."

"I told you, my lord, he's too trusting. Go see Baronet Darcy. He'll tell you. He used to be a witchfinder. That's why that . . . woman . . . moved here. To wreak vengeance on behalf of her coven."

"Vengeance for what?" I said.

"I don't involve myself in wickedness. All I know is that since the witch came, bad things have been happening."

"Like what?" Tom said.

"Disease. Rotting crops. Terrible storms. It's the witch's work, mark my words. Though this time, she's gone too far. Her evil has awakened the White Lady."

I thought of what Robert had told me. *His cattle, falling ill to the quarter evil. Lean years of harvest. And the storm. The storm that wrecked our ship.* I shivered. "You still haven't told us who the White Lady is."

"It's an old tale." Rawlin spooned the last of the stew

into his mouth, then sat back in his chair. "Some two hundred years ago, a knight came to Devonshire. His name was Sir Tristram, and he made his home in the village of Hook Reddale. A prosperous little hamlet, some ways to the north.

"Everyone loved Sir Tristram. He was the truest of knights: brave, loyal, kind, pious. Rich, too. But unlike your typical lord—uh . . ." He looked at me uncomfortably. "I'm sure . . . I mean, I have no doubt—"

"Just go on," I said.

"Well . . . he used his wealth to help the town. Anyway, he had a pair of sons, twin boys, but his wife died giving birth to them. So he petitioned the king to allow him to marry a woman he'd seen while at court: a lady of unearthly beauty, dressed in the purest of shimmering samite.

"Now the king knew this woman, and he was troubled. 'This lady is not for you,' he said. 'I have in mind the daughter of Islington: She is beautiful, and sweet, and faithful to God and Crown.'

"But Sir Tristram's heart was set. The lady in white's beauty had won it, and he would have no other. For a full month did the king try to convince Sir Tristram to choose someone else, for he loved his loyal knight, and he knew the soul of the lady in white. But Sir Tristram would not relent. So the king did. 'You shall have her,' he said, 'though I pray God forgive me for this mistake.'

"Sir Tristram married her, then returned home. Over the years, he'd built a tower at the center of the village, so when his lady became his bride, she could stand atop it, and see the land all around, and know how good and peaceful it was. And when they returned to the village, the lady did go up that tower, and her heart did soar. But not because she saw the beauty of the land. No, she saw only its wealth.

"She knew then, that wealth must be hers—not as is shared between a husband and wife, but all for herself. She knew Sir Tristram's only family was his twin boys, so that very night, she poisoned them all with their drink. He died, his boys with him, and now she owned everything.

"The king despaired; though he had no proof, he knew what she had done. But the Divine Lord, who sits in judgement of all, took His own revenge. The lady's parents, whom she had brought with her to Hook Reddale, were cursed with pestilence, while the lady herself remained untouched. Her parents died, and the villagers fled.

"Now she was alone—truly alone, for she could not

even retreat to the satisfaction of her wealth. Not a soul in the kingdom would take it; for they knew God had cursed every penny. Her stores ran low, her clothes turned to rags, until she had nothing remaining but that samite dress. Realizing what she had done, the lady donned that gown, ran to the top of the tower, and threw herself from the parapet.

"But God had cursed her well. Though her body broke, death was denied her. She lay there, pleading for mercy, but none were left to come to her aid. Until she heard another voice call.

"It was the voice of evil. The voice of the Devil. It called to her from the water. 'Come to me,' it said. 'Serve me. And you shall live forever.'

"And, so, abandoned and alone, she began to crawl. Inch by inch, she dragged her broken body through the snow to the river. And she disappeared under the waves.

"For most, that would be the end of the story. But evil kept its promise, and in the most wretched way. For the lady did *not* die in those icy waters. The power of the Devil kept her alive, lost and alone, hungering for warmth. She tried to leave the river, but discovered that her spirit kept her bound to the water. And when the snow falls, the White

Lady walks the rivers still, calling to young children who, in their innocence, cannot understand the lies that lurk within her embrace. She feeds on them, feeds on their souls, until they are nothing but hollow husks."

Rawlin drained the last of his ale and wiped his mouth with the back of his hand. "That's where those children are, my lord. Do not look for them. For that witch O'Malley has called upon the White Lady. And the White Lady gives nothing back."

CHAPTER
21

TOM LOOKED TERRIFIED. SALLY, her face pale, took my hand, holding me so tightly it hurt my fingers.

"Surely," I said, "there must be something we can do to save them?"

The storyteller regarded me curiously. "Why do you care?"

"What do you mean?"

"They're not your children, my lord, not your charge. Why would you set yourself against the wraith?"

Because I have no choice, I thought. If it was souls the White Lady was taking . . . well, where was mine?

"Has anyone seen her?" Tom asked breathlessly.

"You don't look upon the White Lady, boy. Not if you want to keep your soul. But a man in the hamlet where the blood mark was found said he saw a light near the river that night."

"Did he try to follow it?" I said.

"He knew better than that."

"But if no one can look upon the White Lady, how can we stop her?"

"You can't," he said. "All you can do is go after the witch. Put an end to her black magic. That might send the White Lady back to sleeping."

"But the children—"

"Are gone. Forgive me, my lord, but you didn't hear me. I told you: The White Lady gives nothing back." He sighed. "A boy not much older than you once thought different. No one thinks so anymore."

"What happened?" Tom said.

The man settled back in his chair. "It was a long time ago, not long after the lady cast herself into the river. Everyone knew the village was cursed; none would go near it. But this boy was foolish, and he dreamed of easy riches. 'Look,' he said, 'Hook Reddale was abandoned, the people taking nothing when they fled. So the village will be full of things to sell.' He thought of the knight's tower; imagine the weapons he could find for the taking!

"The boy was married. His young wife begged him not to go. 'Think of me,' she said. 'Think of your children.' But the boy wouldn't listen, and one gray morning, he stole off to the village of Hook Reddale.

"He found it just like he'd imagined: as if all the people in town had simply vanished. He went to the tower, standing at the village's heart, and there he found his dream: old, polished guns; fine English longbows; swords of tempered steel.

"He took one of those swords and brought it home. He showed the weapon to his wife. He thought she'd be pleased; the blade was worth more than everything they owned. But she begged him to take it back.

"He refused. When she told the rest of the village what her husband had done, they came to persuade him as well. 'That blade is not worth anything,' they said, 'for no one will buy it.' The boy didn't care, because secretly, he'd already decided: The sword was too beautiful to sell. He'd return to get another. This one, he'd keep for himself.

"He polished it, put it aside, then went to bed. In the

morning, when he rose, he went to work his lord's fields, as usual. He planned to go back to the village afterward, to plunder all that he could. But as he was leaving his home, he caught a glimpse of the sword, resting against the wall. So he stayed, and he polished it once again.

"The same thing happened, day after day: He planned to return to Hook Reddale, and instead spent the evening with his sword. Until one night his wife awoke to discover he hadn't come to bed. She rose and found him in the cellar, polishing the weapon. And he was talking to it.

"She confronted him. He scoffed at her and put the sword away. But the next night, she found him doing the same thing. He was talking to the sword—and more frightening, she discovered he was *listening* to it, as well.

"She begged him to throw it away. He didn't laugh this time. He simply put the sword down and came to bed. That wasn't enough for his terrified wife.

"'You'll get rid of that sword tomorrow,' she said.

"'Yes,' he said, and she thought that was the end of it. And, in a way, it was. For that night, the boy rose from his bed. He went downstairs, took up his sword, and murdered his wife. Then he gave it one final polish and went down to the river. He lay in the water, the sword on his chest, and was carried away—into the woods, which glowed with unearthly light."

Rawlin's voice faded, until there was nothing but the crackling of the fire.

"I see my story has quieted you," he said. "I'm sorry if I've given you troubled thoughts. But there's nothing to be done here. What the White Lady claims, she will keep. Even to the basest metal. You cannot take from her. Not a blade—and certainly not a child.

"So go home, my lord. Go home to where you'll be safe. And pray you never hear of the White Lady again."

TUESDAY, DECEMBER 22, 1665

i   t   p t   e q   nr   e r
u   b   d u   q   d   s   u

CHAPTER

22

IF RAWLIN HAD MEANT TO SCARE
me, he'd done a marvelous job. I tossed and turned all
night, and when I finally did begin to drift off, only the
icy plain of my nightmares waited for me. It woke me with
a gasp.

I sat there, on my bed, in the dark, helpless. Rawlin's
words had turned everything upside down. Robert had said
Sybil would help me—had already helped me. But if Rawlin
was right, then she'd been duping the farmer all along. After
all this time, could she actually be responsible for his troubles:
cursing—or even poisoning—his cattle, and then coercing
his payment to "fix" it? And what did that mean for me?

She took something from you, Rawlin had said. *I guarantee it.*

I didn't know what to do anymore. Yesterday I was desperate to see the old woman. Now I was desperate to leave. Part of me wished I'd gone with Captain Haddock, just escaped this whole hexed shire—except, of course, I *couldn't* escape. I could *leave,* but my stolen memories wouldn't follow me home.

And if I did go, what then of the missing children? *Five of twelve,* Rawlin had said. Seven more children to disappear. The visions in my dreams had made it clear: We were bound, those children and I, in ways I didn't understand. And to understand them, I'd need to talk to Sybil.

But what if she really *was* a witch?

"It's not just me who thinks so, my lord," Rawlin had said before he'd left. "There are many angry folk about. She'd do well to flee, before they bring her to trial. Or worse."

I thought of those dead cats, lying in a heap outside the village. I knew, now, what had happened to them. The villagers had rounded up every one in Seaton and butchered them. They were afraid the cats were familiars.

Rawlin had a similar warning for me. "Think twice about consorting with the witch, my lord. Folks won't look on it too kindly."

But I *needed* to see Sybil. I needed my memories back. I needed to know what she knew.

You must go to Crook's Hollow, Master Benedict said. *You must see that mark first.*

Why? I asked.

Symbols are keys to the unknown. Every symbol is placed for a purpose. You cannot unlock this mystery without knowing what it is.

I rose, sleep lost for good. I looked over at my roommates with envy. Tom slumbered on the palliasse in the corner, Moppet sprawled on his back like he was a mattress. Her arms hung down, her drool soaking into the cloth of his shoulder. Late last night, out of nowhere, the poor girl had broken into tears again. She wouldn't speak; she'd just sobbed in Tom's arms until she'd cried herself to sleep.

I watched her body rise and fall with Tom's breaths and thought of the one thing she'd been able to say.

Puritan.

After Rawlin had left our room, I'd told Tom and Sally about the strange reaction I'd got downstairs when I'd asked about Puritans. They'd both seemed puzzled, until Sally realized our mistake.

She smacked her forehead and groaned. "I forgot about your disguise. We scared them."

"But I didn't do anything," I said.

"You didn't have to. They think you're Lord Ashcombe's grandson."

"So?"

"Lord Ashcombe *hates* Puritans. After the king returned, he wanted to execute them all."

"What does that have to do with me?"

"What would you think if Lord Ashcombe's grandson showed up unannounced and started asking where the Puritans are? I doubt they even believe our shipwreck story anymore. They probably think we were sent here by your grandfather to investigate the town."

This was a disaster. If Puritans were involved, we needed to know how—and how Moppet, the missing children, and my memories were tied together. But now they'd be sure to keep their heads down, if not flee the village entirely. Or worse: come after us.

I watched the girl sleep and wondered. *If she's not from this area, then where did she come from? How did she get here? And how is she involved in all of this?*

The blood mark, was all my master would say. *You need to see that symbol.*

I spoke to Willoughby at the first sliver of sunrise. He marked the location of Crook's Hollow on my map: along the river, a half mile north of Robert's farm. We set out, Tom plowing a path in front like yesterday. Moppet rode on his shoulders, directing him with an imperious finger, while Bridget swooped overhead.

As for Sally, the visit to the Blood and Barrel seemed to have awakened something musical in her. She sang us some jaunty catches as we walked, trying to get us to join in.

"You're cheerful this morning," I grumbled.

"Why shouldn't I be?"

"Because according to Rawlin, we're off to find the Devil's mark, a corrupted ghost, and quite possibly a witch."

"Would being gloomy help?" she asked.

"I suppose not."

"There you are, then."

Between songs, we spoke of idle things to pass the time, and I glanced every so often at her left hand. Since last night, I'd been watching her, and I saw that she avoided using it as much as possible—and when she had to, she barely moved it. After a few hours, when we stopped to take a break, I asked Tom about it while Sally sipped from the river.

"She got hurt when we were in Paris," he said quietly.

"What happened?"

"A man hit her on the head. It left her out cold for several days. When she woke, she'd lost some memories, and she couldn't really use her hand. She won't admit it."

"Whyever not?"

"I think it's because she knows if anyone finds out, she won't be able to get work. She was a chambermaid for one of the Court ladies. If she's a cripple, she won't be able to go back. No one would take her."

Now I understood her silence. But she couldn't conceal an injury like that forever. "Even if she gets her old job back, they'll find out eventually."

Tom shrugged. "I guess she's trying not to think about it."

I regarded her thoughtfully. "Just because her hand doesn't work now doesn't mean it'll never work again. She should be *trying* to use it. It's the best thing for an injury like that."

"You already told her so."

"She didn't listen?"

"She screamed at you. Then she cried. Then she ran away. You can try again, if you like. Though you might wait until we're not in the middle of nowhere. I don't want to hunt for another lost friend."

I wasn't all that keen on any screaming. I resolved to bring it up later. Much later.

Crook's Hollow was a simple place. Like every other hamlet we passed, it was that same mix of old stone and cob. Here, the dwellings had been built in a row, opposite a string of ancient houses that had collapsed long ago. A track of muddy white furrowed through the snow between them.

Beyond the houses, in an unfenced field, a man stood watch over a score of sheep, the animals rooting in the snow for something to eat. When he spied us coming, he waved, and we trekked through the field to join him. He nodded a friendly greeting. "Good day to you."

"Is this Crook's Hollow?" I asked.

"It is. Are you looking for someone?"

Sally stepped forward. "I'm the Lady Grace," she said, "And this is the Baron Ashcombe."

He bowed in surprise. "My apologies, my lady; my lord. I didn't recognize you."

That puzzled me—was there some reason he *should* recognize me?—and then I realized what had confused him: my clothing. My sapphire silk shirt and breeches, markers of my lordship, were concealed behind the simple sheepskin coat Robert had given me, and my fine leather boots were buried in the snow. Without those, I supposed I looked like an ordinary boy. Which I was, really.

"I'm John," the man said. "John Morrow."

"Joseph Rawlin told us," I said, "that a child went missing by the river a few days ago."

John's face turned grave. "Allan Cavill's boy. David." He looked at me hopefully. "Have you seen him?"

"I'm sorry, no. But I was told a mark was left behind."

The man shuddered and crossed his fingers. "God save us."

"Can we see it?"

He seemed shocked. "You don't want to look at that, my lord. It blackens the soul."

"I don't know if I have to worry about that," I said bitterly.

"My lord?"

"Never mind. We'd like to see the mark, nonetheless. Perhaps it might help us find the missing children."

And though he seemed surprised by that, too, he was

grateful. "We'll gladly take any help you could give. Times have been terrible hard round here of late. Kate!" He shouted toward the house. "Call your brother to tend the flock, and come with us to the river."

A girl of about Sally's age appeared at the door. She threw a cloak around her shoulders and hustled a younger boy out to take care of the sheep.

"My daughter," John said, and he told the girl who we were. "She's the one what found the mark. Don't stare, girl."

Kate, gawking at Sally in awe, bowed her head, chastised.

"Can you tell us what happened?" Sally said kindly, and her demeanor eased the girl's shyness. As we walked toward the water, she explained what she'd seen.

"It was dinnertime, my lady, already dark. I called for the children, but David didn't come. I knew he'd been playing by the river, so I went down. And I found that."

She pointed to the riverbank. A large, flat stone lay on the snow, a foot from the edge of the water.

The girl wouldn't go any closer. John stayed with her, hands placed protectively on her shoulders. So the rest of us went down to the stone by ourselves. I studied it, but it didn't seem like anything special to me, just a simple slate of red sandstone.

"I was told there was a mark on it," I said.

Kate nodded. "I knew the stone was strange as soon as I saw it. It hadn't been there before, and it was too big for David to carry. When I turned it over, I saw the mark."

"I flipped it back, my lord," John said. "It's not safe to keep evil exposed."

Tom worked his fingers under the edge. It was heavy—too heavy, as the girl said, for a boy of five—but it flipped over readily enough in Tom's hands. I stood back, and we stared at the blood mark below.

CHAPTER

23

SALLY STOOD CLOSE TO ME, HER
shoulder pressed into my arm. Tom crossed his fingers.
Moppet peered over Tom's head curiously, but otherwise
showed no reaction.

"What is that?" Tom said, shaken.

I knelt next to it. "I don't know."

It was a strange collection of slashes, loops, and curves, like some ancient, alien script. On one side was a small star; on the other, a . . . I wasn't certain what. It looked a bit like an alembic—an alchemical still—with a stoppered tube at the top. As for the mark itself, it was unquestionably drawn with blood, now dried, some of it flaking off into the snow.

What is this? I asked Master Benedict, but he didn't answer.

I called over to John. "Has anyone seen this mark before?"

He shook his head. "The vicar said we should throw it in the river."

"Why didn't you?"

"Well . . . I thought . . . no one here knows anything about magic. What if we needed it to get David back?"

Kate whispered something to him.

"Hush, girl," he said.

Sally spoke up. "What did she say?"

"Nothing to trouble yourself with, my lady."

"I wish to hear it, Mr. Morrow," Sally said, somewhat sharply.

John flushed. "She said someone should ask Old Sybil. She's a . . . woman . . . around these parts. She . . . knows things."

"The cunning woman," I said.

John hesitated. "Some call her that, my lord."

"And what do you say?"

He shuffled from foot to foot, uncomfortable. "She's never harmed us, far as I know. But Allan Cavill says she's a witch. He says she's responsible for his missing boy."

Rawlin had certainly agreed. "Where's Mr. Cavill now?"

"Hunting, my lord. Food's hard to come by in winter, 'less we want to cull the flock."

I returned to the mark on the stone. I wanted to study it, but given John's nervousness, I didn't think it wise to linger, and the stone was too big to carry.

"Do you have a spare cloth?" I asked him. He took me back to the house and gave me an old shirt with a hole in the side. I gave him a penny for it.

"You should have a new shirt for that," he objected, but I waved him off. I was only going to ruin it anyway.

I told Sally to keep them distracted with questions while I returned to the river's edge. Using the ink from my sash, I copied the symbol onto the shirt, then tucked it under my coat so they wouldn't see what I'd done. Then we took our farewell and headed south.

Sally was surprised. "Are we not going to see Sybil?"

"We are," I said, though by now I'd lost all enthusiasm for it. "But first we need to go back to Robert's farm."

"Why?"

"I'm not sure," I said. "But I think there might be something we need to see."

I studied the mark as we walked. I had the feeling I'd never seen it before, yet something nagged at the back of my mind. Something familiar.

Try looking at it a different way, Master Benedict said.

I wasn't sure what he meant. I tilted my head, and— wait a minute. . . .

"Come look at this," I said.

We all stopped. Tom and Sally peered over my shoulder as I flipped the cloth over and held it up. "What does this look like?"

"I don't know," Sally said. Tom shrugged.

"Look carefully. Look at this part." I pointed to the mark at the end, just before the star.

Sally blinked. "Is that a letter?"

"An *n*," Tom said thoughtfully.

"I think it is. And look at the mark before it—could that be an *a*? I think this is a word."

"In English?"

"I don't know. It's definitely the Latin alphabet."

"It could be a word of magic," Sally said.

"Or of evil," Tom said.

What would be a word of evil? I examined the letters—assuming that's what they were—and tried to work out what they spelled.

The first symbol curved a bit, like an elongated *S*.

Then a loop with a tail—an *o*? Or an *e*?

I couldn't make out the next letter. A *D*? Or maybe it was a combination of letters? Ending in an *a*?

The long stroke in the middle looked like an *l*.

Then came an *n*—maybe an *h*—an *a*, and finally the *n*.

"That stroke above the first part of the word," Sally said. "Maybe that's a dot. For an *i*, or a *j*."

Could be. I put all that together, and got:

"Does that mean something?" Tom said.

I shrugged. "Not to me."

Neither of them had any idea, either. Which left us back at nowhere.

We trudged on.

It was a strange feeling, going back to Robert's farm. Waking up there and not knowing anyone had been terrifying. Now it was the only place that felt familiar. In a way, it was like I was going home.

I think Moppet felt it, too. She began to fidget as we climbed the hills, paying close attention to the passing landscape. When we crossed a pair of tracks, she looked down from atop Tom's shoulders and pointed.

I nodded. "Those are ours, from yesterday."

She seemed more excited now. She kicked her heels like Tom was a horse, urging him on. He whinnied, and she laughed in surprised delight.

"You're really good with her," I said to him.

"She's easy to be good with." He reached up and tickled her as we walked. She giggled as she fended him off, and when he put his arms down, he looked sad. "I miss my sisters."

"Molly," I said suddenly.

Tom stopped, stared at me. "Yes," he said.

A searing pain shot across my forehead. I gasped. I could see names, as if written in flame on my mind.

"Cecily," I said. I pressed my hands to my temples, trying to fight the burning. "Isabel. Catherine. Emma. And Molly."

"That's it. That's them!" He grabbed my shoulders. "You remember!"

The *pain*. My skull pounded, my brain blazed. I crumpled.

"Christopher!"

Tom picked me up; Sally brushed the snow off my collar. Moppet, back on the ground, looked over at me, her expression serious. I drew deep, cold breaths, until the fire quelled in my head. I felt like throwing up.

"Are you all right?" Tom said.

I nodded. Even that made my stomach lurch.

"You remembered," Sally said.

"I didn't," I said.

"But you know their names," Tom said.

"And that's *all* I know. Just names. I don't know those

girls. What they look like, what they sound like . . . they may as well be the king's personal guards, for all I remember."

Still, as the nausea faded, I wondered if this was a good sign. The names of Tom's sisters were the most personal things I'd recalled yet.

Tom pulled me from my thoughts. "Someone's coming."

It was Wise. He crested the hill, longbow in hands, a rabbit skin slung over one shoulder, its carcass on the other. Smiling, he waved for us to join him, and we made our way back to the farm together. Robert was just as pleased I'd returned—and even more relieved to see Moppet.

"We looked everywhere for you," he chided the girl.

I apologized; of course he'd have been worried. "I should have sent word."

"I'm just glad she's well, my lord. And apparently in good hands."

I introduced Tom and Sally, using our disguises. I felt bad lying to him—if anyone deserved the truth, it was Robert—but if people found out we'd been playing at lordship, we'd be in big trouble. As for Robert, he was delighted I'd found my friends, and, when I told him I was the Baron Ashcombe, he was even more delighted I now knew who I was.

"Told you you were a lord," he said cheerfully.

"Uh . . . yes."

"And your memories . . . ?"

I shook my head.

"Well, let's hope Sybil can help," he said.

Tom, Sally, and I exchanged a glance.

Robert frowned. "What have people been telling you?"

I expected he already knew the answer. "That she's a witch."

"She's not," he said. "She's never done anyone any harm."

"What about me?"

"You? Sybil saved you. From your illness."

"It was suggested," I said, "that *she* took my memories."

"Why would she do that?"

"I don't know. But you said she wants something from me. Maybe this is her way of guaranteeing she'll get it."

Robert looked troubled by the notion—though not quite prepared to believe it. "My lord . . . I know what people say about Sybil, but she's done nothing but good for this farm. I beg you, have a care with your words. If you were to say she was a witch, that she'd stolen your soul . . . an accusation from you would carry weight."

That hadn't occurred to me. If Baron Ashcombe were to say Sybil O'Malley had cursed him, never mind a trial, she could be lynched. It was alarming to realize I held Sybil's life in my hands—and I'd never even met the woman.

I'd clearly need to watch what I said. In the meantime, I hadn't returned to Robert's farm just to ask about Sybil. "When Emma Lisle disappeared," I said, "did anyone find a blood mark? Something like this?"

I showed him the cloth. He studied it, frowning, then passed it to Wise, who shook his head. "No one saw any blood at all."

I spotted Tom looking thoughtfully back the way we came. "What is it?"

"Well," he said, "at Crook's Hollow, the blood mark was hidden. I mean, it was in an obvious place—a strange stone sitting in the middle of nowhere—but you wouldn't see the mark unless you turned it over."

That was a good point. Maybe we'd missed something. "We should check back at the river."

All of us went. By now, the snow next to the bank had been well trampled. "Do you remember seeing a stone of any kind?" I asked Wise.

He shook his head.

I hadn't seen one, either. But Emma had disappeared during the storm. If there was a stone, it would be hidden under the snow.

We'd need to start shoveling. Emma's bucket was still here; one of us could use that, and we'd need more tools for the rest. Wise began the trek back to the barn to get them. I went for the bucket.

Then I stopped. "Wise."

He turned.

I pointed at Emma's bucket. "You said this was just sitting there? Next to the river?"

He nodded.

"Did you touch it? Move it aside?"

He shook his head.

I went over to the bucket. I picked it up.

And there, underneath it on a stone in the circle in the snow, was the very same mark, written in blood.

CHAPTER
24

I PICKED UP THE STONE.

It was red sandstone, flat and heavy, though smaller than the one at Crook's Hollow. The symbols here were clear, unsmudged, protected from falling snow by Emma's bucket.

Wise and Robert were shaken, Robert especially troubled.

I got the sense he was rethinking what he'd said about Sybil. And he didn't like what it meant.

I didn't, either. Because now we knew the children were not only taken, but stolen for some terrible purpose.

It was time to ask Sybil what it was.

Robert's instructions were clear: Follow the river north and turn east when you see the tree that looks like a squashed giant. We did as told, and as we neared the place, Tom stopped so short I bumped into his back.

"Look at that," he said.

Before us stood the tree. Its trunk was broad and squat, aged bark twisting in knots and gnarls, forming a wizened, bearded face right in its center. The branches split overhead. Two great limbs stretched from each side, arms with a thousand knobbled fingers. A dead, blackened patch marked the split, as if a lightning strike had burned the wood away. At its bottom, the tree's roots dug into the ground, tortuously twisted feet.

We stared at the Squashed Giant—and the longer we did, the more it seemed to stare back. The branches swung in the breeze, the wood creaking, its fingers reaching for our necks.

We moved on hurriedly. Tom led us east, into the woods. Soon we came to a small clearing, where Sybil's hut stood.

"Hut" was too generous a word. A ramshackle blend of cob, wood, and a handful of errant stones made Sybil's home look less like a house and more like an animal's nest. Smoke rose from the chimney, curling through the canopy of snow-laden trees.

I took a breath. "We should prepare before we go in."

"How?" Tom said. "By coming to our senses and running away?"

"Maybe you should take out your sword."

Tom lowered Moppet from his shoulders and pulled away the sheath covering Eternity's hilt. He drew the blade from its scabbard, gripped it in both hands.

"What now?" he whispered.

There was nothing else to do. We went inside.

CHAPTER
25

WHAT SURPRISED ME MOST WAS
the smell.

The interior of the hut was a simple affair: a straw mattress; a three-legged table, the fourth replaced by the sawed-off branch of an oak; a collection of ceramic pots stacked around the wall. Herbs hung from the ceiling, slung over strings drawn from corner to corner. A cauldron bubbled in the lumpy clay hearth, boiling over a crackling fire, and while I supposed a cauldron was what a witch's hut *should* have, what struck me the most—and most confusing—was the scent that filled the air.

The herbs. The heavy, earthy smell of drying leaves and

gnarled roots. It was . . . familiar. Warmth spread inside me, not from the fire, but from my heart. I reeled, dizzy.

Home

Master Benedict said.

Home

I thought.

Do you remember? came the whisper

and for the briefest moment, I caught a glimpse of a shadow by the fire: a lanky old man, absurdly tall, bent over the flame

then it was gone. The spinning in my head slowed, and I caught sight of the woman behind the cauldron. She was old, yes, but not tall. She was barely bigger than Sally, and frail, like a breeze would break her in two. And there was a weariness in her expression that made me think, in some way, she'd already been broken.

She turned to meet her intruders. Her gaze lingered on Tom's blade, then Sally's dress, and then, strangely, on my snow-stained boots. When she brought her eyes to mine, they were full of bitterness, so sharp it cut to the bone.

Her accent was Irish, a thick Emerald Isle brogue. "Did they send you to kill me?"

"We don't wish anyone harm," I said, cautious.

"So you always enter a home uninvited, sword in hand?"

Tom flushed and lowered his blade.

"What do you want?" Sybil said.

"My name is Christopher Ashcombe," I said. "I'm the Baron of Chillingham. My grandfather is Richard Ashcombe, the King's Warden."

"I know."

"You do?"

"We've met before."

I glanced at Tom, then Sally. "When was this?"

She smiled thinly. "You might not remember it. You were asleep at the time."

I wasn't in the mood for jokes. "What did you do to me?"

"Depends. What's wrong with you?"

I *really* wasn't in the mood for jokes. "Robert said you asked me to come see you."

"So I did. And now I'll ask *you*, again: What's wrong with you?"

I didn't see any reason not to tell her the truth. "I can't remember things."

"What kinds of things?"

"Everything that matters. I can't remember who I am."

She studied me for a moment. "Interesting."

I knew she was toying with me, and though I was afraid, it made me angry. "Robert said you spoke to me while I was out. What happened? Tell me what you did."

"Or you'll do what?"

I stood there, surprised by the truth of her response. What would I do? What *could* I do?

Sally placed a hand on my arm. "Christopher told you: We're not looking for anyone to get hurt. We just want him to get his memories back. And the missing children returned to their homes."

Sybil didn't answer right away. She plucked some holly from one of the strings overhead and held it over the cauldron, as if to add the leaves to the brew.

"The children," she said.

"Yes," I said. "They've disappeared."

"I know that."

"The locals blame you."

"Of course they do."

"They say you're a witch."

"I am not."

"They say you summoned the White Lady."

She didn't answer.

"Well?" I said. "Did you?"

"What do you know of it?" she asked.

"I've heard the stories. And I've found the marks."

She looked up from the cauldron. "What marks?"

"The blood marks," I said. "Where the children vanished."

I pulled the cloth from beneath my coat and handed it to her. She stared at it.

"Do you know what it says?" I said.

She frowned. "Says?"

"Yes. It's a word. I think this is an *n* and this an *a*—you see?"

She stared at it some more. "Where did you find this?"

"At Crook's Hollow, where David Cavill disappeared. It was written in blood, hidden under a stone. I then found the very same mark at Robert Dryden's farm, under the bucket Emma Lisle left behind."

Sybil studied my face, her expression inscrutable. Then she handed the cloth back, turned away, and returned to her cauldron.

"You know something about what's happening," I said. "Don't you?"

"I know many things."

"Stop playing games. It's not just my memories. These are *children* that are missing."

"What do you care?"

"You're the second person to say that to me," I said, frustrated. "What's happened out here? Does no one care about anyone but themselves?"

She whirled, eyes blazing. "Forgive me, 'my lord.'" She spat the honorific like it was poison. "Your kind serves no one *but* themselves."

"You don't know him," Sally said.

"I know all I need to know, 'my lady.' You're all the same."

"Christopher's never harmed anyone," Tom said. "He *helps* people."

Sybil sneered at him. "Oh, so the servant *can* speak."

"Enough," I said. "I told you the truth: We didn't come here to fight. I just want my memories back. If you won't help me, then at least help the children. Tell us what you know."

She slumped, then, and turned away, defeated. "I can't."

"Why not?"

"Because I have nothing to do with missing children."

"The villagers think—"

"What they always think," Sybil snapped. "They come for my help when the sickness fills their chests, then come for my head when the rot takes their crops. I told you: I am no witch. I have nothing to do with this. *You* do."

I blinked, startled. "Me?"

"That's why you were brought here."

"I came because Robert said you needed to see me."

"I don't mean my home. I mean *here*. To this land of evil." She eyed me up and down. "You were in a shipwreck."

"I—yes," I said, unsettled. "Robert told you."

"I knew it already. That shipwreck was no accident."

"What do you mean?" Tom said, scared. "There was a storm—"

"Yes," she said. "A storm. A storm that wasn't natural. A storm carried by the thing that hovers over your master. Can you not see it? The hollow black bird that sits even now upon his shoulder?"

My mouth worked, but I could barely get the words out. "You can *see* it?"

"It was the demon that called the storm," Sybil said. "It broke your ship and brought you to these shores. The demon clung to you, took your soul—your memories—and nearly took your life. Robert called me, and I saved you. But your salvation did not come without price."

She threw the holly into the cauldron. "It was the Spirits of the Wood who intervened. Takes more than these old bones to wrench your soul from a demon's talons, you see." She smiled, but there was no humor in her eyes. "The Spirits agreed to help, but only if I bound you with a *geas* in return."

My head reeled. Sweat trickled down my neck, ran down the back of my shirt. I had to grab Tom's arm to steady myself.

"I don't understand," Sally said. "What's a 'gesh'?"

I knew. Sybil had used the old Irish word, but in my broken memory, I knew. "It's a curse," I said. "A *geas* is a compulsion. A vow, forced upon someone through magic."

Sybil nodded. "You are remarkably well educated in such things, Baron. Now you will *feel* them."

"Why would the Spirits do this?" Tom said, horrified.

"Because your lord has something they need."

"What could he possibly have?" Sally said.

"Children are missing. The young baron here is the one that must find them. That is what the Spirits told me. It is him. And only him." She turned back to me. "That is your *geas*. Find the children. Find them, return them, and your curse will be lifted."

Tom raised his sword, and though his voice—and his hands—trembled, I think he really meant to use it. "Let him go."

She spat at his feet. "Do you threaten me, or the Spirits? Do you think your magic blade will cut them down? Then go ahead, servant. Kill me. Then no one will be left to release your master. He'll be lost forever."

"But *why*?" I said. "Why did they choose me? And how am I supposed to work without my memories?"

She shrugged. "I'm just the messenger. As for your memories, those are not important. You have everything you need—in fact, *only* you do. No one else who lives here can do what you can."

"I don't understand."

"Think about it," she said. "Think of all the people you've met since you awoke. And you will have the answer."

"But—"

"I have nothing more to say to you. The task the Spirits gave you is simple. Find out what's happening to the children. Then save them. Do this, and the Spirits have promised they'll return your memories. Fail, and not only will your past fade, so will your present. You'll forget how to read. You'll forget how to speak. You'll end up no smarter than a tree."

She laughed bitterly. "If that happens, my lord, come back to me. I'll plant you in my garden and water you. Until then? Get out."

CHAPTER
26

I COULDN'T STOP SHAKING.

I stood outside Sybil's hut, boots sunk into the snow. Sally had an arm around me, a hand on my chest. Bridget kept walking over my feet. Tom and Moppet stood silent and helpless.

And I couldn't stop shaking.

Lose my memories forever, I thought, and suddenly my stomach churned. I ran, stumbling, through the trees.

"Christopher!" Sally called.

I kept going. I heard the crunching snow under my heels, ragged breath in my ears, my voice in my head. *Lose my memories forever.*

My guts rebelled. I fell into the roots of a tree and vomited.

Then Sally was there. She knelt next to me, held me close. "Don't be afraid," she said. "We'll get you through this."

And Tom was there, too, hand on my back. Bridget landed on my shoulder, nuzzling at my hair. I took her and held her, and now I couldn't keep in the words.

"I'm going to lose everything," I said.

"You are not," Tom said. "We walked forever to find you. We won't let you go again."

"You heard what Sybil said."

"She said if you solve the puzzle, find the children, you'll get your memories back. So that's what you're going to do."

He had such utter confidence in me. All I felt was despair. "I can't."

"You can," Sally said. "In fact, you've already begun."

I didn't know what she meant.

"You recognized the blood mark was a word," she said. "It was your idea to go back to Robert's farm, and you found the mark everyone else had missed. And what happened in between? *You remembered the names of Tom's sisters.*"

I looked up at her.

"You've started searching for the children," Sally said,

"and your memories have started to come back. Just like the Spirits promised. All you have to do now is keep going."

I wanted to believe. But the question I'd asked Sybil still hung in my mind: How could I succeed without my memories?

You already have the tools you need, Master Benedict said.

What tools? I said. *I don't know anything. I can't even tell what this blood mark says.*

Who could?

His question made me pause.

None of the locals had recognized the mark was a word. Even Rawlin, who knew the entire story of the White Lady, had simply called it "the blood mark." I'd assumed Sybil, at least, would know it. But even she'd been surprised when I pointed it out.

I didn't think she was lying about that. At the very least, she did seem to genuinely want the children found, so if she knew what the word was, she'd have told me. And yet I recalled what she'd said. *You have everything you need—in fact,* only *you do. No one else who lives here can do what you can. Think of all the people you've met since you awoke. And you will have the answer.*

She knew *something* she wasn't telling me. And I couldn't understand why. *No one else who lives here can do what I can.* Tom thought that meant I was good at puzzles. But I couldn't shake the feeling Sybil had meant something else.

Think of all the people you've met since you awoke. And you will have the answer.

I did as she said. There was Robert and his family, Wise, Jane, and Moppet. Then there was Willoughby, his daughter, Captain Haddock, and Rawlin. In Crook's Hollow, John Morrow and his daughter. And then there was Sybil herself. Tom and Sally, too—in a way, I'd just met them as well.

Was one of these people behind the children's disappearance? Is that what Sybil had meant? If so, why not just tell me? Or better yet, do something about it herself? If the Spirits of the Wood could curse me with a *geas*, why not curse the actual villain instead?

I shook my head. I didn't know enough about spirit magic to figure that out.

Think of all the people you've met. . . .

Other than the fact that they were all locals—except for Tom and Sally, and maybe Moppet—I couldn't see the common thread between them. Robert was kind. Wise was a mute. Willoughby, servile. Haddock, self-serving. And so on, and so on.

This was getting me nowhere. And we had to go somewhere—literally. It wouldn't be long before dark. Returning to Seaton was probably our best option; there I could ask Rawlin if he knew someone who might decipher—

"Of course," I said.

"Of course what?" Tom said.

Rawlin had already given me the answer, last night. *Go see Baronet Darcy. He used to be a witchfinder.*

"The baronet," I said. "If he hunted witches, he's practiced in rooting out evil."

"I'd imagine so."

"So let's visit him. His estate is just north of here. Maybe he can decipher the blood word—and he can put us up for the night, too."

Tom frowned. "A baronet's home is not an inn. You can't just barge in and demand a bed."

"Actually, I can. But I won't need to. He'll offer one. In fact, he'll insist upon it."

"Why would he do that?"

"Because I'm a baron, remember? I outrank him."

. . .

Robert was right: The Darcy estate did look like a castle.
The house was surrounded by a thick stone wall, fifteen feet
high. The wall had seen better days; age had crumbled it
here and there, collapsing it completely to form a hole in
the stone twenty yards from the spiked iron gates. The gates
themselves were closed, which made it unconscionably rude
for us to use the gap in the wall, but we did so anyway. It
was getting dark, and we were cold, and I'd rather beg a
baronet's forgiveness than freeze to death.

Lanterns hung outside the entrance, illuminating
the house with gentle flames. Shadows danced over the
stonework, and above it all stood the most impressive fea-
ture: the tower. It rose two floors higher than the rest of
the building, the torches overhead turning it into a land-
locked lighthouse, pushing back against the encroaching
night.

But it was too cold to stand around admiring the view.
Tom thumped on the heavy doors and waited. After a second pounding, we were greeted by a prim-faced steward
who seemed annoyed that we'd roused him. His expression
grew even more cross as he looked at Tom, with Moppet
sitting on his shoulders, and me and Sally beside him. No

doubt he thought we were beggars. I don't think it helped that I was holding a pigeon.

"Can I assist you?" he said, sounding certain he couldn't.

"Inform Baronet Darcy," I said in my haughtiest voice, "that the Baron Ashcombe is here, with the Lady Grace."

The steward balked. I understood his hesitation: We'd arrived without announcement, without a coach, without an entourage. We were more likely to be criminals than lords.

I worried he might refuse us, but discretion won out. It would be worse to insult a lord than let in a thief. "Of course," he said, and he led us into the warmth.

The entrance hall took my breath away. It was eighty feet long, and three stories high, the upper story painted with a mural of the assassination of Julius Caesar. The ceiling was painted, too, a window into heaven: cherubim and seraphim flying through puffy white clouds, God sitting above them all on His radiant throne. Below our feet, black-and-white stone stretched away, with a dozen other paintings, sculptures, and busts arrayed on the path to the staircase, rich red carpet over Italian marble.

I tried not to gawk—Baron Ashcombe wouldn't—as the steward took our coats and bade Sally and me wait in the drawing room. As our retainer, Tom would have to retire to the servants' wing. Moppet—who stared at the wealth around her like it was the king's own palace—naturally went with him. I gave her Bridget to hold on to as well.

"Make sure my man is well fed," I said, as superior as I could. Tom threw me a grateful look.

"Of course, my lord," the steward said, and he installed us in the drawing room before going to get the baronet. He should have brought us refreshments, but he didn't; apparently, I'd locked myself into a battle of bad manners with the Darcys' steward.

I tried to decide—would Baron Ashcombe chastise him?—until I saw Sally's arched eyebrow.

"If you're finished playing," she whispered.

"Just acting the part," I said, face growing hot.

We waited, with little to do but admire the room's décor: masterwork paintings and Oriental rugs, silver curios and velvet chairs; and we waited so long I began to think something was happening here that went beyond mere rudeness.

A baronetcy was the lowest titled rank in the kingdom— low enough, in fact, that baronets were not considered part of the peerage. Despite their title, baronets were commoners, ranked just above knights, and to be addressed as "sir," not "my lord." Baronet Darcy might rate higher than any of the local folk, but even given that our visit was unannounced, it was unacceptable for him to make us wait. I began to get nervous—had I got something wrong?—until the baronet entered. Then I saw the cause of the delay.

The man could barely walk. His round face, pale and sweating, screwed up in pain every time his right foot touched the ground—which it mostly didn't, as a tall, burly, finely dressed man with long, curly black hair kept his arm around him, so the baronet could lean on him like a crutch.

Baronet Darcy smiled through the pain. "Welcome, Baron," he boomed, his voice rich and full. "It's so good to see you—"

He stopped, leaning heavily on the man at his side. He looked around the room. "Pardon me, my lady," he said to Sally, "but where did the baron go?"

Had my *geas* rendered me invisible, too? "I'm Baron Ashcombe," I said.

He looked at me and frowned. "No, you're not."

CHAPTER
27

SALLY AND I FROZE. IF WE WERE discovered playing at nobility, it would be the hangman's noose for all of us.

No, I thought. *We have the king's permission. Lord Ashcombe will vouch for me.*

Except Lord Ashcombe was at least a fortnight away. If Baronet Darcy took matters into his own hands . . .

Begging for mercy would fail, I knew. And the true explanation would sound outlandish. No, the only way forward was boldness.

I squared up to him. "I beg your pardon?"

My attitude flustered him. "Young sir . . . Baron

Ashcombe is the King's Warden. I've met the man."

Now I understood. My heart slowed as I explained what Sally had told me. "You mean my grandfather, Richard. He's the marquess now. I inherited my title this summer."

"Oh." He turned beet red. "Oh my goodness. I'm so very sorry. Out here—I hadn't heard—"

"Quite all right," I said, and in truth, as my heart stopped racing, I was delighted he'd made such an error. It would make him far less likely to question any future mistakes I might make. Plus, he'd be considerably more eager to help me.

Though, at the moment, he was the one in need of assistance. He'd gone pale again, and not because he was embarrassed. "Are you all right?" I said.

"Of course, of course." He tried to smile; it came out as a grimace. "Just a small problem with my foot. A touch of gout."

I answered without thinking. "You should take off your boot. Have your servants bring lemon juice, and if you have natron, stir in a spoonful and drink it. Also, if you can get them, soak your foot in the salts rendered from Epsom's springs."

He looked somewhat startled. "My goodness, Baron. You know a remarkable amount about treating gout."

Uh . . .

Sally recovered for me. "His father had a steward who suffered from it. Christopher was very fond of him."

"Of course, of course. Well, I'm most grateful for your advice. Apothecaries are—ah!—scarce around these parts. Please, sit. We were about to go to table for dinner. I do hope you'll join us?"

He hoped correctly. The day had left me famished.

"Cooper!"

The steward entered.

"Set two more places for dinner. And where's Julian?"

"Just returned, sir," the steward said.

"Tell him to join us." The steward left as his master was taken over to the couch. "Julian is my son," the baronet said. Then he paused. "Oh, look at me. I haven't even introduced myself. Lady Grace"—he attempted an awkward one-footed bow—"and Baron Ashcombe—Christopher, was it?"

I nodded.

"I am Edmund Darcy. This quiet fellow"—he indicated the curly-haired man helping him sit—"was once my sharpest assistant, now my greatest friend. Álvaro Arias. He's come to visit, all the way from the Continent. To my shame, I've reduced him to a crutch."

Álvaro bowed to us with grace. "Don't be ridiculous, Edmund." I caught an accent, Spanish. "That's what friends are for," he said, and I couldn't help but think of Tom.

He knelt to pull off Sir Edmund's boot. The baronet sweated as Álvaro yanked at his heel. "So, Baron, what brings you to . . ." He trailed off as his eyes rolled back in his head, and, finally, he passed out.

Sir Edmund sagged as Álvaro held him in the chair, shouting for the steward. Sally and I rose immediately to help. As we did, I could see why he'd lost consciousness. His gout was shocking. His foot was so red and swollen I didn't understand how they'd got the boot on him in the first place. The agony must have been unbearable.

Cooper hurried in, followed by a pair of servants carrying mulled wine and pastries. "Bring some snow," I commanded them.

Álvaro propped Sir Edmund up; Sally fanned his face. When he awoke, he was beyond embarrassed. "What a welcome," he said.

"Think nothing of it." I caught myself before saying *I'm used to such things*, though somewhere, in the back of my mind, I thought, *I* am *used to such things*.

I stopped. I pressed ever so lightly on the memory; it

made me dizzy. I pulled back before I passed out, too, but before I relaxed, I caught an image. I was caring for . . . some old man? He . . . also had gout?

Trying to remember made the world swim. I had to let the image go. But my pulse quickened. *My memories: I think they're coming back. Just like Sybil promised.*

The servants returned with a bowl full of snow. Álvaro was trying to get Sir Edmund to sip from the wine. "Press the snow to your face," I said. "You'll feel much better."

He did, apologizing so much it became boring. "So," he said finally, "to what do I owe the pleasure of your arrival?"

Sally told him about our visit to Paris—painting it as a trip to see distant cousins—and then explained we'd been in a shipwreck, washing up on shore.

Álvaro was amazed. "You survived *that* storm? *Madre de Dios.*" He made the sign of the cross. "The saints are watching over you."

"Does your grandfather know what's happened?" Sir Edmund said. "We should send word."

"I've already done that," I said. "Though it'll be a couple of weeks before I hear from him."

"That soon? In this snow?"

"I hired a ship."

"Oh. Clever. Well, I'm sorry for your troubles, but I'm delighted you've come. Please, Baron, it would be an honor if you would consider my home as yours for the duration of your stay. Did I tell you I met your grandfather once?"

He had, but he seemed particularly proud of it, so I let him continue.

"It was after His Majesty's glorious return to the throne. King Charles granted me my baronetcy, and I had occasion to talk with the baron—sorry, the marquess—about the merits of the cavalry charge."

I knew nothing about the merits of the cavalry charge, other than that trampling someone with a horse while chopping off their head sounded rather effective. I got the feeling that the real Baron Ashcombe would know much more about it than me, so I changed the subject.

The baronet's comment about the king reminded me of what Moppet had whispered in our room last night. "What do you know about Puritans?"

He seemed surprised by the tangent. "Quite a bit, actually. I had occasion to deal with several during the Interregnum."

"Have there been Puritan troubles around here?"

"Lately? Not that I've heard. Devonshire has been

peaceful since the fall of the Commonwealth. Is something going on?" he said, curious.

My answer was cut off by a boy of around sixteen entering the drawing room; Baronet Darcy's son, Julian. He had a round, ruddy face like his father's, cheeks still reddened by the cold. His boots left wet prints on the marble behind him.

"Father!" he said, his voice high, his words rushed, excited. "I shot a deer—" He spotted us. "Oh! Hello."

Sir Edmund introduced us. Julian lit up when he heard my name. "Ashcombe? Like Richard Ashcombe?" He stared at me with awe.

"My son will have many questions for you. But not *too* many," Sir Edmund said to the boy, with a chiding look. "Julian will escort you to table. I'll be along in a moment."

Slowly, Álvaro helped Sir Edmund to his feet. As commanded, Julian led us to the dining hall.

"My father thinks I talk too much," he said cheerfully. "What's it like, being the King's Warden's grandson?"

"It's—"

"I bet you're good with a sword. Are you good with a sword? I want to learn, but my father won't let me. He says fighting's for common folk."

I thought of pointing out that, as a baronet, his father *was* common folk. I let it pass. "I've—"

"Oh! Could you teach me? The sword, I mean. I want to fight for the king, like your grandfather. I bet you'll get to do that, too. I want to become a knight. It's nice here, but I don't really have any friends. I want to see the world."

The way he changed subjects made my head spin. Talking to him was like having a conversation with a butterfly.

"My father had adventures once," Julian continued. "He lived in Essex. That's where I was born. Oh!"

He stopped and pointed to a doorway, the upper stones rounded in an arch. Beyond it, I could see a spiral staircase leading upward.

"That's the tower," Julian said. "Have you been up yet? You can see for miles around. Though we're not close enough to see the ocean. Can you believe I've never even been on a boat? You can't take a boat along the river, it's too shallow, but the ocean's so close—I mean, not close enough to see, but it's close—I should have been on a boat by now, don't you think? So will you?"

I blinked. "Will I what?"

"Teach me the sword. We have a whole bunch in the armory. We could have a lesson now!"

"Um . . . I think your father wanted us at dinner."

"Oh. Right. After, then?"

I was beginning to wonder if I could fake using a sword when Sally saved me. "Why don't you have your man Tom teach him?" she said. "Tom was trained by Sir William Leech himself."

"Really? Sir William Leech?" Julian sounded impressed. "Who's that?"

"A . . . very good swordsman," she said.

He seemed overjoyed at the idea. He rattled on about— well, many things; I couldn't keep up. He was an odd sort of fellow, like a little boy trapped in a young man's body, and I found talking to him a bit unsettling. At the same time, I began to feel sorry for him. It was clear he was painfully lonely.

Still, I was relieved when his father finally arrived. Sir Edmund hobbled in, Álvaro holding him so his foot wouldn't touch the ground. Seeing the friendship the Spaniard offered made me think of Tom again, and that made me even sadder for poor Julian, living here all alone.

"Christopher's man is going to teach me the sword," he said proudly.

His father gave me an embarrassed glance—and not, I

suspected, just because his son had used my name instead of my title. "I see. Now, Julian, go call Cooper and have dinner brought in, won't you?"

The boy bounded away. Once he'd left the room, Sir Edmund said, "My apologies, my lord. Julian gets ideas in his head. I promise, he won't trouble you during your stay. He mostly likes to wander the countryside, anyway, hunting and exploring, visiting with the villagers. I'll make sure he's not a bother."

"It's all right," I said, though I wondered how I'd survive a fortnight's worth of Julian's enthusiasm. "I was just as excited to learn the sword."

"Ah. Yes." Sir Edmund shifted uncomfortably. "Then I'll definitely keep him out of your hair. I'd rather not go giving him ideas; next thing I know he'll have up and joined the army." He sighed. "I suppose all children dream of adventure. I did, once, too. But with that excitement comes a darkness, and, well . . . Julian's not meant for such things."

His talk of darkness seemed to carry a great weight behind the words. I itched to ask him about his days as a witch-hunter—and more important, about the blood mark—but Julian bounded back into the room, servants carrying our dinner behind him, and I knew I'd have to wait until the meal had finished. Talk of witches and blood was too vulgar for a baronet's table.

Sir Edmund spoke a lot during the meal, in part, I think, to quell his son's incessant questions. Álvaro ate in silence, letting Sir Edmund do the entertaining—which the baronet was clearly eager to do. He told me a little about the area, but he was far more keen to steer the topic to my supposed grandfather. He seemed rather excited at the prospect of the King's Warden visiting his home.

He's eager for the prestige, I realized. He kept dropping names: Lord Ashcombe, the Duke of York, the king. And though the furnishings, the clothing, the silver settings that surrounded us already displayed his wealth, he kept slipping in statements of how rare this particular painting hanging behind us was, or in what exotic land the goblets on the table had been made.

I remembered what he'd said earlier, about his baronetcy. It wasn't hereditary; he'd got it—most likely bought it—from the king five years ago. *He didn't grow up with money,* I thought. *Or status. But he likes it.*

He will want something from you, my master said. *Your presence is an opportunity for him.*

If he planned to use me to ingratiate himself with

Lord Ashcombe, he was going to be sorely disappointed. For the moment, however, this would be useful: I could ask quite a bit of the man, with the promise of favors to be returned in kind. I waited, my patience strained, until the meal wound down and he asked what I thought of Devonshire.

Finally. "It's beautiful," I said, "and the people are as kind as any I've met. Though your troubles have come to my attention."

"Troubles?"

"With the children."

Sir Edmund looked at me blankly.

"The children?" I said. "The missing children?"

Sir Edmund looked over at Álvaro. His friend seemed just as puzzled. "Children are missing?" Álvaro said.

I remembered the way Sybil had sneered, spitting my title back at me. I began to understand her reaction. Here was the wealthiest man in the county, living in comfort, trying to worm his way into the peerage—yet oblivious to the trouble outside his own gates.

"We've heard nothing of this," Sir Edmund said. "Julian? Do you know of any missing children?"

Julian nodded. "Little Jack disappeared from Kingston

Osdale. I helped look for him, but there was nothing we could do. He fell into the river."

"How do you know that?" I said.

"His tracks through the snow. They went straight to the water's edge. He must have slipped on a rock and drowned."

Exactly what I'd thought, before I'd seen the blood marks. "Did they find his body?"

"No."

"Then he didn't drown."

Sir Edmund looked at me curiously. "Why do you say that?"

"Because it's not just Little Jack that's missing. It's Emma Lisle from Robert Dryden's farm, and Allan Cavill's boy from Crook's Hollow, and at least two others. Something's taking them."

"Some . . . *thing*? Do you mean an animal? There are wild dogs about."

"Not an animal," I said. "The villagers claim it's the White Lady."

The room went quiet. Sir Edmund and Álvaro glanced at each other. Julian studied his plate.

"What have they seen?" Álvaro said.

"A light, at night. And I found a blood mark at two of

the sites, and I bet if we went to the others, we'd find the same mark there."

"This blood mark," Sir Edmund said. "What does it look like? Some kind of symbol?"

"It's a word."

He looked startled. "A word?"

"I've made out some of the letters. But I can't quite figure out what it says."

I pulled the cloth from beneath my sash and pushed it over to Sir Edmund. The baronet looked at it, as if unsure what to do. Then he unfolded it.

And he gasped.

CHAPTER
28

SIR EDMUND JERKED BACK FROM
the table. His chair toppled, and he went with it. Though
clearly in pain, he slid himself backward on the rug, eyes
wide.

Álvaro sprang to his feet, his own chair tipping, rattling against the stone. He gripped his knife, looking from
the blood mark to me. In his eyes was a silent, merciless
threat.

I rose. Sally grabbed my arm, fingers squeezing my
wrist. We stared, Álvaro and I, at each other across the
table. Julian remained seated, looking at his plate as if there
was no other thing in the world.

"Stop!" Sir Edmund shouted from the floor. "Everyone stop. Álvaro. Álvaro!"

The Spaniard turned his head toward Sir Edmund but kept his eyes on me.

"Help me up, please," Sir Edmund said.

Álvaro seemed to weigh something in his mind. Slowly, he placed the knife on the table. Then he went to Sir Edmund and lifted him to his feet.

"It's all right," Sir Edmund said, wincing. "I was just startled." He nodded toward the blood mark. "You don't have any idea what that is, do you?"

"I told you," I said, "that I know it's a word. But I can't decipher it."

"Then count yourself blessed, my lord. Because if you *had* deciphered it, you'd have placed your soul in eternal peril."

"You can read it?" Sally said.

He nodded and motioned to Álvaro. "We've seen it before. It's not merely a word. It's a name. It's the signature of Leviathan, the beast of the water."

Now I could make it out. What I'd thought was an elongated *S* was actually a lowercase *l*. The loop with a tail was an *e*, not an *o*. Then *v*, and *i*, and the rest. Leviathan.

The serpent, rising from the sea to devour God's creation.

And still Álvaro stared at me like I was his prey. Sir Edmund patted his arm. "There'll be no need for that, old friend. Lord Ashcombe is fine. Get the poker. From the hearth. It's all right."

The Spaniard hesitated, but he did as Sir Edmund asked. He slipped the poker under the cloth, lifting it from the table.

"What are you doing?" I said.

"Burning it," Sir Edmund said.

I started to object—I might need to study that blood mark yet—but the look in Álvaro's eyes told me not to argue. Careful not to bring it near anyone, he swung the poker into the fire. The wool shriveled on the logs, crisped in the heat, turned to ash.

"Before I was awarded my baronetcy," Sir Edmund said, "I used to be a witchfinder."

"That's why I came to you," I said, still wary under Álvaro's gaze. "I'd hoped you'd be able to tell me what the word said. More important, what it meant."

"Evil," he said. "It means evil." He sighed. "There is a great deal of it in these hills. I didn't know that when I made my home here. I thought I'd left all that behind."

He stared into the fire, watching the wool burn. Then he spoke. "Julian. Go to your rooms."

I thought Julian might object, but he didn't. He stood, not meeting anyone's eyes, and left.

"Come with me," Sir Edmund said. "I have something to show you."

Álvaro took his arm, and we made our way through the halls to the baronet's study. Álvaro led Sir Edmund to a chair, but the baronet steered them past it to the desk, its drawers and cabinets carved with ornate, lifelike leaves.

"You'll find this interesting, Baron," Sir Edmund said. He pulled out a small, purple leather bag from the center drawer and held it out to me.

I reached for it, expecting him to hand me the bag.

Instead, at the last second, he turned it upside down and dropped what was inside onto my palm.

It was a light, knobbly cylinder, not quite an inch long and dusky brown. It took me a moment to realize what I held.

"It's a bone," I said.

"Yes," Sir Edmund said, relieved. "A finger bone of Saint Benedict, patron against demons. My most prized possession."

I looked up and saw Álvaro had finally relaxed. And I understood what Sir Edmund had just done.

"This was a test." I held up the bone. "You gave this to me deliberately. You were testing me."

"Evil often recoils at the touch of the sacred." He took the bone from me with delicate fingers and placed it back in the bag. "I apologize, Baron; I meant no insult. But you are clearly unaware of the danger to which you subjected yourself when you copied that signature."

"I didn't know that's what it was."

"That's no salvation. Evil takes hold most easily when it remains in the shadows." He motioned for us to sit. "Like the witch in the woods to the south."

"You mean Sybil O'Malley," I said.

"You know of her?"

"I went to her hut."

Sir Edmund looked horrified. "Why would you go there?"

After their reaction to the blood mark, I certainly wasn't going to tell them I'd lost my memories. "I've been investigating what happened to the missing children. A man in Seaton claimed Sybil was the cause of it."

"A likely suspicion. Young children are frequent victims of witches. Their blood is of great use in dark magic. And their fat is an ingredient in the flying ointment." He shifted in his chair. "You mentioned the White Lady earlier. An alliance between them would benefit both. Sybil O'Malley gets the body, the White Lady takes the soul."

The thought of it made me shudder. "Sybil claims she isn't responsible. She says she's not even a witch."

"And you believe her? My lord . . ."

"Speak plainly, Sir Edmund."

He did. "You have no idea of the forces you are investigating. Your grandfather may have trained you in the arts of combat, but those are only useful against earthly foes. You are now dealing with the world of spirits. A thousand mortal swords couldn't protect you.

"Álvaro and I spent our lives fighting them, and barely did we survive. Your aim is noble, but—forgive me—your naiveté will cost you far more than your life. The notion that Sybil is innocent is absurd."

I wasn't sure I disagreed. "Do you remember Robert Dryden?"

"Dryden? Oh—yes," he said. "He came for help when his cows fell ill, I think. I gave him some money."

"He claims Sybil only uses white magic, to help people."

Álvaro scoffed.

"With respect, my lord," Sir Edmund said, "what would he know of it? *All* magic is black. The very power of it corrupts the soul. Common people often treat with witches, thinking them mere 'cunning folk.' It only gives them the opportunity to work their spells with their victim's permission. They'll all turn on you, in the end."

I remembered what Sybil had said, her words bitter. *They come for my help when the sickness fills their chests, then come for my head when the rot takes their crops.*

"Robert Dryden," Sir Edmund continued, "may mean well, but all he's doing is placing his soul at risk. I hunted witches for years—studied under Matthew Hopkins, the Witchfinder General himself—and they are the most deceptive of sorts."

"I heard about the witch trials," Sally said. "Weren't many of the claims false?"

"*Most* of them were. That's part of why fighting witches is so difficult. Their craft is tricky to ascertain. Sometimes people are frightened, and they confuse normal events with black magic. Others are malicious, using the courts to inflict pain on those they dislike. There were a thousand trials before the Interregnum. Five hundred of them resulted in conviction. I believe that number is too high by at least double—if not more."

"But then . . . you're talking about hundreds of innocent women put to death."

"Not just women. A great number of the convicted were men. But, yes, I believe hundreds of innocents were executed."

Sally's face darkened. Sir Edmund put up a hand. "I share your anger, my lady. Too many of those who pressed claims of magic had neither the knowledge nor the temperament to be witchfinders. But I promise you, no innocent creature ever went to her death when *I* was at trial.

I investigated forty-seven cases, and only found eleven in league with evil. A proportion far smaller than others."

"What happened to them?"

"Hanged, of course."

"How could you know they were guilty?"

"I have a method of discovery that is foolproof."

"A bone dropped in the hand?" I said.

He flushed. "No, my lord. Much more worthy. If you indulge me a moment, I'll show you."

CHAPTER
29

SIR EDMUND STOOD. WITH ÁLVARO'S help, he made his way back to the desk.

"What do you know of tests for witches?" he asked.

"Nothing," I said.

"Well, there are several of them. Many of the simpler tests require contact between the accused witch and one of her victims: If a person ensorcelled is touched by the witch, the spell will break. So investigators might bring someone having fits to the trial, then force the witch to lay a hand on them. If the fits stop, then this is proof that the witch cast the spell, and she will be found guilty."

"What if the 'victim' is faking?" Sally said. "Couldn't

they just pretend to have a fit until the accused touches them?"

"Yes," Sir Edmund said. "Which is why I never used a touch test of any kind. There are other, similar examples, but I rejected them, too, as none of them satisfied me as unfalsifiable. No, there are only two tests I know of that cannot be faked.

"The first is called dunking. The accused is stripped, tied with each hand to the opposite foot, and thrown into water. If they are innocent—well, no one can swim when so bound, so they will sink to the bottom. If they are evil, however, then the water, in its purity, will reject them. In other words, the witch will float. If this happens, the accused is proven to be a witch, and will be hanged."

Sally looked appalled. "But if they're innocent—"

"They'll drown, yes. It's an effective test, but a cruel one, for it condemns the innocent and guilty alike. Many courts have outlawed it for just this reason. Certainly, I never employed it, and fought against its use wherever I could. It was only the second kind of test that I performed."

He reached into the drawer that held the bag with Saint Benedict's finger bone. This time, he brought out an engraved, jeweled silver box. Álvaro helped him hobble back to us, where Sir Edmund rested with obvious relief in his chair.

"When a woman becomes a witch," he said, "she gains a familiar: a demon who comes to her in the shape of an animal, often a cat. To seal their pact, the familiar feeds on the witch's blood. Where the demon feeds, its polluting evil creates a mark—a witch's mark—on the body. This mark will be darker than the surrounding skin, and it has the curious property that it cannot feel pain, and will not bleed except when fed upon by the familiar. It is from this fact that we define what is, in my opinion, the only worthy test of a witch."

Sir Edmund opened the box. "It is known as pricking. A witch is examined by a physician for possible witch's marks. Once the physician has ruled out all natural blemishes, the questionable ones are tested with this."

He pulled out a silver cylinder around three inches long. It was hexagonal in shape, with small circles engraved along each side. At one end was a finely detailed silver crown, with six crosses fused to the metal below it. At its other end was a needle, an inch in length.

Carefully, almost reverently, Sir Edmund handed it to me. "This is a pricking needle," he said. "And it is utterly infallible. You place the needle's point against the mark you wish to test, and plunge it in. If the accused is innocent, the pain will be agonizing, and the wound will bleed. But if they are a witch, then the needle will cause no pain, and there will be no blood. Pain, of course, could be faked. But no bleeding? After being stuck with this? Impossible."

I turned it over in my hands. The needle glinted in the light. A curious sensation came over me: a *desire* to use it, to test it against some witch, to prove their wickedness—

"You feel it," Sir Edmund said.

I looked up and found him gazing back at me, eyes alight.

"That needle," he said. "Its blessing. You feel it, don't you?"

The silver, warmed by my touch, seemed alive under my skin. Was I imagining it? Or could I really feel its power?

"May I see it?" Sally said.

I handed it to her, not really wanting to let it go. She studied it, gripped it like I had. Then she placed the needle against her palm.

Sir Edmund started. "Do be careful, my lady. The tip is incredibly—"

She pressed the needle in. Her eyes widened, and she gasped as it slipped into her skin.

"—sharp."

Álvaro snatched the needle away. A dot of blood swelled in Sally's palm.

The baronet called the steward for a cloth. "I'm dreadfully sorry, my lady. I should have warned you."

That wouldn't have made a difference. She'd stuck herself with the point deliberately. I looked at her, but she wouldn't meet my eyes.

"I hope your fears are put to rest, at least," Sir Edmund said to her. "This needle permits no errors. No frightened farmers, no petty grievances could fake this pure and public test. And I performed the test myself, so none could attempt trickery by sleight of hand. Not even Álvaro, whom I trust beyond measure, was allowed to handle it."

Sally pressed the cloth into her palm to stop the bleeding.

"Have you tested that needle on Sybil?" I said.

"She will hardly consent to its use without a trial," Sir Edmund said.

"Why not arrange one?"

"I can't. The assizes will no longer sit for witch trials. They now require a confession to bring someone to court. Which misses the point entirely!" he huffed. "And as you can see"—he waved at his gout-addled foot—"I am in no condition for a trial. I told you before that the darkness finds its way into you. This is how it has cursed me. And because of my infirmity—and the cowardice of the assizes—Sybil O'Malley summons the White Lady to do her bidding. And evil walks the land again."

"If you were able," I said, "how would you stop her?"

He thought about it. "It would have been easiest to have condemned the witch before her summoning. But with the White Lady already freed, that is no longer sufficient. At this point, you'd have to destroy the wraith herself."

I shivered. "How can you destroy a ghost?"

"By understanding their nature. Ghosts are not a natural part of this world; they belong to the hereafter. For a spirit to remain, something must bind it to the mortal plane. This is usually accomplished via some artifact of the ghost's earthly trauma. Something meaningful to the White Lady when she was still alive."

"What would that be?" Sally asked.

Sir Edmund shrugged. "There's no way to know. It could be anything: a piece of jewelry, a beloved possession, a favored garment worn at the time of death."

"How would you find it?" I said.

"You would feel it. If you got close enough, it would radiate evil. Your body would rebel with terror. Only the stoutest of hearts could even approach it."

"And then what?"

"Burn it. Cast it into fire hot enough to melt steel. But you'd have a much larger problem before that. Touching the artifact will summon the spirit. That's probably what the witch used to bind her to her power in the first place. So if you found the item, you'd have to find some way to evade the wraith as well. And, of course, you'd be in the lion's den, so to speak; the artifact would most likely be found near the source of her misery."

I recalled what Rawlin had said. "That would be the abandoned village. Hook Reddale."

Sir Edmund paled. "A terrible place. I went there once—at least, I tried. I couldn't even approach it. I tell you, Baron, I've faced a dozen screaming witches, each promising eternal torment, each with the power to provide it. I stood against them all. But the terror I felt when I approached that village . . . it frightened me in a way nothing has before."

His story made my stomach flutter. I understood now why the Spirits of the Wood had bound me in their *geas*. How desperately I wished to give up this insane quest, to go home and never return. If I could have, I would have. And when I remembered the missing children, my wish filled me with shame.

"So," I said. "You know where Hook Reddale is."

He nodded. "I was able to discover its location by matching the clues in the story to the land. All you need to do is follow—"

Suddenly he stopped. "Why are you asking this?"

Because I have no choice. "Children are missing, Sir Edmund."

"And you mean to rescue them."

"If I can."

"You can't. Have you not been listening? You are wholly unprepared to fight this kind of evil. Even I would not face it."

"I wouldn't have to go alone," I said. "My man has a holy sword, handed down from knights of ancient blessing. And while I understand your affliction keeps you bound here, perhaps Señor Arias would be willing to—"

"No," Álvaro said. For the first time since I'd met him, he looked scared. "Listen to Edmund. This is not a place for you."

Sir Edmund shook his head in agreement. "I cannot permit it."

I felt foolish arguing—I didn't even want to go. None-theless, I let my voice go cold. *You are the blood of Richard Ashcombe,* I reminded myself. *You do not require his permission.* "You seek to command me . . . *sir?*"

Sir Edmund flushed. "Of course not, my lord. But you are my guest. I cannot, *will* not, send you to your doom. What would I tell your grandfather when he came looking for you? He would side with me, I think. If he does not, well, then it is for *him* to take responsibility."

He sighed. "Please, I wish for us to be friends. My home, my grounds, my things are all yours, for however long you remain. But I cannot countenance any expedition to that cursed village. I beg you, my lord: Ask me no more."

CHAPTER
30

SIR EDMUND DID HIS BEST TO
lighten the mood after our argument, but there wasn't
much I was interested in hearing. I pleaded weariness from
a long journey, and he apologized for keeping me up. He
had Cooper show us to our rooms and apologized once
more for the dark turn the evening had taken.

"Think nothing of it," I said. "It was improper of me to
press you as I did."

Cooper installed me in my quarters. Part of me—most
of me, really—wished I could just stay here. The room was
lavishly comfortable, appointed in damask and brocade. The
bed, seven feet wide, was soft and inviting, drawn round by

Oriental water-lily curtains. And I hadn't been lying: I *did* wish for sleep. But I had work to do.

Poking my head out the door to see the hall was empty, I snuck down to Sally's bedroom. She let me in, frowning. "If anyone catches you here," she said, "we'll be the source of endless gossip."

I knew I should care about that, but I didn't. I was stuck in the middle of nowhere, playing a role that didn't fit me, with a mind that didn't even remember who I was. I barely felt like I was real.

"What do you think?" I said. "About Sybil being a witch?"

Sally chewed her fingernail. "I don't know." I was a bit surprised at her reticence; downstairs, she'd pressed the man stronger than I had. "She said she wasn't."

"She's not likely to confess it, though, is she? Especially if she's really behind all this."

"No, but . . ." She trailed off again.

"What's going on?" I said.

Sally's eyes flicked toward me. It seemed like she wanted to tell me something. Her room had a pair of high-backed cushioned chairs by the fireplace; I sat on one and waited.

She took the chair opposite. We remained for a while

in silence, until she finally pulled her hand from her mouth and looked ruefully at her fingers.

"I've completely destroyed my nails," she said.

She laughed a little, but it was forced. I just waited. And when she spoke again, there was no humor in her voice.

"There was a girl," she said. "In Cripplegate. Alice Goodall. She was a few years older than me. She was beautiful. All the girls looked up to her, and the nurses thought she was God's little angel. She might as well have been the queen. And she hated me."

"Why?"

Sally shrugged. "Because I was half French? Because I was new? Because I was different?" She stayed like that, wondering, and realizing, maybe, that she'd never really know. "Alice tormented me. She'd bring me in, let me be part of her circle. Treat me like I was her friend, even her confidante. Then she'd be cruel to me. She'd shut me out, make the rest of the girls not talk to me.

"You and I met during one of those times. I had the flux, but none of my 'friends' would visit me. The nurses assigned you to care for me. You made me—"

soup, I thought

"—soup."

My chest tightened. I'd remembered.

"Anyway," Sally continued, "she did this over and over. I was always afraid—each day, I didn't know if she was going to be kind or cruel. I think she liked that best of all."

Sally trailed off, lost in her memories. "One night, it became different. Alice and I were supposedly friends again. I was in bed, drifting off to sleep, when suddenly she was standing over me. She leaned down and whispered, 'I know what you are.'

"I didn't know what she meant, and I said so. So she said, 'I figured it out. You're a witch.'

"I just froze. The nurses had told us about the witch-hunts. How so many girls had been caught up in wicked-ness, and hanged for it, and how we should run from the promises of black magic. And here this girl was, this angel, promising to tell everyone I was a witch. And I knew if she did, they'd believe her. She'd *make* them believe her."

"You were children," I said. "No one would have taken her seriously."

"Are you sure? It was Reverend Glennon who told me, later, how many innocent girls—not just women, but girls—had been executed by outright lies. I was so scared,

Christopher. Alice never threatened me with it again. But I remember. I always remember."

She drew a breath. "I was innocent. What if Sybil is, too?"

I had my own doubts. And yet . . . "There *is* black magic happening here. The children are proof of that."

"That doesn't mean Sybil's responsible for it."

But she did lie, Master Benedict said.

About being a witch? I said.

About you.

I frowned. What did he mean?

"Christopher?"

Sally was looking at me strangely. I held up a hand. What had Sybil said about me?

You have everything you need—in fact, only you do. No one else who lives here can do what you can.

Not that, Master Benedict said.

Then what else did she say?

Think of it this way, my master said. *What* didn't *she say?*

Now he was being utterly cryptic. How was I supposed to know what she didn't say?

Think, Master Benedict whispered.

So I did. *I told Sybil who I was. She said she knew. I told her what had happened to me. We talked about the missing children, and I showed her the mark. She refused—*

The strangest image came to me then. A man . . . in a bird mask?

My chest tightened—*the Raven!*—but it wasn't, and somewhere inside, I knew it wasn't. I clung to the image, fighting off the dizziness that threatened to overwhelm me, until I saw the man clearly.

He wore a wide-brimmed hat and a long leather robe with some kind of insignia on his chest—a cross? A triangle?—I couldn't quite make it out. He held a silver rod. At the end of it was a grinning gargoyle's head, its wings spread in flight. But it was that mask, that leather mask, that I couldn't take my eyes off.

It's not the Raven, I thought. *It's a—*

Plague doctor. The man was wearing a plague doctor costume.

So why did it make me afraid?

"Do I know a plague doctor?" I asked Sally.

She went white. "Why?"

"For some reason, I see him in my head. He's wearing a bird mask, and he has some kind of staff—"

"That's Melchior." Sally shuddered as she told me his

story, what had happened between us during the plague.

I frowned. I felt like there was a puzzle being worked on in my head—and somehow this strange bird man was the answer. If only I could just *remember*.

Hold on to that feeling, Master Benedict said, *and think of Sybil. Where is the lie?*

What the plague doctor evoked was fear. What did he have to do with the cunning woman? I returned to my memory of the hut.

Sybil refused to tell me what she knew about the missing children. I got angry with her, and she got angry back—

That was it.

"Sybil," I said slowly, "said the Spirits of the Wood told her I was the only one who could find the children."

"Because you've solved problems like it before," Sally said.

"How did she know that?"

"The Spirits must have told her."

"Then why didn't she know who I was?"

"What do you mean?" Sally said.

"Remember how she kept sneering at me? The way she said 'my lord'? She hates the nobility."

"So?"

"So I'm *not* nobility. I'm just pretending to be. If the

Spirits told her what I'd done, who I was . . . why didn't she know I wasn't an Ashcombe?"

Now Sally paused, too. She didn't have an answer.

Neither did I. That was the most puzzling thing. Sybil had been adamant she wasn't a witch. She'd been equally adamant that I, and I alone, could solve this mystery. But she'd also thought I was Baron Ashcombe. So . . . was the *geas* a mistake? Could the Spirits even *make* a mistake?

There was something else going on here, something strange. And why was I seeing this Melchior?

Think about it, she'd said. *Think of all the people you've met since you awoke. And you will have the answer.*

The solution was there. It had to be in there.

But I couldn't find it.

"What do you want to do?" Sally said.

I couldn't tell who was right. Sir Edmund? Sybil? Neither? I pushed my thoughts aside, frustrated. At the moment, that didn't really matter. The White Lady. *She* was the one we really had to stop.

And that meant we needed to go to Hook Reddale.

"Sir Edmund said he'd discovered it by matching clues in the story to the land," Sally said. "Maybe we could work it out, too."

I'd been thinking about that. Rawlin had told us Hook Reddale had a tower in its center. And when the White Lady signed her evil pact, she'd crawled from the tower into the river.

The river had to be the Axe. Which meant we could find Hook Reddale by walking its streams until we spotted the tower—which had to be still standing, or Sir Edmund wouldn't have known it was the right village.

Of course, that left us with a different problem. The Axe was *long*. And, as my map made clear, it branched in several places. Sir Edmund had found Hook Reddale, but he'd been living here for years. He'd had all the time in the world to go exploring.

"Exploring," I said suddenly. "That's the answer."

"You know where Hook Reddale is?" Sally said, surprised.

"No," I said. "But I'm pretty sure I know someone else who does."

I stayed up, pacing in my room to keep myself awake, until I was sure everyone had retired for the night. Then I crept down the hall. The coat of arms on one of the doors—a yellow shield, a unicorn rearing in the center—made it easy to tell which were Sir Edmund's quarters. I went to the door beside it, where a smaller shield was affixed, and knocked faintly.

A voice came from inside, high and fast. "Who is it?"

"It's Christopher," I whispered.

I heard the shuffling of bedsheets, the creak of the floor. When the door opened, Julian Darcy stood in his bed-clothes, lantern in hand. "You shouldn't be here," he whispered. "Father doesn't like it when I'm up late."

"Sorry. I couldn't sleep," I said. "Listen, I was planning on seeing some of the countryside tomorrow. I figured you must know the area well."

He beamed. "Of course. I'll show you the hamlets, and where the best hunting is—do you shoot? I can teach you. And there's a cave by the river; I think people used to live there a long time ago. There's some painted handprints—"

If I didn't cut him off, he might keep talking until dawn. "We can do all that. But I was really hoping to see Hook Reddale."

Julian went quiet, just like at the dinner table. He looked at me, scared. "I don't know where that is."

"I think you do," I said. "In fact, I *know* you do."

"No."

"Your father told us you like to go exploring."

That confused him. "So?"

"So your father knows where Hook Reddale is. He wouldn't want you stumbling into such evil; he would have warned you to stay away from it. But he can't warn you off if you don't know what you're supposed to avoid."

Julian sounded desperate. "You can't go. You can't. The White Lady lives there."

"That's why I have to find it. We have to stop what's taking the children."

"You can't. You shouldn't even try. Please, please stop trying." He changed his tone. "Look, there are lots of great places to see around here. The land's beautiful. And we can spar! Your man Tom can show me how to use a sword, and I'll teach you the bow, and—"

"No," I said coldly.

"But—"

Inside, my spirits fell. If Julian was too scared to tell me where Hook Reddale was, I'd have to force it out of him. I knew how to do that. It's just that it would be cruel.

"I will not train with you," I said, "because I do not spend time with cowards."

His face fell. "What?"

My heart sank along with his. Still I pressed. *"Children are missing, Julian. Not soldiers, not men. Children. And you can't even speak a few words?"*

He bowed his head. "You can't stop the White Lady. If you keep investigating this, you'll die."

"At least I won't die a coward."

Julian leaned his head against the door. I don't think I'd ever felt so wretched.

"Two miles north," Julian said, "the river branches. Take the path to the northwest. After another mile, a stream branches southwest. Follow it, and you'll see the tower."

I drew a breath. "Thank you. Listen . . . ," I said awkwardly. "I'm sorry about . . . You're not a coward."

"Yes," he said. "I am." And he shut the door.

I heard the key turn in the lock. I knocked, even more softly than before. "Julian?"

He didn't answer, so I went back to my room. I changed into the bedclothes Cooper had left for me—Julian's old things, I imagined—then lay in bed, alone, afraid, and ashamed.

WEDNESDAY, DECEMBER 23, 1665

Ni i   tem p t m es q d   n r ve e r;
equ   b co d um qu d on sc   u

CHAPTER
31

WE LEFT BEFORE THE DAWN. I
didn't want anyone to see us, especially Julian, who might
already be regretting giving me the location of the abandoned village and thinking of telling his father my plan.
I did speak with one of the servants—I had to order a girl
to collect Tom, Moppet, and Bridget from the quarters
below—and no doubt the maid would tell her master that
we'd left. But she'd wait to do that until he'd risen, too late
for him to stop us.

Sally suggested I not even tell Tom where we were
going. After the shameful way I'd extracted Hook Reddale's
location from Julian, I refused to keep Tom in the dark.

"It'll be easier," she warned me.

"He deserves to know," I said.

She raised an eyebrow. "Which one of us has no memories?"

That was a low blow. Regardless, once we'd begun following the river north, I told him.

He stared at me like I'd gone mad. "We're going *where*? To do *what*?"

"It's the only thing I can think of," I said.

Tom looked up at Moppet, sitting on his shoulders as usual. "He got worse," he said. "I thought if he lost his memories, he'd be more sensible. He actually got *worse*."

This didn't seem all *that* different from the things Sally had told me I'd done in the past. Tom disagreed. "The cemetery, in Paris? That was bad. But at least there the dead *stayed* dead. How are we supposed to fight a wraith?"

"Actually," I said, "from Sir Edmund's description, I'm wondering if the White Lady's a revenant."

"I don't even know what that is."

"It's like a wraith. But with a burning sense of vengeance."

Tom stopped speaking to me. He marched ahead through the snow.

Sally shrugged. "Told you."

· · ·

The natural route the river carved led us straight to the village.

The fluttering in my stomach almost made me wish it hadn't. The weight of where we were going seeped into our bones with each step. Tom went silent, and Bridget, who'd flapped away from Moppet's arms at the first branch of the river, was nowhere to be seen. Even Sally's songs faded with the gray of the day.

Sybil had said the storm that brought me here was cursed. I could feel it lingering in the sky, the thick, heavy clouds its curse made real. As I looked into the gloom, I realized I hadn't seen a single second of sun since I'd awoke. I wrapped my coat around my body, stamping my feet to fight the chill.

But it wasn't until we saw the tower that I began to shiver.

Hook Reddale was as gray as the sky overhead. What few buildings still remained among the ruins were the ones built of stone, and those had mostly crumbled into half houses and shapeless heaps, overlain by a thick blanket of snow, unmarked by any sign of people.

And in the middle of it all stood the tower. The tower

the knight had built for his love, the tower she'd thrown herself from, the final step into the darkness that had turned a murderess into the White Lady. Stained and weathered, it rose four stories high. Shriveled, blackened vines curled around its base, crawling over the rocks into the arrow slits, all the way to the battlements at the top. A single iron-reinforced door of cracked wood and rusted, crumbling metal faced the trees, offering the only way in.

I had no doubt the tower was the most likely place to find any remaining artifact of the White Lady. Yet I shuddered when I thought of walking inside. Sally suggested we look in the surviving houses first. "We might find something useful," she said.

Both Tom and I thought she was just trying to put off the inevitable—and both of us were perfectly fine with that. We chose the closest house that was still intact. The door, hanging precariously from one hinge, creaked as we pushed it open, groaning as we woke it from its centuries-long slumber.

The interior was just as ruined as the rest of the village. Heaps of snow lay below the windows, blown through where the shutters had rotted and fallen long ago. A tattered banner hung from one water-stained wall, its lower half chewed into threads. The furniture was ravaged, too: wood gnawed from table legs, cushions torn apart, the straw and stuffing beneath stolen away for rats' nests. A shelf against the wall sagged and split, spilling ceramics, broken, to the floor.

Sally linked her arm in mine and pressed close. "Look," she said.

She motioned to the table in what had once been the dining room. A large wooden bowl rested in the center, with smaller bowls set around it, a thin black film of decay covering them all. Knives—or what had once been knives—lay beside them, the blades barely recognizable beneath the rust.

"They left their things," Sally said. "When they fled the village, they just left their things behind."

I imagined their terror, and my own heart thudded in response. Tom looked miserable, like he'd rather be anywhere but here. Moppet, surprisingly, seemed the least perturbed. She regarded the rot around us with distaste, but not fear. If anything, she seemed mildly curious. Could she not feel it? The presence? Its wickedness?

"What now?" Sally said.

"Let's look around," I said.

"For what?"

I wasn't really sure. "See if anything's been disturbed recently. Just *don't* take it."

No one needed the reminder. Even if one of us was foolish enough to test the village curse, there wasn't anything left worth stealing. None of us dared climb the rotting stairs. Nor did we try the cellar, where what little light spilled down revealed that water had seeped through the foundation. A half dozen barrels, and what looked like the edge of a wine rack, were frozen in a black sheet of ice. In an old bedroom, I found a candle whose wax had survived the centuries. I didn't bother with it; I didn't have any way to set it alight.

I rejoined the others by the entrance. "Anything?"

They shook their heads.

On to the next one. I stepped outside, planning to check the house across the way. Just then, Tom grabbed my arm. *"Christopher."*

He pointed with a shaking finger. My own panic rose as I saw what he'd spotted.

Footprints.

CHAPTER
32

A SET OF FOOTPRINTS TRACKED across the snow. They led straight from one of the flat-roofed houses to the tower's door. And they hadn't been here before.

Someone—or some*thing*—had joined us.

"Tom," I began, but he was already ahead of me. Steel slid against leather as he pulled Eternity from its scabbard. The tip of the blade trembled in his hands. *A holy sword, handed down from knights of ancient blessing,* I'd told Sir Edmund. I wondered if it could harm the undead.

I drew my vial of oil of vitriol, though I didn't know how effective that would be, either. Sally placed a hand against my back as she looked around the village for other signs of life. Tom pushed Moppet behind him. She seemed confused at what was happening, though she sobered at Tom's caution, his naked sword a clear sign of danger.

"What do we do?" Tom whispered.

Run, I wanted to say. But those footsteps were why we'd come. "The house first," I whispered back.

Cautiously we went forward. When we got to the house, I motioned to the windows.

Tom took the one on the left. I took the right. Slowly, I peeked inside.

Nothing.

Like the place we'd just left, this house held nothing but rotting furniture and snow. I saw no sign that anyone had been in there.

So who—or what—made those tracks?

Whatever had come from the house, the tower was where it was now. We'd delayed as long as we could. It was time to face it down.

We stepped forward, eyes everywhere. I listened, but I heard no movement, no voices—just the slow, squeaking crunch of our boots. We walked beside the footprints, careful not to step into them, afraid of walking in the White Lady's shoes.

I glanced up at the tower, at the arrow slits that ringed it. And I froze.

"Did . . . did something move inside?" I whispered.

Tom shook his head, uncertain.

"I didn't see anything," Sally said.

A shape flitted over the tower. I ducked before I saw: It was Bridget. She'd flown to the battlements from the woods.

She swooped down. Moppet, scared now, held out her hands to catch her, but the pigeon only circled us, cooed in alarm, then flew toward the woods. Was my imagination running away with me? Or was the bird trying to warn us of something terrible waiting inside?

I didn't really need a warning—I was already sure something terrible was in there. Yet still we inched forward, until we reached the door.

The footprints ended here, as if someone had stood there and waited. I had a crazy thought—*do we knock?*—then we moved to the sides, pressed against the wall.

I reached for the handle. Tom, terrified, drew back his sword, ready to strike. I took hold of the rusted iron ring. Then I pushed.

The door groaned. Its moan rolled over the hills, breaking the silence like thunder. I cringed, ready.

Again nothing. Nothing called to us; nothing came out, except the stale musk of mold and the coppery tang of rust. I edged my head around the door and peeked inside.

The tower was dark, the only light spilling through the arrow slits, giving the circular chamber a hazy glow. In the gloom, I could see a table in the center, a single chair of matching wood toppled next to it, the cold, empty hearth behind. A spiral staircase wound along the far side of the wall, disappearing into a narrow opening in the ceiling.

I looked at Tom. "Ready?" I whispered.

His eyes bulged. *Me?* he mouthed.

You're the one with the magic sword, I thought. But it wasn't fair to send him where I didn't want to go myself. I ticked a count off my fingers.

One.

Two.

And three. I swung inside, vitriol gripped in my hand. Tom rushed in behind me, sword back, point forward, ready to thrust.

And still we saw nothing.

Sally and Moppet shuffled in behind us. I motioned to the stairs. There wasn't enough room for two at a time, so I went first again, until I could just peek into the floor above.

I found myself in what remained of the armory. A rack of rusted weapons ringed the tower. There were swords, double handed and single, and polearms with wickedly curved bills; their wooden poles had cracked under their weight, leaving rusty blades corroding on the stone. A dozen longbows remained, strings hanging rotted from a single end. The crossbows had already snapped under the tension, half of them fallen to rest beside the broken halberds. Next to the stairs, four ancient firearms rested, and it was these that caught my eye most of all.

They were arquebuses: the earliest kind of firearms, not seen in over two hundred years. Little more than metal pipes with straight wooden handles, they had no triggers, just a pan for holding gunpowder. An arquebusier would have to light it himself to fire it. I was utterly fascinated by the sight of such ancient weapons, and if I hadn't been terrified, I might have stopped to take a look.

Yet still we found no evidence of anyone inside. We continued up to the third floor, and here we found a cache of old shields, rendered useless by time.

The final floor was empty. The stairs ended here, the only way up a ladder rising to a hatch in the roof, locked with a rusted iron drawbar.

That would lead to the battlements atop the tower. Tom leaned in close. "Are they up there?" he whispered.

"Not unless they're not human." The drawbar locked the hatch from inside.

Tom's eyes went wide. He shook his head and backed away. But we had to look. Carefully I climbed the ladder; amazingly, it still held my weight. Tom gripped Eternity so tight his knuckles turned white. I took hold of the bolt and pulled.

It wouldn't budge. I tugged at it, yanked as hard as I could. The rung beneath my boots cracked under the pressure, and I leaped up higher, bent over, head pressed against the ceiling. But I couldn't move the latch an inch. Time had rusted it shut.

I motioned for Tom to try. Reluctantly he took my place. The rungs creaked threateningly; I had to support his weight with my shoulder so the ladder wouldn't split. He took hold of the bolt. His muscles strained, his face turned red, and still it wouldn't move.

The sound of wings flapping made me turn. Bridget squeezed through one of the arrow slits. She hopped down to the floor and marched toward me, cooing.

I picked her up. She flapped her wings again, cooing, insistent.

"I think she's trying to tell you something," Sally whispered.

If that was true, I had no idea what it was. I stroked her feathers to calm her.

Tom jumped down from the ladder. "It's completely stuck," he whispered. "Unless we break it off, we can't get up there."

"Then whoever came in here . . . ," Sally said. "Where did they go?"

You're missing something, Master Benedict said.

I frowned. What had I missed? We'd been through the entire tower except for the battlements, and unless we climbed from the outside, no one could get up there. There wasn't any place in the tower for someone to hide. Unless . . .

A secret passage?

I wondered. It wasn't uncommon to build an underground tunnel, through which defenders could sneak in supplies while under siege.

That's not it, my master said.

Then what am I missing? I said. *There's nothing in here but rusted weapons.*

You're looking at what's there. What isn't *there?*

The strangeness of the question made me pause. Why

would I look for what *isn't* there? What did that even mean?

We went down the spiral stairs, back to the bottom, searching. I didn't see anything I hadn't seen before.

I shook my head. This was getting us nowhere. We were supposed to be looking for—

"The artifact," I said. "The artifact that binds the White Lady to the Earth."

"What about it?" Sally said.

"It isn't here."

"How do you know?"

"Because of what Sir Edmund told us. He said we'd feel it. That we'd go numb with terror."

"*I'm* numb with terror," Tom said helpfully.

I was afraid, too. But no more so than I'd been outside. I was sure of it now: There was no artifact here. There was nothing at all except the remains of the knight's weapons. In fact, I couldn't see any evidence anyone had even been in here. Just our tracks—

And it hit me.

I stared at the stone below our feet. "Where did the footprints go?"

"What?" Sally said.

"The footprints. The ones that led us here. They came right up to the door, and then stopped."

"Because they came inside."

"All right. So then where did the footprints go after that?"

Tom tried to remember. "There weren't any footprints inside."

"Exactly."

"But . . . why would there be? There isn't any snow in here."

"No, but look." I pointed to the floor. Boot prints tracked all over the stone. "When we came in, our boots were wet. We've been leaving prints everywhere we go. So where are the prints of whoever came in before us?"

"You think a ghost would have wet boots?"

"If she didn't, then where did the prints outside come from? Tracks out there should mean tracks in here."

But there hadn't been any. I realized something else, then, too. "The door. When we opened it. It creaked."

"So?" Sally said.

"Did you hear a creak when we were checking out the house?"

She frowned. "No."

"No prints," I said. "No noise. They didn't open the

door." Which meant either they'd never come inside the tower, or— "There *has* to be a secret passage."

Tom looked around dubiously. "I don't see anywhere a passage would go."

He was right. Though the walls were thick stone, they were too narrow to fit a person. So if they hadn't come inside . . .

Where had they gone? Had we missed some tracks? Had the person doubled back?

I opened the door to the tower and looked at the footprints we'd followed here. They were easy enough to distinguish, made by hobnailed boots. I could see where the nubs of the nails had pressed into the snow.

They came from that house, I thought. *And then they tracked here. The person stood outside the door, and—*

"LOOK OUT!"

Tom didn't even give me time to flinch. He grabbed my shoulder and pulled me inside, nearly wrenching my arm from its socket.

I felt something slice across my forehead and heard a crack against the stairs behind me. Then I went flying, sprawling hard on the stone.

The fall rattled my brain. "What—?"

"Get away!" Tom shouted, and Sally dove next to me, landing with a squeal. Tom dropped Eternity, the blade clattering on the floor. Still dazed, I saw something fly through the door, and again came the crack from the stairs. I looked over, staring dumbly as something bounced off the stone.

It was a pair of . . . sticks? One had bronze-colored turkey feathers attached. The other had a broadhead blade—

An *arrow*?

Tom crouched, shielding Moppet with his body as he kicked at the door. I saw one more arrow thud into the wood before it slammed shut. Tom slipped the bolt, sealing us in. Then he stared at me, wide eyed.

An *arrow*.

Someone had shot an arrow at me.

Three arrows, in fact. And one of them had just about got me. I pressed my fingers to the sting in my forehead. They came away wet with blood.

"The woods," Tom said. "Someone shot at you from the trees."

"Who?" I said, dazed.

"I couldn't see them. They were wearing a hood. I just saw them let loose an arrow, and then I threw you down."

He'd saved my life.

"We have to get out of here," Sally said.

"How?" Tom said.

My master returned. *How, indeed?*

There was only one way from the tower: the door. The door, where I'd nearly been skewered.

Yes, he said.

And the footprints . . .

"The tracks," I said. "They led us right to the tower."

We'd thought that meant the person had gone inside. Instead, they'd stopped at the door.

But how could footprints go nowhere? Whoever had made them hadn't turned around; we'd have seen it. Unless—

"Oh no," I said.

Unless he'd walked *backward*. Walked backward, stepping in his own tracks. Then it would *look* like he'd entered the tower, even though he'd never gone in. We'd follow him, and then—

I understood.

"We were led here deliberately," I said. "This tower is a trap."

CHAPTER

33

"WE HAVE TO GET OUT OF HERE," Tom said, panic rising.

"We can't," I said. "That's the point. He's cut off the only way out."

"What about the battlements?" Sally said. "If we could pry off the latch—"

"It's fifty feet up, with nothing to climb down. We'd break our necks."

I cursed. We'd been drawn into this snare so easily. We couldn't even fight back; all we had was Tom's sword. Whoever was shooting at us was in the woods; we'd never reach them without getting hit.

"What about the weapons upstairs?" Sally said.

I doubted they'd be of any use; they were too old. None-theless, we returned to the second floor, where I looked skeptically at what time had left us. "Let's try a bow."

Tom pulled one from the rack. He placed the curve behind his thigh and slowly began to bend it into shape. The wood creaked, protesting at its first strain in two hun-dred years.

I looped the string, still attached at one end, around the other. As slowly as he'd bent the bow, Tom relaxed the pressure.

The string shattered into fragments. The bow snapped back, cracking the wood across the middle, and giving Tom a whack on the thigh that left him limping.

Heart sinking, I scanned what was left. The crossbows were in even worse shape than the longbows. The arquebuses were rusted so badly that they were as likely to explode as fire. I found a pair of spears we might be able to throw, but the odds of hitting someone in the woods were so unlikely, they might as well have been useless.

"Forget it," I said. "We'll kill ourselves with these before we do anyone else—what are you doing?"

Sally crept to one of the arrow slits. "Seeing if the archer is—eek!"

She dove for the floor. An arrow buzzed her head, slicing through a stray curl of hair before snapping on the wall opposite.

Tom's eyes were wide. "That's a good shot."

Too good. Through an arrow slit? I shivered as I remembered the broadhead whistling past me. If Tom hadn't yanked me out of the way . . .

Despair filled my guts. He might have saved me, but we were completely stuck.

Tom helped Sally from the floor. Moppet cowered behind him, holding Bridget. "Did you see the man?" Tom asked Sally.

She nodded. "He's in the trees to the south, in a brown cloak."

"Is he alone?" I said.

"I think so."

We peeked through different arrow slits, checking all around. No one shot at us there, and I saw no one else in the trees. It seemed clear: We were held here by only one man. That was better than facing an army—but not much better. The archer still cut off our only escape.

"Could we wait him out?" Tom said.

"We have no food," I said. "We can't open the top

hatch, either, so we can't even get water from the snow."

We were in trouble. If the archer had supplies, he could keep us pinned for days. At the moment, he seemed restless, almost desperate, firing arrows at impossible targets. If he got clever, he'd hide among the trees, make us think he'd left. Then when we tried to sneak out . . . we'd never know if he was watching.

What's more, we had the cold to consider. There was a hearth in the tower, and in the table was wood, but we didn't have any way of starting a fire. Since we'd planned to travel only in daylight, I hadn't thought to bring a lantern or torches. If it were warmer, we'd last a few days, even without water. In this weather, once night came, we'd freeze.

"We're going to die here," Tom said, panic rising again.

"Just . . . let me think," I said.

"Think of what?"

I didn't know. We couldn't run, and we couldn't hide, which meant our only option was to fight. But what could we fight with?

I was so distracted I barely realized my fingers had already started searching my sash. Yes—my ingredients had helped us escape the starving dogs. Maybe I had something that could help us escape this man, too.

The question was: What? I had plenty of ingredients that could cause him harm, but he was too far away for me to hit him. For an escape, I'd need—

Saltpeter.

I pulled out the vial of saltpeter. Mixed with sugar, it would make smoke. If we laid down enough smoke, then . . .

I shook my head. I didn't have anywhere near enough ingredients to make the kind of smoke I'd need to obscure the tower. The wind would just blow it away.

Of course, saltpeter had other uses. With charcoal and sulfur . . .

"Come on," I said, and we hurried back to the second floor. Sally waited by the arrow slit, Moppet curled safely behind the tower wall, while I inspected the four arquebuses that remained.

The barrels had rusted badly. The wooden handles had half rotted off. I took one of the guns and tested it, pressing the barrel against my knee.

It snapped. Rusty shards broke away at the flash pan, sending splinters of metal bouncing off the stone. I threw the weapon away and took another one. This one cracked, too, though closer to the muzzle this time.

"What are you doing?" Tom said.

I grabbed a third arquebus. "Looking for something that can make a big boom," I said, and I strained the barrel again.

It held.

"This one," I said.

"You want to shoot him?" Tom said. "With that?"

"Unless you have a better idea."

"What are you going to shoot him with?"

I pointed to the crate of bullets.

"A rusty bullet in a rusty barrel?" Tom said. "Will that even fire?"

I wasn't sure it had to. "I have an idea."

"Oh no."

I let that go. "The man outside led us here deliberately. He knows there's only one way out. We delayed his plans— he obviously meant to shoot us when we left the tower—but he has to know the weapons in here are useless, and you can't get to him with your sword. He must feel safe. So what if we start shooting back?"

"You'll never hit him with that," Tom said.

"I don't know that I have to. We were supposed to be easy prey. If bullets start flying at him, he might think twice about sticking around. We don't need to kill him. We only need to scare him off."

"Do you really think that will work?" Sally said.

I wasn't sure. Tom wasn't wrong: I had a better chance of having the barrel blow up in my face than have it fire. I didn't even really know how to shoot.

Still, it gave us something. "And you two scoffed at me," I said as I pulled the ingredients for gunpowder from my sash.

Tom scowled. "The fact that we keep ending up in places where we *need* gunpowder is not something to be proud of."

I brushed the dirt from one of the flagstones. Then I measured out the sulfur, charcoal, and saltpeter. "Make sure we don't lose sight of him."

"Easy for you to say," Sally muttered, as another arrow clattered in the slit.

"You see?" Tom said to her. "This is why I'm always complaining."

I mixed the ingredients, and within a few minutes I had a little pile of gunpowder. Now it was time to prepare the weapon.

There was a ramrod, still intact, in the rack; I ran it through the barrel. An alarming amount of rust flaked out. I drove it in again and again, until I'd removed most of it. The pile of rust didn't fill me with confidence.

Nor did the bullets. Half of them had been reduced to little more than pebbles. I chose the largest, most intact ball from the center of the crate. Then I loaded the arquebus. I packed most of the gunpowder in, then a small ball of wool torn from the inner lining of my coat to use as wadding. The ramrod shoved the bullet in last. Then I filled the flash pan with what remained of the gunpowder. All I needed now was—

"Oh no," I said.

"What's the matter?" Sally said.

"I need to set off the gunpowder," I said. "But we don't have any fire."

CHAPTER
34

TOM LOOKED PUZZLED. "WHAT'S wrong with the flint on the gun?"

"There isn't one." I showed him the weapon. "When this arquebus was made, they hadn't invented the flintlock. You shoot these by lighting the powder in the flash pan. But I don't have any way to do that."

"There's a flint and tinder in your sash."

"There is?"

"Of course. How else could you set so many things on fire?"

I searched for the flint. I couldn't find it. Eventually, I just took the sash off and dumped all the tools from the pockets. There were the spoons, the knife, the lens, the tweezers—but no flint.

Tom frowned. "You always have one—I'm telling you." He rooted through the collection. "Half your things are missing."

"You probably lost them," Sally said, "when you went overboard."

This was unfair. I had everything, everything except one stupid way to light the gunpowder.

But you do have one, my master said.

I do? I considered the tools again, and—

The lens?

The magnifying lens could focus the sun's rays well enough to start a fire. Except we didn't have any sun. It had stayed hidden behind the clouds since I'd woken.

Look closer, Master Benedict said.

At what? I said. *There's no flint, no fire, and no sun. How else could I light something?*

How indeed, he said, as if he were disappointed.

I wasn't sure why, but it made me feel embarrassed. Without the sun, there was no way these tools could create fire. Unless I'd missed something in—

The sash.

Of course. Of *course.*

I rooted through the sash, searching for the vial. I'd seen it. I knew I'd seen it.

"What are you looking for?" Tom said.

"Nitrum flammans," I said, and I pulled the vial triumphantly from the sash.

"Is that Latin?" Sally said.

"Yes. It means 'flaming niter.' It'll make fire—*without* fire."

"He's like King Midas," Tom said to Moppet. "Except instead of gold, everything he touches explodes."

"Do you want to get rid of that archer or not?"

Tom threw his hands up and walked away.

"If you two are *finished*," Sally huffed, dodging another arrow.

Annoyed, I grabbed my arquebus and stomped upstairs. "I'll get the best angle from the fourth floor. Tom, you wait on the third floor, by the arrow slit. When I call, give me a musketeer's order. Sally, stay here and keep the man distracted."

I went all the way to the top. Then I knelt beside the arrow slit and peered through.

The man had shifted. His face was still hidden by his hood, but he was standing in the open now, beside the tree.

He'd nocked an arrow, and every so often he raised his bow, but he'd finally stopped shooting at the tower. This was good: If he'd stopped wasting arrows, he'd realized he didn't need to be so impatient. We were no threat to him from inside.

Or so he thought. I propped the arquebus with its muzzle resting on the arrow slit. Then I opened up the vials.

First, the nitrum flammans, Master Benedict said. *Grind it into a fine powder.*

I took a single white crystal from the vial and used the heel of my boot to grind it on the flagstones.

Next, the zincum india.

Dull gray, the zincum was already a powder, so I measured the same amount as the nitrum flammans and stirred them until they were well mixed.

Place the mixture on top of the powder in the flash pan.

I did.

Now, my master said. *Take the spirit of salt and carefully—carefully—drip the smallest of drops onto the mixture.*

Then what? I said.

Close your eyes. And pray.

I worked the stopper from the spirit of salt. I poured a single drop into one of the silver spoons, then held the spoon ready, the arquebus lifted into position.

I stared down the barrel at the archer. He remained, waiting.

"All right, Tom," I called down softly. "Give the order. And make it *loud*."

Tom did loud very well. His bellow rattled the walls. "READY."

The archer started. He raised his bow, but his hands wavered. His head shifted under his hood, confused.

"LEVEL."

The arrow came loose. It sped toward the tower; I heard it clatter off the walls somewhere below. The man nocked another and drew it back.

"FIRE!"

Please work, I thought, as I dripped the spirit of salt onto the mixture.

It took only an instant. The nitrum burst into a bright white flame. The powder beneath it ignited. Smoke and light blinded me. And then—

BOOM

The arquebus kicked backward, knocking me flat. Smoke filled my vision, my nose clogged with the acrid stink of gunpowder. I lay there, dazed, until Tom's voice finally cut through the haze.

"Christopher!" I heard his boots thumping on the stairs as he ran. "We did it! We *did* it!"

I coughed. "I got him?"

"I don't know," Tom said. "But look!"

I peered out. The archer wasn't there anymore. I could just make out a line of tracks, leading away from his former spot by the tree.

"We scared him off," Tom said.

I lay against the wall and hugged my arquebus.

CHAPTER
35

WE DIDN'T DARE LINGER. WE HUR-
ried downstairs and opened the door to the tower.

"Wait," I said. "It might be a trick. Tom, wave your sword."

Eternity was already in his hands. Slowly, he brandished
it in the doorway.

No arrows came this time. I craned my head around the
opening, Tom's hand on my collar, ready to pull me back.

Still nothing. Carefully, I ventured out. The only sign
of life was Bridget, flapping down to land in the trees. We
really had scared him off.

Tom was ecstatic—and more than ready to flee. "Let's
get out of here."

"Hold on," I said. "I want to see where that archer ambushed us."

"Why?" Tom complained, but he followed as we made our way through the snow. He kept hold of his sword, so this time, Moppet had to walk. She clung with a tiny fist to the back of his coat.

When we got to the tree, I saw the archer had come prepared. After all the arrows he'd fired at us, another fourteen remained, bronze feathers up, broadheads plunged into the snow behind the trunk. A small leather satchel rested beside them; inside I found a dozen strips of dried mutton. With the snow, he'd had food, water, and ammunition.

"Look at this," Tom said, amazed.

He showed me the side of the tree facing the tower. At shoulder height, a rusted iron ball was wedged inside the wood, slivers of bark punched away.

My heart swelled. What a shot! "Fifty yards away," I said proudly. "With a two-hundred-year-old arquebus! And I *still* almost got him."

Tom looked suitably impressed. Sally rolled her eyes. "Don't we have more important things to do?"

I felt she was spoiling the moment, but she did have

a point. The archer was gone, but now we had something much more valuable: his tracks. The man's boots had matted the snow around the tree, but when he'd fled, he'd left a clear trail for us to follow.

"Let's see where they go," I said. We kept one eye on the tracks, the other on the trees in case the archer returned. His steps were long, skidding here and there—he'd been running—but it was clear from the footprints that his hobnail boots had made the tracks that had led us to the tower.

Now they led directly to the river. And, curiously, they went *into* the river.

"Did he run to the other side?" Tom said.

We looked, but we didn't see any tracks leading away. They just . . . stopped. Like the missing children's.

"Maybe he had a boat," Sally said.

The trees would have easily kept one hidden, but the water seemed too shallow, even for a rowboat. And if he'd had one, we'd have seen evidence that it had been here: marks from the hull sliding through the snow, or a stake pole, or tracks next to a tree where the boat had been tied. There was nothing. As far as I could tell, the tracks simply went into the river and vanished.

Tom's eyes went wide. "You don't think . . . ?"

"The White Lady?" I said. "No. That was no ghost shooting arrows at us."

On the contrary, it was clear now. Our enemy was mortal. What I didn't know was *who* they were, why they were doing this. Or where they'd gone. Why would someone walk into the river—

"The tracks," I said suddenly.

"Which tracks?" Tom said.

"The ones that led us to the tower. Come on, let's go back."

We returned to Hook Reddale, following the river downstream. Tom objected, but I wasn't nearly so scared this time. I thought of how hard my heart had been thumping as we'd entered the abandoned village before. I'd been afraid of the supernatural. Now I realized: I'd really been scaring myself.

And that's exactly the point, I thought. *The legend of the White Lady. It has everyone so scared.*

That was part of the key. The other part we found in the village. I stayed along the river, eyes on the snow. And there they were. "Look."

Two sets of tracks emerged from the water: one going

toward Hook Reddale, one leading back. They led to and from the flat-roofed house where we'd first seen the footprints.

The tracks stopped at the back wall. The stones had wet marks on them, and, at the top, some of the snow had been disturbed.

"Give me a boost," I said to Tom. Dutifully he hoisted me so I could see the roof. Some of the timbers had collapsed on the north side. Tracking around it were the hobnailed-boot prints, heading right for the front edge of the house.

"That's how he tricked us," I said, as Tom put me back down. "He came from the river and hid atop the roof, watching us. When we went into that first house, he hurried toward the tower, making the tracks. Then he walked backward, stepping in his own footprints, so we'd think someone had gone inside."

After that, he'd gone back to the river—

I stopped, my mind racing. And again, that strange image of the bird man came to me: the plague doctor, Melchior. This time, I understood why.

Fear. And deception. Everything we've heard is a lie.

I looked at the hobnailed prints. The tracks. The river. The White Lady.

And now I knew. I knew who was taking the children and how they were doing it.

"Come on," I said, and I rushed back to the river.

"Hey," Tom said. "Where are you going?"

"To the woods," I said. "We have to go see Sybil."

CHAPTER
36

WE HURRIED SOUTH, FOLLOWING the River Axe.

It took us hours, every minute a question: What if the archer came back? In the trees, we jumped at every snapping twig; on the open hills, we ran until our lungs burned, until we were in the woods south of the Darcy estate, where we finally spotted the Squashed Giant.

The morning's events had me keeping an eye out for tracks in the snow. So it was as we moved toward Sybil's hut that I noticed there were a lot of them, heading toward her house. Someone—several someones—had come to see her, and recently. We followed them, cautious.

And then I saw the blood. "Tom."

He pushed Moppet behind him. As he drew his sword, I approached the bloodstain, studying the tracks.

They told the tale well enough. There had been a fight. The snow by the trees was flattened, trampled by at least a dozen boots. Near the center, a crimson patch stained the white, bright red dots flecked all around. The blood trailed away, sliding in a smear through the snow toward the hut.

Slowly, carefully, we followed it. It led through the trees, all the way to the door of Sybil's house. The thinnest wisp of smoke curled from the chimney.

From the tracks, it looked like the victors hadn't followed whomever they'd stabbed. Still I waited, listening, before going inside. All I heard was the wind rustling the branches, Bridget cooing overhead, and the distant chitter of a single, lonely starling.

The door to the hut was ajar. I motioned to Tom. He pressed the tip of Eternity into the wood and pushed it open.

"Hello?" I called.

No response.

I decided to chance it. Back pressed against the cob, I peeked through the doorway.

There was only Sybil inside. She lay slumped by the hearth. The wood in the fireplace had burned to ash, the remaining embers giving off a faint glow.

"Sybil?" I said.

Her voice was weak. "Welcome back, Baron."

We went inside, knelt beside her. She remained still, head bowed, hands to her stomach, stringy gray hair covering her face. When she looked up, her skin was as white as the ash beside her.

She saw Tom gripping his sword. "If you returned to use that, I'm afraid you're too late."

She lifted her hands. They were painted dark in the glow of the embers, the same dark stain swelling on the front of her dress.

My heart sank. "Let me see."

She waved me off. Red drops flicked from her fingers, spotting the wool of my coat. "No point."

"A surgeon—" I stopped myself. Where would I find a surgeon? Was there even one in Seaton?

"It wouldn't help," Sybil said. "My guests did too good a job."

"Who were they? Who did this to you?"

"It doesn't matter."

"If we're going to stop the kidnappers," I said, "I need any evidence I can get."

"It wasn't the kidnappers. Quite the opposite."

The opposite? She must have meant . . . "One of the parents? Of the missing children?"

I remembered what John Morrow had said when we'd visited his village. *Allan Cavill says she's a witch. He says she's responsible.*

"Was it Allan Cavill?" I said. "His friends?"

She coughed and grimaced. Blood stained her teeth. "I will give you no testimony, Baron. It was not the kidnappers who did this, and that is all you need to know. When you have your own children, you will understand." She sighed. "Why are you here?"

"I . . . I need your help."

It felt shameful, asking for help while she bled to death in her own home. Still, for the first time since we'd entered, I saw life in her eyes. "You've discovered something."

"The White Lady has nothing to do with the children," I said. "The kidnapper's just using her legend as a cover."

She closed her eyes. "So I suspected. How is he taking them?"

"The river. That's why there are no tracks. He walks

through the water, leaving the snow undisturbed. Once he has the child, he walks back through the river until it's safe to return to land."

"Clever," she said. "Do you know who he is?"

"I think so. He has to be someone the children know and trust."

She looked at me sharply. "Why do you say that?"

"*Because* there aren't any tracks," I said. "It's fine for the kidnapper to disguise his path by only walking in the river. But what about the children? They haven't been leaving tracks, either. That means he hasn't had to chase them down. They just walk into the river when he calls them. They wouldn't do that for a stranger. It has to be someone they know."

I drew a breath. "I think it's Julian Darcy."

Sybil looked startled. She hadn't been expecting that. "Why do you say it's him?"

I told her of the trap that had been set for us this morning. "We couldn't see the archer's face, but he looked to be around Julian's size. And he's a hunter; he knows how to use a bow."

"Many people do. None of that is proof."

"No, but this is: Julian was the only one who knew we were going to Hook Reddale."

Sybil listened while I told her what had happened at the Darcy estate. "Sir Edmund wouldn't tell me where the village was, and his friend Álvaro refused to go there. When Julian tried to warn me off, too, I thought it was because he was scared of the White Lady. Now I realize: He was actually scared I'd discover that there *was* no White Lady.

"He tried to get me to stop investigating the children's disappearance. When he saw I wouldn't, he told me where Hook Reddale was—not to help, but so he could set a trap.

"And there's more. That blood word I found: Sir Edmund and Álvaro knew what it said. That made sense: They were witch-hunters; they'd studied evil. The thing is, Julian *also* knew what it said. Because *before* his father explained what it was, Julian turned his head away. He wouldn't look at any of us. I thought it was because he was afraid. But now I see: He was *ashamed*."

Sybil shook her head. "Julian might not have been the only one who knew you were going to Hook Reddale. He could have told someone else, after you left his room. He could have gone and told his father."

"Maybe," I said. "But it wasn't Sir Edmund who attacked us; his gout won't let him leave the estate. And it wasn't Álvaro, either. He's too tall to be the archer we saw."

She frowned. "Who is this 'Álvaro'?"

"Álvaro Arias. He's an old friend of Sir Edmund's. An assistant, from his witchfinding days."

Her expression darkened. She spat, and what came out was mostly blood.

"You didn't know," I said.

"I never met the man."

"Not Álvaro. Sir Edmund. You didn't know he had gout."

She said nothing. And the final piece fell into place.

"You thought it was him all along," I said. "*That's* what you meant when you told me only I could solve this puzzle. It wasn't because I was good at puzzles. It was because *the only one who could investigate Baronet Darcy was someone of higher rank than him.*"

Sybil smiled, proud, defiant. "I knew you were the one. You weren't from here, so you hadn't grown up with the fear of the White Lady. You could face her down—and Edmund Darcy, too. When I saw you'd already begun to crack the mystery, found the blood mark, spotted it was a word . . . I knew it would be you. Because it *is* Edmund Darcy behind this. It *has* to be."

She coughed, even more violently than before. Spasms wracked her body. We leaned in to help her, but there was nothing we could do. She stayed like that, heaving ragged, bubbling gasps until she found her breath.

"You are wrong about Julian," she said.

"There can't be anyone else who—"

She held up a hand. "I'm not saying he's not involved—though if he is, it's not in the way you think."

She had to clear her throat. "I know the boy," she said. "He's foolish, and his brain is addled in many ways. But he's not evil. If anything, he's obsessed with being 'good.' I don't mean 'a good person.' I mean a hero of old, like one of King Arthur's Knights of the Round Table. If Julian really is involved with the children's disappearance, then I guarantee you: He's only doing his father's bidding. The man has convinced his son it's the noble thing."

Tom frowned. "How could kidnapping children possibly be noble?"

"I don't know," Sybil said. "You'd have to ask the baronet."

"Why are you so sure it's Sir Edmund?" I said.

"I know the man. He's a fraud. And a murderer."

I stood there, still. "Why would you say that?"

"Because he killed my daughter."

And although the room was already cold, a new chill filled it, sinking deep into my bones.

"Edmund Darcy is not from Devonshire," she said. "He used to live in Essex, which is where I lived after I got married. My husband, God rest his soul, died when the plague of thirty-six spread through the land. But, before his passing, he and I had a daughter.

"Her name was Alyson. Oh, Baron . . . she was beautiful. As beautiful and sweet as the summer sun."

Her voice trailed off. She stayed like that, quiet, her mind lost in gentle memories, until another fit of coughing brought her back.

Sybil wiped her mouth. Her fingers trailed blood across her cheek. "Yes. She was beautiful. But she was cursed. She had the great misfortune to fall in love with the son of a marquess—and the even greater misfortune for him to love her back. For this was a match that could never be.

"The daughter of a local baron, you see, had already set her sights on the marquess's son. When he told the girl that he loved my Alyson—that he'd rather renounce his title than marry anyone else—she went to Edmund Darcy, witchfinder. She accused Alyson of witchcraft, said she'd cast a spell on the boy. His love for a peasant girl could only have been black magic."

Sybil grabbed my arm, her grip strengthened by rage.

"She was guilty of nothing, Baron. *Nothing.* I swear on all that is holy, she was no witch. When the bailiffs took her away, I went to Edmund Darcy. I fell to my knees and begged him to see that Alyson was innocent.

"Darcy listened to me. He listened, and he nodded, and he promised me a fair trial. He showed me the needle he would use to prove her innocence. 'Do not fret, good lady,' he said. 'The truth will out. My methods of testing are infallible.'

"So came the trial. I watched as that foul girl spilled her lies, and I waited for Darcy to step forward. When it came time, he grilled Alyson mercilessly. She professed nothing but innocent love.

"Then came the testing. Darcy explained that Alyson had a blemish on her hip which might be a witch's mark. He could test it, and prove guilt or innocence once and for all. I was not afraid, Baron. It was a birthmark, nothing more!

"Darcy showed us all the sharpness of his pricking needle by plunging it through a strip of thick leather. Then he plunged the same needle into Alyson's side. But there was no pain. And when he drew the needle out, there was no blood."

She clenched her fists. "It was impossible. Impossible.

Yet it was all the proof the assizes needed. My daughter was dragged away and hanged. I watched her die, Baron. She was only fourteen years old. And I watched her die."

Sybil lay her head against the hearth and closed her eyes. "They burned her body, afterward, as a witch. Didn't even leave a grave I could visit. I went to see Edmund Darcy. All he could say was 'Madam, the test cannot lie.' But, suddenly, he seemed to have all this money. When he'd first arrived at Colchester, he'd stayed in a meager inn. Now he moved to the most expensive rooms in the city. It was fraud, Baron. He murdered my girl with a fraud. And he did it all to make himself rich.

"I knew, now, what he was. So I began to watch him. And I saw. More and more, he brought accused witches to trial. And always, always, always it was the same: The rich were proven innocent; the poor were always guilty. And when the assizes finally refused to hear any more witch trials, Edmund Darcy left town, his wealth grown without bound.

"I lost track of him—until our king's return. I saw in the news-letters that one Edmund Darcy of Essex had bought himself a baronetcy and moved far from his crimes, where no one would remember him.

"But *I* remembered, Baron. I remembered. Now *you* must remember. For Alyson. For all the girls who died at his hands, and for all the children gone missing. *Remember what he is.*"

She fell silent. I knelt there, beside her, mind churning.

"I don't doubt your story," I said. "But even if Edmund Darcy was a fraud, why would he steal children now? What possible purpose would it serve? And why would he force his own son to do it?"

When she answered, her voice was weak. "I don't know. All I can tell you is that it must be for money. All Edmund Darcy is loyal to, all he believes in, is money. Find the money, and you will find his guilt."

She slumped. "Now go. You have my story, Baron. Go and put things right."

"Wait," I said. "Please . . . I'll do as you ask, I swear it. But you have to ask the Spirits to release me from the *geas.*"

"I can't," she said.

"I promise I'll—"

"I can't release you, Baron, because the Spirits cast no *geas.*"

I sat back, stunned. "But . . . you said . . . the storm. The shipwreck. My memories. The Spirits told you—"

"I spoke to no spirits." She sighed. "I am a sinner, Baron. There are so many sins of which I am guilty. But I know nothing of spirits. I'm just an old healer woman, with a passing knowledge of herbs."

"But . . . the witches' marks on Robert's door. The charm at my feet. You made those. Didn't you?"

"I made them because the people believe. And if they believe I'm a cunning woman, then maybe it will spare me from being called a witch."

"No. You knew. You knew things about me. The storm. The shipwreck. The demon. The . . . the Raven."

"I knew you were in a shipwreck because Robert Dryden told me you were. I knew you were tormented by a demon raven, because when I came at Robert's call, you screamed about it in Latin, in your dream."

"But . . . *why* would you do this to me? Why would you lie?"

"So you'd search for the children. No matter where the hunt took you, no matter how much danger you were in. If you could only save yourself by finding the children, then you would never stop, never rest, until you'd exposed the culprit, and condemned Edmund Darcy."

She sighed. "Add that to my sins, Baron. I manipulated

you with a lie of my own. Perhaps your memories have gone because you *are* cursed. Or perhaps your memories were taken by your illness, when you lay abed those two weeks. Either way, I had nothing to do with it, and I cannot heal you. I am sorry, Baron. I wish that I could."

I slumped next to her, crushed by despair. But I asked her no more questions, and she offered no more comfort. We just sat there together, quietly, until the end.

CHAPTER
37

FOREVER, I THOUGHT. *THIS IS FOREVER.*

I cast those words into my mind as we trudged through the snow. *Are you there, Master? Are you listening? Why didn't you save me? Why didn't you help?*

He wouldn't answer.

"Are you all right?" Tom said.

I stared into the distance. Nothing but endless snow. "No."

He shifted Moppet on his shoulders as he walked beside me. "Are you worried about your memories?"

"What memories?" I said bitterly.

"Some of them have returned."

I didn't answer.

"Sybil thought maybe you lost them because of your illness." Tom nodded toward Sally, who followed some twenty feet behind. "Maybe your memories are like her hand. You just have to use them, and they'll get better."

"You don't know that," I said. "When Sally was injured in Paris, she lost memories, too. Most of them never returned. So what if this is it?" I waved my hands over the hills. "What if this is all that's left to me? To live the rest of my life as a stranger. No family. No home."

"You have a home."

"You mean the shop? Blackthorn? A home isn't a *thing*, Tom. It isn't wood and bricks and mortar. It's the people in it, and the things that happen there. It's the place that, even when it's empty, it's not really empty, because the memories you have fill it with love. I understand that now. I understand it because I *have* no memories. And I'm starting to think I never will."

"I don't believe that," Tom said. "You *have* been remembering things. Little things, yes. But it shows Christopher Rowe is still in there. We'll help you get the rest of them back, one way or another."

"And if you can't?" I said. "What happens then?"

"Then we'll still be here. Sally. Bridget. Isaac. Even Lord Ashcombe. We'll help you make new memories, make a new home. And even if all those others fall away, *I'll* still be here. We're friends forever, Christopher. No matter what."

I looked up at him, at this stranger who'd pushed relentlessly to find me, even when all hope was lost.

And as we walked—for at least a little while—I no longer felt so alone.

We stood on the banks of the River Axe. As I watched the water flow, I felt like I was watching my own mind: shifting, changing, ever impossible to grasp.

"Which way?" Tom said.

I sighed. "North."

"North?" Sally said. "You don't mean . . . back to the Darcy estate?"

Tom looked at me like I'd gone mad. "You do remember Julian tried to kill us, don't you?"

"Yes," I said. "And I'm willing to believe what Sybil said about Sir Edmund, too. But if we're going to stop them, we need proof."

"You're a baron," Sally said. "Any court in the land would take your word over Sir Edmund's."

"I'm a *pretend* baron. I can't go to the assizes and tell them I'm an Ashcombe. What happens when we finally go to trial? Besides, for all my suspicions, we don't really *know* Julian's the one who shot at us, or that Sir Edmund's forcing him to kidnap children. And if they are the ones behind it, we don't know why, or who else is involved. Álvaro, for example—what's his role in all this? Is he working with them, or is he in the dark? What about the locals? Do any of them know the truth?" I shook my head. "We need real evidence if we want to put a stop to this."

They couldn't argue with that. Still, Sally wondered, "What do you hope to find?"

"I'm not sure. But Sybil claimed Sir Edmund was a fraud. So let's start there. Let's see what we can discover at his estate."

"Hold on," Tom said. "If they *are* behind everything, and it really was Julian who shot at us, aren't they just going to kill us when we return?"

"On the contrary. If they're the villains, then the estate's about the safest place we can be."

". . . Are you feeling all right?"

"Think about it," I said. "They could have murdered us in our beds last night. Why didn't they?"

"You want me to explain the minds of madmen?"

"I don't think they're mad. Look, suppose Sir Edmund and Julian are the kidnappers. What if the others in the house—the servants, if not Álvaro—don't know what's going on? What would happen, then, if we died in the baronet's home? How would he explain it? Don't forget, I told Sir Edmund Lord Ashcombe is coming to get me. What do you think the King's Warden would do if he arrived only to discover his grandson was murdered at their estate? No, as long as we don't push them into a corner, our lives there are safe. It's when we *leave* the estate we'll need to worry."

That did still leave a question, however. I had no idea how to prove Sir Edmund was behind the kidnappings. I wasn't even sure how to prove his witch-hunting was a fraud.

"I think I need to see that needle again," I said. "And I need to examine it without Sir Edmund there. We need a distraction."

"Do you have anything in your sash that would make me sick?" Sally said.

"Many things. How sick do you want to be?"

"Well, don't kill me. And I'll need to get better quickly."

I thought about it. "Syrup of ipecac is the easiest."

"What will that do?"

"Make you throw up."

She deflated. "I hate throwing up." I gave her the vial. She walked away, grumbling. "The things I do for you."

I looked over at Tom. "It was *her* idea."

Cooper let us back in. "Sir Edmund is in the drawing room, my lord," he said. "He's been worried about you."

We left our coats with Tom. According to our plan, Tom would pretend he and Moppet were heading to the servants' quarters but would instead wait for us near the entrance, just in case we needed to make a quick escape—or worse, the sort of help only his sword could provide.

"We must see Sir Edmund immediately," I said to the steward. "I have strange news. Is Julian around?"

"No, my lord. He's out, as usual. Shall I send him to you when he returns?"

"Yes," I said, though I didn't really want that. The fewer people around, the better.

Cooper escorted Sally and me to the drawing room, where Sir Edmund was chatting on the couch with Álvaro. "Baron!" he said, relieved. "Thank goodness. I had no idea what happened to you." He looked at me chidingly. "Though I have my suspicions."

"Your suspicions are correct," I said. "We went to Hook Reddale."

He huffed. "My lord . . . you placed yourself in great danger. To say nothing of the Lady Grace. Why—look at her, she's positively green."

He wasn't just saying that. Sally's skin had taken on a distinctly greenish hue. "I'd better sit," she said, her voice warbling.

"Here, here. Have my seat." With a grimace, Sir Edmund stood to give Sally his spot on the couch. Álvaro helped him to the neighboring chair while Sally took his place, holding her stomach.

"Are you unwell, my lady?" Sir Edmund said, with genuine concern. "You didn't . . . did you see . . . ?"

"The White Lady?" I said. "No. We found a different sort of villain. Someone shot at us."

"*What?*"

This was the tricky part. I couldn't lie about what had happened at Hook Reddale. After all, if Sir Edmund *was* working with Julian, he'd already know his son tried to kill us. A lie would make him realize he was a suspect. Instead, I told him the story we'd worked out on our way here.

"I think we stumbled upon a band of brigands," I

said. "I suspect they've made a base in the abandoned village."

Sir Edmund looked shocked. "But . . . the White Lady. Surely no one would test her wrath by living there."

I shrugged. "Perhaps they're only using it to stockpile supplies. But there's no doubt someone is running about the village; we saw their tracks. And the arrows that nearly killed us came from no wraith."

"It's almost impossible to believe. There must be some sort of—my lady?"

Sally had half risen from the couch. She clutched her stomach and moaned. Then she vomited all over Sir Edmund's rug.

Everyone stood, alarmed. "Cooper! Cooper!" Sir Edmund called, and he limped to Sally's side. He'd gone as pale as she had. "She's afflicted by the curse of Hook Reddale."

"No," Sally croaked. "I have . . . another affliction. Christopher . . . please . . . my medicine . . ."

She bent over in Sir Edmund's arms and vomited again.

"Where is it?" I asked her.

"I don't know," she gasped. "It wasn't among my things. I must have left it in my chambers this morning. It's in my little orange bottle—" She retched. A thin string of bile dripped from her lips.

"Your servants," I said to Sir Edmund.

"Of course, of course," he said, and he turned to Cooper, who'd just arrived. "Rally the household. Search the lady's quarters for her medicine. It's in an orange bottle."

"I'll go, too," I said. "I've seen the bottle before."

"Of course, of course. Hurry, my lord."

Sally heaved again as I ran out with the steward. Cooper collected everyone he saw along the way, until I was leading a small army in livery. We made it all the way to the stairs before I skidded to a stop.

"Wait," I said. "I just realized: My man might have her bottle. I'll ask him. You search her chambers. Look everywhere. What you're looking for is about three inches high, and orange, with a cork stopper. You can't miss it."

"Yes, my lord," Cooper said, hurrying them all upstairs.

And finally, at last, I was alone.

CHAPTER
38

THERE WAS NO TIME TO WASTE. I
had, at best, a few minutes before the servants would
return empty-handed.

I sprinted to Sir Edmund's study and flung open the
drawer in the desk. The velvet bag with the bone of Saint
Benedict was there, next to the silver box. Hands trembling,
I pulled the needle out.

The silver cylinder glinted in the lamplight; the needle
looked almost alive. The crosses around the top winked in
the flame. And as I looked closer, I noticed a faint engraving
along one of its hexagonal edges.

I hadn't seen that before. I peered at it closely and could just make out the words.

Et cognoscetis veritatem, et veritas liberabit vos

It was Latin. A quote from the Gospel of John. *And you shall know the truth, and the truth shall set you free.*

It was almost obscene. If Sir Edmund were a fraud, then—

I blinked. Suddenly I felt dizzy.

Those

Et cognoscetis veritatem

words. I'd seen

et veritas

those words

liberabit vos

before.

My knees buckled. The world spun, too fast.

But those *words*. Not on the needle. Where had I seen them?

On a shelf, a memory whispered.

Yes. Yes. They'd been written on a bookshelf, the inscription burned into the wood. But not here. Not in Seaton. Not in Devonshire. It was before. Before the shipwreck.

The bookshelf. It opened. There was . . . a staircase? Down? And . . . a man?

Yes. A man. An old man. Not Master Benedict. But I felt something.

Friendship.

Love.

The books, in the bookshelf. The book . . . *seller.* His name . . . Tom had said it.

Isaac.

I remembered him. I remembered *him.*

My heart swelled. *Isaac. I know you.*

The dizziness remained. I fought it. And still I remembered—

Running. I was running—why was I running?—

I fell against the desk.

Stop, Master Benedict said.

I can't. I can't. I'll lose it.

You must stop. You don't have much more time.

I heard footsteps. I dove behind the couch as a pair of boots clomped past the door.

The memory. I didn't want to lose the memory. It felt so *good* to remember. But the pain . . .

The pain?

The pain was in my finger. I lay there, breathing, as the world stopped spinning, and looked down to see I'd stabbed myself with the pricking needle.

I pulled it out, wincing. Blood welled on my skin. I sucked on my fingertip, the flesh throbbing in time with my beating heart.

Well, there was no doubt the thing was sharp. It had bled Sally, and now me. And yet Sybil had claimed the needle was a fraud.

He plunged the same needle into Alyson's side, she'd said. *But there was no pain. And when he drew the needle out, there was no blood.*

This needle couldn't help but draw blood. Could Sybil

have been wrong? Could her daughter really have been a witch after all?

If she wasn't, then Sir Edmund must have cheated. But how could he do that with a needle this sharp? I could only think of one way—and that was to make sure the needle never went in at all.

And now I remembered something Sir Edmund had said. *I performed the test myself, so none could attempt trickery by sleight of hand.*

Sleight of hand?

What if *he* was the one playing the trick? What if he'd never stabbed the accused at all? If he'd turned the needle to the side, slipped it past the skin, it would still look to the court like he'd plunged it in.

No, that wouldn't work. The court might not see his deception, but the supposed witch would. She'd know he hadn't pricked her. All she'd have to do was turn her body and call for him to do it again. They might disbelieve one girl, but all eleven he'd condemned? Impossible.

It had to be something else. I rooted through the desk again. Behind Saint Benedict's finger bone, I found a sheaf of papers. A quick glance at them showed—

That was interesting. They were receipts. All of them

listed payments to Edmund Darcy, all from men living in Essex, most of whom were members of the peerage: barons, counts, marquesses, even a duke. The amounts weren't small: dozens of pounds. In a few cases, hundreds.

My mind raced. Sybil had claimed Sir Edmund was selling innocence—or guilt—according to someone's ability to pay. Could he have been so foolishly arrogant as to have kept evidence of his own crimes?

I scanned them more closely, and I saw: He might be arrogant, but he wasn't foolish. All the receipts said things like *for services to the town of Chelmsford* or *for efforts in prosecuting the evil from our lands.* There was no evidence here. If Sir Edmund was a fraud, I thought, what a delight these papers would bring him every time he looked at them. They would be a record only of his cleverness.

I put the papers back in the desk. My time was running out, and I hadn't found anything at all.

Forget everything else, Master Benedict said. *The needle is important.*

He was right. If there was fraud, the needle had to be the key. I studied the thing again, turning it over, close enough to the lamplight that its heat seared my cheek. I'd missed the engraving before. Maybe I'd missed something else.

But what could that be? The silver was polished, pristine—

No. Wait.

It was *not* pristine. The silver was scratched. Near the top, between the arms of one of the crosses, I saw faint grooves. They curved from the cross's vertical arm to its horizontal.

It looked like wear. Yet nowhere else on the silver did I find similar marks.

Why on earth would such a spot show wear? And why would the grooves be—

Curved, I thought.

I placed my thumbnail on the leg of the cross. I pushed it in the direction of the grooves.

And it turned.

A faint *click* rattled inside the cylinder. I stared at it. Then, slowly, I placed the needle against my palm and pressed.

The needle slid in.

Not into my hand. Into the cylinder.

I let go. The needle sprang back out.

The test, I thought. Heart thumping, I pulled the collar of my shirt down until my upper ribs were exposed. I laid the point of the needle against my chest, like I was an accused witch, on trial. Then, with a quick prayer, I drove the needle in.

It was strange. I could feel the prick of the needle on my flesh, the press of the cylinder surrounding it. It *felt* like the needle had gone into me. But there was no real pain, just the discomfort of the point against my skin. And when I drew the needle back, there was no blood, just a faint indentation where it had pressed.

Fingers shaking, I turned the cross back to its original position. I tested the needle again—and now it wouldn't budge.

This was it. This was how he'd done it. The cross on the end was the trick: By turning it, it switched the needle from fixed to collapsible.

There was nothing holy here. It was pure evil. Sir Edmund, false witchfinder, deciding with a flick of his thumb whether the girl before him was innocent or guilty. And if he chose guilt, the poor accused wouldn't even know how she'd been duped.

Sybil was right. Sir Edmund was nothing but a fraud.

CHAPTER
39

I HAD HIM. THIS NEEDLE WAS PROOF, pure and undeniable, that Sir Edmund had committed terrible crimes.

And yet I didn't know what to do.

He needed to account for the lives he'd taken. But those crimes were twenty years old. The problem now was the missing children. How could I prove he was part of *that*? I didn't even know why it was happening.

And I didn't have any more time to think about it. I made sure the pricking needle was back in its locked position, then replaced it in its box. I exited the study, listening. It sounded like the servants were still up in Sally's quarters, searching for a bottle that didn't exist. That wouldn't last for long.

I made my way back to the drawing room, forcing myself to walk slowly. And yet the slower I went, the more I imagined I could feel a bow being drawn, a broadhead aimed at my spine. The sensation got so strong I had to turn and look.

The hall was empty. I took a breath. *Stop panicking,* I scolded myself. *They may want to stop your investigation, but what you told Tom and Sally is true. They can't attack you here. It would bring down the wrath of Lord Ashcombe.*

Then I paused. They couldn't attack us here . . . if our deaths were seen to be foul play. But an arrow in the back wasn't the only way to get rid of someone. I thought of my master's poisons, hidden in that cherrywood box at the Blue Boar Inn.

I shook my head. Sir Edward couldn't poison us. How would he explain all our deaths?

My blood froze as I realized: Our own deception would provide him with the means.

I sprinted back to the drawing room. Sally was lying on the couch, looking miserable. Sir Edmund and Álvaro hovered over her, the Spaniard pressing a cool, damp cloth to her forehead.

"We can't find it," I said, letting my real panic show

through. "Your medicine isn't here. Are you *sure* you had it with you yesterday?"

Sally glanced over at me.

"I mean, really, *really* sure?" I said.

She got the hint. "I . . . don't know," she said. "I didn't see it yesterday, but I didn't need it."

"So where's the last place you saw it? Somewhere *else*?" I prompted.

She paused. "I had it in my room at the inn," she said finally.

I turned to Sir Edmund. "We have to return to Seaton."

"My lord," he said, startled. "The lady is in no state to travel."

"She'll be in a worse state if she stays," I said. "She must have that medicine. We have to go."

"It's too far. Too late in the day. And the snow is too deep to take you in my carriage. If your servant goes to collect it—"

"He can't. As you said, it's too late in the day. By the time he reaches Seaton, it'll be too dark for him to return. He'd have to wait until morning—and she could die by then. We'll have to chance it."

"Wait—"

The last thing I was going to do was wait. I didn't want to give Sir Edmund an opportunity to think of a good reason to leave Sally here. Ignoring their protests, I scooped her into my arms and ran from the drawing room.

"Baron!" Sir Edmund called. Álvaro tried to help him follow, but with his foot, he couldn't keep up.

I whispered as I reached the entryway. "Tom!"

Tom stepped around the corner. Moppet clutched the leg of his breeches, Bridget nestled in the crook of her arm. Tom's hand was over his shoulder, already gripping Eternity's hilt.

I shoved Sally into his arms and grabbed our coats. "We need to go."

We bolted from the estate and ran along the river, Moppet hanging off Tom's back. I didn't dare slow until we'd reached the woods. There we stopped, puffing, Sally lolling in Tom's arms.

"Are you still sick?" I asked her, worried. "The ipecac should have worn off by now."

"Oh, I'm feeling better," Sally said cheerfully. "I just like being carried."

Once we were certain we hadn't been followed, we stopped running. A few hundred yards through snow was bad enough; we couldn't possibly keep it up over miles. Still, the fear in our guts kept us moving, heads on a swivel, searching the woods for buzzing arrows.

"I thought you said we'd be safe at the estate," Tom said.

"That was before we showed up claiming Sally was sick." I cursed. "We gave him the perfect way to poison us. If Sally's 'strange illness' were caught by the rest of us, if we were trapped by snow in Sir Edmund's house without medicine . . ."

Tom's eyes widened. "So Sir Edmund really is behind this?"

"I'm almost sure of it. At the very least, Sybil was right: He's a murderer." I told them what I'd discovered about the pricking needle. They listened, faces grim. It was terrifying to realize we'd stayed the night with a killer.

"We still need to figure out what he's doing with the children," Sally said. "How are we going to do that from Seaton?"

"We're not going to Seaton. We'll follow the river south until we pass the bridge at the fork. Then we'll use the same trick Julian's been using: We'll walk through the water to cover our tracks."

"To where?"

I could only think of one place to hide.

. . .

It was well past nightfall by the time we reached Robert's farm. With the cloud cover, we had no moonlight to guide us. Fortunately, the river laid out the path, or we'd have been lost. As it was, we slipped and stumbled through the snow until the farm's lights glowed with blessed relief.

When we thumped on Robert's door, he was surprised but pleased. "My lord! How—" He broke off as he looked us over. "Are you all right? You look terrible." He flushed. "Er . . . I mean . . ."

"No need for explanation. We feel terrible," I said. "Would we be able to stay in the cob house tonight? I'll pay you."

He was offended I'd even suggested it. I thanked him profusely as he escorted us to the house. "I'll bring food, and more blankets," he said. "Anything else you need?"

I shook my head, and he left. Tom looked wearily at the palliasse Moppet had slept on when she'd been here. It was far too short for his height.

"Take the bed," I said.

"You know I can't do that," he said. "You're the lord."

"Just take it. Robert's not likely to cause a fuss, and I'll handle any questions. You've earned it."

Tom didn't argue further. He groaned as he collapsed,

facedown, on the mattress. Moppet curled up next to him. Sally flopped onto the palliasse, just as weary. "I *hate* throwing up," she said.

I sighed. All that was left was the chair, so that's where I stayed. I was still there when Robert returned, his arms full with bowls of piping-hot stew. He regarded the strange scene with some puzzlement. I shrugged and was grateful he didn't ask any questions.

Tom was too tired to sit up, even to eat. He just turned his head and poured the stew sideways into his mouth. It made me feel like laughing. Though not for long.

We were safe for the night. Soon enough, however, tomorrow would come, and I had no idea what we were going to do. A smear of stew still on his face, Tom fell asleep. Moppet was already slumbering, Bridget beside her.

Sally drowsed on the palliasse, barely able to keep her eyes open. "Are you going to bed?" she mumbled.

"Soon," I said.

"Do you want the palliasse? We can trade in the night."

"All right."

"Make sure you wake me."

"I will," I said, and I listened to her breath, slowing until the dreams took her.

Master? I called. *Are you there? I need you.*

No one answered.

Please, Master, I said. *I'm lost, and I don't know what to do. Please. Please come back to me.*

But all I heard was the crackling of the fire.

THURSDAY, DECEMBER 24, 1665

Ni il a tem pert m es   q od non r ve etur;
eque ab cond um qu d on sc tur

CHAPTER

40

NOTHING.

I had nothing.

I spent the whole night trying to piece together what we'd discovered. Trying to somehow make it all fit. But it didn't make any sense. What do you do when you can't find the answer?

You flop around aimlessly, I thought. *Like I've been doing all night.*

But somewhere in the back of my mind, different words whispered. *You step aside and let your mind find the answer for you.*

I'd heard that somewhere before. From . . . Tom?

No, not Tom. From Master Benedict.

Yes. He'd said that to me. But not since I'd awoken.

He'd said it *before*.

I sat up, excited. I'd remembered something else.

Yet the joy of it didn't last long, for it got me no closer to solving this mystery. No closer to saving the children—my friends—myself—from danger. Sybil blamed Sir Edmund, who was admittedly a fraud and murderer. I was sure it was Julian; he'd known we were going to Hook Reddale, he knew how to use a bow, and most important, the children knew him from his regular visits to their hamlets. The most likely truth was that it was both of them, working together. Sir Edmund directing his son, Julian actually taking the children.

So what about Álvaro?

He was the piece I couldn't get a grip on. Sir Edmund had said Álvaro was his old assistant. Was Álvaro a true believer, then? Or did he know Sir Edmund was a fraud?

He must have seen his master getting wealthier and wealthier during the witch trials. Did he know Sir Edmund was selling innocence? Or did he simply think it was just rewards for the best witchfinder in the country?

Even now, I couldn't place him on either side. On the one hand, Sir Edmund had made a point of saying that no

one—not even Álvaro—was permitted to handle the fraudu-
lent pricking needle, which made me think he'd been duped
like everyone else. On the other hand, the timing of his
appearance—"visiting for the winter" just as children started
to disappear—struck me as too much of a coincidence to be
believed.

I didn't know what to think. Sybil had been no help;
she'd said she never met the man. This was the most frustrating of the missing pieces, because the more I thought about
it, the more I was sure Álvaro was the key to unlocking this
mystery. If he was one of the kidnappers, then the reason for
his arrival would explain why it was happening. But if he was
not . . . I remembered the zeal with which he'd pulled his
knife at the sign of evil. He'd be an incredibly powerful ally.

I buried my head in my hands. Sir Edmund, Julian,
Álvaro—I had no proof of *anything* regarding the children.
And even believing at least some of them were guilty, that
left another question I couldn't answer.

Why steal children at all?

Sybil had promised that Sir Edmund's motive was
money. It's all he cared about, she'd said. Except that didn't
make sense. Sir Edmund had made his money taking bribes
from the wealthy; the children who'd vanished were poor.

What profit could those children provide? Ransom? For what? A pail of milk?

You can't answer that, Master Benedict said, *until you answer a different question. What happened to the children?*

I frowned. *What do you mean? They were kidnapped.*

Yes. But what happened to them afterward?

I was shocked to realize we'd never considered that. At first, we'd wondered *who* had taken them. When we'd thought it was the White Lady, we'd just assumed they were dead. Once we discovered it wasn't her, however, we'd asked *why* the children were taken. And in trying to answer that, we'd missed the most important question of all.

Where had they gone?

If the Darcys were behind it, they had to have hidden the children somewhere. Could they have locked them away on the estate?

No, that didn't make sense. Sir Edmund had to be keeping the kidnappings a secret from his servants; otherwise, he'd have murdered us in our sleep instead of having Julian ambush us at Hook Reddale. So the children had to be elsewhere, where none of the servants could find them. An interesting idea came to me.

What if he'd hidden them in Hook Reddale?

The lie I'd told Sir Edmund about stumbling upon a brigand camp actually made a certain sense. If you didn't believe in the White Lady, the abandoned village would be the perfect place to hide. No one would ever look for you there.

Except that couldn't be it. When we'd gone there, the snow hadn't been touched. No one had been in Hook Reddale since at least the snowfall. We'd have seen the tracks.

A terrible thought occurred to me: What if the children weren't being kept anywhere? What if they were . . . I mean, if the Darcys had no problem killing *us* . . .

I shuddered. That was too terrible. I didn't want to believe it.

But then where?

Think of Julian, Master Benedict said. *What did he say to you? When he told you about going outside?*

I tried to remember.

I'll show you the hamlets, he'd said, *and where the best hunting is. . . . And there's a cave by the river—*

I sat up, startled.

A cave. The perfect hiding place. It was hidden. It was sheltered. Depending on how well sheltered, you could keep a fire by the entrance and keep the children warm enough to survive; no one passing would see the light. The Darcy estate was right *next* to the river. The children might be just a few hundred yards away.

Then I remembered: There were caves all over this area. I sank into my chair, deflated. I'd hoped that maybe I could find them on my own. But the truth was—if the children were even alive—I had no idea where to begin.

There's still one more piece you're missing, Master Benedict said.

I knew what he meant almost as he said it. It was right in front of me, sleeping next to Tom on the bed.

Moppet.

She'd arrived at Robert's farm, seemingly from nowhere. Where had she come from? And how was she linked to the children who'd vanished?

After three days with the girl, it was hard to believe we still knew nothing about her. Though she clearly adored Tom—and at least seemed to trust me and Sally—two words were all she'd ever given us. "Monmon," when she first saw Tom. And "Puritan," when she'd become so scared she'd cried.

"Puritan" had to be the key. But I couldn't understand how it fit. At first, I wondered if the Darcys were involved with some Puritan plot. I dismissed it when I remembered that Moppet hadn't seemed troubled at all by being at the estate. Though it occurred to me: Moppet had never actually seen the Darcys themselves. She'd stayed with Tom, in the servants' quarters, the whole time.

I shook my head. We'd been flailing around for too long, and now we were out of options. We had to convince Moppet to tell us what she'd meant. As I sat there, thinking of how to do that, there came a faint knock on the door.

"Come in," I said softly.

The deep red of sunrise spilled through the doorway, making me squint. I hadn't realized it was morning. I shielded my eyes, then let my hand fall, let the rays warm my cheeks. Finally, the clouds had parted.

Wise brought us breakfast, more flat bread slathered with clotted cream and strawberry preserve. His bow slung over his shoulder, he placed the plates on the table next to me.

"Thank you," I said absently. I didn't have much appetite, even for this.

Wise touched me lightly on the shoulder. He pointed at me, then placed his hand on his chest, concern on his face.

"No," I said. "I'm not all right."

He pointed to my mouth, then to himself. *Do you want to tell me?*

I sighed. "Someone tried to kill us yesterday."

He looked shocked. He spread his hands, a question.

"I don't know who. We couldn't see him." I motioned to Wise's bow. "But he shot at us when we visited Hook Reddale."

Wise stiffened and shook his head. At first, I thought it was because I'd mentioned the home of the White Lady. Then I realized what had worried him.

"I know it wasn't you," I said. "You're too tall. I think it was Julian Darcy."

Wise frowned and cocked his head.

"You don't think so? Do you know him, then?"

He nodded. He pointed to his eyes, then his bow, then outside, and made a motion like his fingers were walking. *I see him out hunting.*

Wise hesitated. He waggled his fingers beside his temple. Then he placed his hand over his heart and shook his head. I think I understood what he was saying. *Julian's odd, but not a bad person.*

"Sybil said the same thing. She thought maybe his father was tricking him into doing it."

Wise's frown deepened, but he didn't respond.

Tom roused with a grunt. He sat up for a moment, bleary eyed. Moppet shifted and wrapped her arms around his waist.

He groaned. "Is it 1666 yet?"

"Another week, I think."

He flopped back down on the bed. "Wake me when the year turns." Moppet snuggled into him.

"Sorry," I said. "We have to talk. Moppet? Moppet."

She kept her eyes shut.

"I know you can hear me, Moppet."

Tom sat up again. Sally woke, too, stretching on the palliasse. "What's going on?"

"We have to talk to the girl."

The girl in question was no longer pretending to be asleep. She clung to Tom, looking scared.

"Why?" Tom said.

"Because I think she knows things. And we can't wait any longer for her to tell us. We need to know them, too."

I leaned forward. Moppet stared at me, eyes so big and blue.

"I know you're afraid," I said. "I am, too. But we really need your help. Not just for us. There are a lot of other little boys and girls out there who are lost. They miss their families, and their families miss them. Will you tell us what you know? Please?"

She trembled, her eyes welling up. Tom cupped her face, turned it toward him, wiped her tears away with his thumb.

"You don't have to be scared," he said. "No one will hurt you ever again. I promise."

He took his sword from where it leaned against the wall. He pulled off the sheath that hid the hilt and drew the blade. He laid it across their laps.

"You see?" he said. "I'll keep you safe. Eternity will protect us."

Moppet stared at the sword. Her eyes tracked along its length, from the shining blade to its brilliant, beautiful moonstone. Then, blinking away tears, she whispered.

"Puritan," she whispered, so faint I could barely hear her. "Hit foreign Puritan."

I rose from my chair. "What? 'Hit foreign Puritan'? What does that mean?"

"Did she say 'hit'?" Sally said. "I thought it was 'hat.'"

That made even less sense. I knelt by the bed, and Moppet shrank into Tom's chest.

"Gently," Tom chided me.

"Moppet," I said, as calmly as I could. "Did you say 'hit' or 'hat'? 'Hat foreign Puritan'?"

Tom frowned. "Christopher."

At first, I thought he was chastising me for scaring the girl. Then I realized he was looking behind me. I turned.

It was Wise. The man had backed up, right against the wall. He stared at Moppet, terrified.

His mouth worked silently. I went to him. "Wise? What's the matter—?"

I reached for his arm. He jerked away from me, raised his hands.

"It's all right," I said. "It's just me."

Wise's senses seemed to return. He stared at me, then pointed at Moppet.

My heart began to race. "Do you know what she's saying?"

He nodded.

"Is it Puritan? Hit foreign Puritan?"

He shook his head.

"Not 'hit'? Or is she not talking about Puritans?"

Wise looked around the room. Suddenly he pointed at the fire.

"Fire?" I said. "Was there a fire recently?"

He shook his head. He moved closer, pointing frantically at the flames.

"Flame," I said. "Smoke."

He shook his head.

"Hearth," Tom said.

"Chimney," Sally said.

Wise slumped. Then he straightened, as if he had an idea. He ran outside, beckoning us to follow.

We did, not even stopping to put on our coats. Robert, coming from the farmhouse, halted in the snow, puzzled. "Something wrong, my lord?"

I didn't answer. The sun peeked over the horizon through a gap in the cloud cover, staining the sky a brilliant red. Wise pointed at it.

"Sun." I thought of what he'd been trying to tell us inside. "And fire. Fire . . . in the sky? A shooting star? A comet? I'm sorry, I don't understand."

Wise looked as frustrated as I was. He thought for a moment. Then, suddenly, he grabbed my shirt. He shook it, rubbed his hand over the material.

"Silk?" I said. "Smooth?"

He shook his head. He yanked my shirt up and began rifling through my sash.

Robert was appalled. "Wise! You can't manhandle his lordship—"

I waved the farmer off, watching Wise carefully. He lifted each vial from my sash, then slid it back again. When he found what he was looking for, he pulled it out and shook it triumphantly.

Pills rattled inside the glass. They were small and blue. I'd seen them the first time I'd searched the sash.

"The blue mass?" I said, confused.

"What are those?" Tom said.

"*Pilula hydrargyri.* They're called the blue mass. They're a remedy for constipation, or consumption, or . . . well, a lot of things."

"What's in them?" Sally said.

"Quicksilver, mostly." I didn't understand what they had to do with anything.

Wise placed the vial next to my shirt. He shook both of them, looking at me intently.

I still didn't get it. The only thing I could think of that was remotely the same was that both my shirt and the pills were—

"Blue?" I said.

Wise nodded, delighted.

"Blue. You're trying to say 'blue.' But what does that have to do with—"

He pointed downward.

"Ground," I said. "Blue ground? Underground?"

He shook his head. Then he grabbed a fistful of snow.

"Snow."

He shook the pills.

"Blue . . . oh, you mean the *color* of the snow. White."

He nodded. And then he pointed back at the sunrise.

"Red," I said.

He shook his head and angled his arm higher.

"Orange?"

He nodded vigorously.

Now I understood. "That's why you pointed at the fire. The flame—it's orange. But what—"

Wise dropped to his knees, drew with his finger in the snow. He leaned back and looked up, so we could see what he'd sketched.

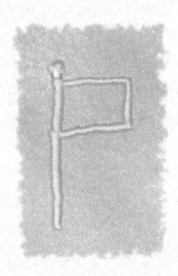

"Looks like a flag," Tom said.

A flag. Blue, white, and—

"Orange." I gasped. "That's the Prince's Flag!"

"What prince?" Tom said.

"Of the Netherlands. William of Orange. It's the old Dutch flag. It used to be orange, white, and blue." I turned to Wise, mind racing. "That's the flag you'd know from your sailing days. But what does that—"

Wise pointed at Moppet insistently. And I finally realized what he'd been trying to say.

"*Dutch?*" I said. "She's speaking *Dutch?*"

He nodded, relieved.

We stared at the girl, stunned. Tom grabbed my arm. "Now you can talk to her!"

"Me? I don't know Dutch."

"I thought Master Benedict taught you every language."

"I can't know *every* language. The closest I know is . . ." I tried different tongues in my head. "German."

She might know that. I knelt in close as she hugged Tom's leg. "*Sprichst du Deutsch?*" I said.

She looked at me blankly.

"I guess not. Um . . . *Parles-tu français?* No? *Parli italiano? ¿Hablas español?*"

Her expression didn't change.

"You know more than that," Tom insisted.

"The rest are classical languages." I supposed Latin was worth a try; if her parents had been educated, she might have learned it. *"Loquerisne latine?"*

She didn't respond.

Tom was disappointed. "You don't speak any Dutch at all?"

I searched my memory. "I might know the *word* 'Dutch.'"

"What's that?"

"Nederlands."

Moppet drew a breath.

I leaned in once more. I pointed at her. *"Nederlands?"*

She nodded. *"Nederlands,"* she whispered.

I stood, amazed. "No wonder she doesn't speak to us. She's not just scared. She hasn't understood a word we've said."

Sally frowned. "We're at war with the Netherlands. What's a little Dutch girl doing wandering alone in England?"

"Maybe she was shipwrecked, like us?" Tom said.

Or maybe . . . ? "Wait," I said. "If she's speaking Dutch,

and she's not saying 'Puritan,' what's she actually saying?"

The closest language I knew was German, and while there were big differences between them, some of the words would be similar. *Puritan,* I thought. *Suppose someone said that to me, speaking German. Then that would be* . . .

Wise tugged on my sleeve. I turned to see he was still kneeling in the snow. While we'd been talking to Moppet, he'd drawn something else. He pointed to it.

And I understood.

CHAPTER
41

"THAT'S IT," I SAID. "THAT'S *IT*."

"What?" Tom said. "The shipwreck?"

"No. What Moppet's been saying. It's not 'Puritan.' It's *Piraten*. In German, that means 'pirates.' It's *pirates*."

Wise nodded, pointing at Moppet. We stood there, stunned.

"*Pirates* are kidnapping the children?" Tom said. "Can that be true?"

"It would certainly explain what's been troubling Moppet," I said. "Think: When did she get the most scared?"

He looked up, surprised. "When we went down to the Blood and Barrel. By the docks."

"Right. It wasn't Hook Reddale. You'd think the home of the White Lady would have frightened her the most. Yet she wasn't scared at all—because she couldn't understand what we were saying. She didn't know it was supposed to be haunted. No, it was the Blood and Barrel, with Captain Haddock and his crew. Nothing frightened her more than them."

"It isn't Captain Haddock that's kidnapping children, is it?" Sally said.

"It couldn't be," I said. "Moppet would have screamed blue murder if we'd taken her to the same pirates that had snatched her."

Robert agreed. "I know Roger Haddock. He may not be a *good* man, but he's not a *bad* one. And he certainly wouldn't kidnap our children. He's absolutely loyal to England."

The farmer looked thoughtfully at Wise. "If it's really

pirates taking the children, then it could only be Barbary pirates. They've raided our coasts for decades." He frowned. "But this is not how they do it. Corsairs attack entire towns. They don't hide and snatch children in secret."

"Wait," Tom said. "If it's pirates, why haven't we seen their ship?"

"There are hidden coves all along the coast. If their ship can sail the shallows, they could have tucked in anywhere for the winter. Unless you stumbled upon them by accident, you'd never find them."

"Then how are we supposed to stop them?"

I was fairly certain that, wherever they were holed up, that's where Moppet had escaped from. But I doubted she'd be able to lead us back. She'd been wandering for days, lost, before Wise found her. She'd never remember where the pirates' cove was.

Which left us with only one alternative. "We have to go back and see Julian."

"Julian?" Sally said. "I thought it was Barbary pirates."

"He has to be working with them. He's the only one who knew we were going to Hook Reddale. No one else could have laid that trap."

Robert looked confused. When I told him what we'd

discovered, he could barely believe it. "Why would Baronet Darcy help Barbary pirates steal our children?"

"I don't know," I said. "But Julian's the key to figuring it out. If Sybil was right, and he's not truly evil, perhaps we can play upon his guilt, get him to confess. I just wish we had some evidence to help break him."

"What about his footprints?" Sally said. "The tracks at Hook Reddale were made by hobnailed boots. If we can match his soles to the prints . . ." Sally trailed off as Wise and Robert pointed to their tracks in the snow. Both of them were hobnailed.

"Most people round these parts have them," Robert said. "Helps with the weather."

But Wise regarded me thoughtfully.

"You have an idea?" I said.

Wise stepped back and unslung his bow. He half drew it, aimed at me, though there was no arrow in the string. He pointed at me, and then his own eyes. *Did you see the man who shot at you?*

"Just his cloak," I said. "He kept his hood up the whole time."

Wise pulled an arrow from the quiver on his back. He held it out.

"We definitely saw the arrows." A little *too* closely.

He pointed at the head, then at the fletching.

"Yes, we saw it. It was a broadhead, for hunting, and the fletching . . ." I stopped. "The *fletching*."

"What about it?" Tom said.

"The arrows Julian shot at us at Hook Reddale. The fletching was bronze. Turkey feather. If Julian's arrows match the fletching, that's our evidence."

Sally objected. "He can't be the only person in Devonshire using turkey feathers for fletching."

"Then we press him on it. Or threaten him with Lord . . ." I glanced at Robert. "Uh . . . my grandfather. But we may not need to. If he's really not wicked, he should feel guilty about what he's done. Let's see how he reacts."

I asked Robert for rations to take with us on our trek back to the Darcy estate. When he left to get them, I turned to Wise. "You've met Julian Darcy, right?"

He nodded.

"Would you be willing to come with us to his estate? It might help convince him to confess if someone he knows appeals to him."

Wise's eyes went wide. He put his hands up and backed away, shaking his head.

I didn't blame him. He'd been terrified when he'd heard Moppet say "pirates"; I couldn't imagine the nightmares he must have about being a slave.

"I'm sorry," I said, trying to calm him. "It was wrong of me to ask."

Wise bowed his head, looking ashamed.

I put a hand on his arm. "You're a good man. You not only saved my life, you've helped discover what's been happening to the children. We'll get them back, I promise."

He smiled gratefully. But he still looked ashamed.

And afraid.

We made to leave for the Darcy estate right away. Wise stopped us, gesturing. It took me a while to figure out what he was trying to communicate. When I did, it made me pause.

I'd forgotten. "Julian won't be at home now. He spends the day outdoors."

I cursed. We could have gone anyway and waited for him to return, but then I'd have to spend time with Sir Edmund. Never mind that I didn't trust him. I didn't want him anywhere near us when we confronted his son.

So we waited. We timed our departure to arrive at the

Darcy estate an hour before dusk. Then we hid ourselves among the trees and watched carefully for Julian's return.

Time passed slowly, the cold seeping through our coats. Still we waited, until—

There. A lone figure in a cloak, trekking along the riverbank, turned and made for the estate.

"Is that him?" Tom whispered.

I couldn't tell. The cloak looked lighter in color than our would-be assassin's, but the archer had been shaded by the woods. He made his way to the main entrance and opened the door without knocking. Just before it closed, he shook off his hood.

It was him. We rushed to the door. Cooper welcomed us, as usual. "Sir Edmund is in the drawing room."

"Actually," I said, "has Julian returned? We were hoping to speak to him."

"Certainly, my lord. He'll be changing now. If you'd like to join Sir Edmund, I'll tell Master Julian you've—"

"That's all right; we'll see him ourselves."

I brushed past the surprised steward and hurried upstairs. Everyone came with me this time, Tom and Moppet included. I didn't want Eternity anywhere but by my side.

I didn't knock at Julian's door. I just burst into his

room like we were old friends. "Julian!" I said cheerfully.

He stood there, startled, right in the middle of changing. He was naked from the waist up, his breeches around his ankles, wearing only his drawers.

"Christopher," he said breathlessly. "And Lady Grace—oh my." He turned scarlet as he hurriedly pulled up his breeches. He grabbed a shirt laid out on his bed and turned away to put it on. That's when I saw them.

His back was covered in scars. A crisscross of knotted flesh marked his skin, evidence of wounds old and healed. But some of the cuts were fresh, swelling, oozing an angry red. I could see the scabs where the blood had clotted. Someone had flogged him, mercilessly. A lifetime of cruelty, etched forever into his back.

Sally's hand flew to her lips. Tom looked away, horrified. Moppet hugged his leg.

I couldn't help but stare. And as I did, a memory returned. I remembered a place of cold stone, of gray walls and darkened rooms. It was

home?

Not home, Master Benedict said

and no, it wasn't. Not anymore. But it had been, years ago. Cripplegate. The orphanage, where I'd lived.

Since you were a baby, Sally had told me.

I remembered it. I remembered the sternness of the masters, and the petty cruelty of the other boys. I remembered the pain of the beatings, for things done and things not done. I remembered my prayers. How I prayed for God to send me a family, how I promised Him anything, everything, if He'd send someone who might love me.

And I remembered thinking: *Forever. This is for forever.*

Then Master Benedict came and rescued me. I remembered that now. I remembered *him*. But I couldn't see his face.

Why couldn't I see his face?

"I wasn't expecting you," Julian mumbled. He buttoned his shirt, still turned away. His scars were covered now, but I felt a great swell of pity for the boy. I had to remind myself: *He tried to kill you.*

Julian buttoned his doublet, still babbling. "I apologize," he said, and he did look sorry.

That's not just an apology, I thought. *That's guilt. And fear.*

"I was just out exploring," Julian said. "I found a new cave; I never thought I'd find one in the western hills, but there it was—"

I cut him off, smiling, as friendly as could be. "Did you still want to learn the sword?"

He looked confused. "I . . . yes. Really? Now? Yes!" His expression kept changing, like he couldn't decide what to feel. Embarrassed? Excited? Friendly? Afraid?

I pretended not to notice. "Then let's go to the armory. We can choose our blades."

The thought of swordplay seemed to resolve whatever struggle was going on inside. He clapped his hands, like a delighted child, then hurried from his room and bounded down the steps.

We had to run to keep up with him. He sped past startled servants to the estate's tower. By the time we got inside, he'd disappeared.

"Up here," he called, poking his head out from the second floor.

We went up, cautiously. But he wasn't holding a weapon, and there wasn't any hostility in his eyes. He still hadn't realized what I planned.

"Here they are," he said, and he waved his hands around the room.

The second floor of the tower was where the Darcys kept their arms. The weapons, in racks around the curved walls, reminded me of the knight's tower in Hook Reddale. Of course, these were in much better shape, and there were fewer of them: four swords, five halberds, three longbows, two pistols, and a single musket.

"They're not much," Julian said apologetically. "Nothing so nice as your man's sword. But they'll be good enough, won't they?"

I froze. Julian had just made a terrible mistake.

Tom was carrying Eternity slung over his back, as usual. But the sword was still in its scabbard, and Tom hadn't removed the sheath that covered the hilt.

So how did Julian know how nice the blade was?

There was only one place he could have seen it: in Hook Reddale, as we'd entered the tower. All doubts vanished. Julian *was* our would-be assassin.

The rest of the evidence was on the wall. Beneath the longbows, slung low from a hook, were a pair of quivers, a score of arrows filling each one. The fletching was unmistakable: turkey feathers, bronze.

Julian reached to take a sword from the rack. I bumped him out of the way. "Allow me."

He looked a little confused at how I'd pushed him. When I turned to him, sword in hand, fear flickered across his face.

There wasn't any more reason to delay. "Julian?"

"Yes?"

"Why did you try to kill me?"

I expected him to deny it. I expected him to protest, to shout, be surprised, be confused, angry, hurt. Instead, he wilted with undisguised guilt.

"I'm sorry," he whispered.

His confession caught me off guard. "You *admit* you shot at us at Hook Reddale?"

"I'm sorry," he said again.

"And the children . . . you've been taking them, too?"

He turned white, so pale, I thought he might faint. "I'm sorry. I'm sorry. I'm so sorry."

I couldn't understand his reaction. Had he gone mad? "If you're sorry," I said, "why would you do it?"

He looked so small. "I didn't want to. I swear I didn't. He made us."

"*Who* made you?"

"I can't tell you."

"Julian—"

"Everyone's going to die." He wrung his hands, eyes shut, as if not seeing would make everything just a dream. "Everyone's going to die."

I grabbed his arm. "Listen to me. We can protect you."

"You can't. You *can't*. He'll kill us all."

"Who will kill us? Your father? Álvaro? The pirates? *Who?*"

"Julian?"

I spun at the sound of the voice. Sir Edmund limped up the stairs, all his weight on Álvaro. Cooper trailed behind them, poking his head just above the floor.

Sir Edmund stared at us. He saw the sword in my hand, his son in tears. "What's happening?" he said, his voice tight.

There was no time for an answer. Because just then, Álvaro's eyes went wide. He cursed.

And suddenly Moppet was screaming.

CHAPTER

42

EEEEEEEEEEEEEEEEEEEEEEEEEEE—

Her shriek pierced my ears like a knife. Tom jumped, startled out of his skin. Sir Edmund stumbled backward and nearly fell down the stairs; only Álvaro's grip saved him from tumbling. As it was, he knocked the Spaniard off balance.

Sally whirled, face white. Against the wall, Julian cringed. I backed away, gripping the hilt of my sword so hard the leather dug into my skin. And through it all came Moppet's scream.

EEEEEEEEEEEEEEEEEEEEEEEEEEEEEEEEEE—

The sound was the worst thing I'd ever heard. It was pure terror, a nightmare made flesh, so anguished it shook me to the core. It evoked something primal, deep inside; all I could do was freeze, all I wanted to do was flee. So when the attack came, I didn't see it happen until too late.

Álvaro shoved Sir Edmund off him. He glared at Moppet with such hatred that it made me shiver. Then he reached for his belt and drew a knife.

I thought he was going to throw it at the girl. So did Tom; he scooped her up and turned, offering his back as a target instead. We were both wrong.

Álvaro spun on his heel. Sally screamed.

"Christopher!"

Then he hurled his dagger.

I saw it coming. Time seemed to slow, the knife hanging in the air. *Why is he attacking me?* I thought crazily, and in the same moment, I understood: the sword. I was the one holding the sword.

I flinched, eyes shutting involuntarily. So I didn't see Sally throw her hand out. I only felt her ram into me, pushing me aside, and then I heard her howl in pain.

We fell. She hit the ground next to me, holding her left wrist, staring in shock at the blade, the blood, the dagger punched through her palm.

Álvaro cursed, this time in Spanish. He reached for a

halberd, the closest weapon on the wall. I tried to scramble to my feet, but Sally had landed on my legs, pinning me to the stone. I struggled to get out from under her.

"Tom!" I shouted.

Tom pressed Moppet against the wall, the girl still screaming in paralyzed terror. When he turned, he looked so angry. I'd never seen him so angry.

He roared. He charged Álvaro, hands outstretched, just as the halberd came free. My guts churned as Álvaro whirled, slicing the wickedly hooked weapon toward my friend.

But the polearm was too long for close-quarter combat. By the time he brought the blade around, Tom had stepped inside the arc. The pole hit him, thumping hard against the side of his chest. Fueled by fury, Tom ignored it, driving forward. He wrapped the Spaniard in a bear hug and lifted him from the ground.

They slammed into the weapon rack. It cracked, sending two more halberds clattering to the floor. Then they fell, too, disappearing as they tumbled down the stairs.

"Tom!" I wriggled out from under Sally, began to rush after him. Then, in the corner of my eye, I saw something move.

Julian, I thought, and I turned. He'd recovered, too, and now he pulled a longbow from the rack.

I launched myself at him, sword still in hand. He drew an arrow from one of the quivers on the wall. He'd just begun to nock it when he saw me coming.

His eyes widened. "No—!"

I cracked him on the temple with the pommel. His head snapped back, crunching against the wall, and he slid down, bow slipping from his hands.

You knocked him out, I said to myself in amazement. Then I sliced the longbows' strings—all of them. If he roused, he wouldn't find another weapon there.

Sir Edmund pushed himself from the floor. Terrified, he ignored the weapons and turned to flee down the steps. Sally, still cradling her wounded hand, kicked at him from the ground, driving her heel into Sir Edmund's gout-swollen foot. The baronet turned white, then collapsed, gripping his ankle, mouth open in a soundless scream.

And all the while I thought, *Tom. He's still in trouble.*

I ran, bounding over the writhing Sir Edmund. I prayed I wouldn't see the worst.

Tom was standing at the bottom of the steps, his back to me. Beyond him, I could see Álvaro's legs on the floor.

"Tom?"

He turned. He spread his hands, upset. "I didn't mean to," he said.

And I saw. Álvaro's head was twisted, bent impossibly backward. The fall down the stairs, Tom's weight landing on him . . . the Spaniard had broken his neck.

I had to look away. I consoled myself: At least it wasn't Tom. "Are you all right?"

He nodded, silent, and came back upstairs, head bowed. Moppet—who had finally, blessedly quit shrieking—hurled herself into Tom's arms, weeping uncontrollably. I hurried over to Sally.

She held her hand, palm upward, the dagger pierced all the way to the hilt. Her face was pale, her breathing shallow.

"I think I'm in trouble," she said. She gave a laugh, then sobbed.

"Don't touch the knife," I said. "Tom, bind the Darcys. And see if you can find a cloth for Sally's hand."

He used the leather bindings on the quivers to truss Julian and Sir Edmund. Then he moved them to the ground floor of the tower, where there weren't any weapons close by. I carried Sally down, her head against my shoulder as she struggled not to cry. For a moment, I worried about the servants—would they come to defend their master?—but the sound of fleeing feet and a glance into the entrance hall showed them all sprinting from the estate.

I laid Sally on the stone. "Thank you," I said.

She sniffled. "For what?"

"What do you mean, for what? You saved my life."

"Oh. That."

I stared at her incredulously. "Sally . . . you *do* know you have a dagger in your hand, don't you?"

She shrugged. "It was a worthless hand, Christopher. It didn't even work anymore." She said it lightly. But her voice caught, and she choked, tears in her eyes. "What am I going to do?" she whispered.

"You're going to get better," I said. "I promise."

She sobbed and buried her head in my chest. I held her close until Tom brought me a cloth. He couldn't find one upstairs—there were only rags for cleaning the weapons, filthy with rust and oil—so he began to tear a strip of linen from his shirt. Then he thought better of it, and tore a strip from Sir Edmund's shirt instead.

I took hold of Sally's wrist. "I need to pull the blade out," I said. "I'll make a poppy infusion for you when it's over. But this is going to hurt."

"It hurts already," she said.

I grabbed the hilt. She gritted her teeth.

"Sally?" I said.

"Yes?"

"Has anyone ever told you you're beautiful?"

She stared at me. "I . . . you . . . I . . ."

I yanked out the dagger.

CHAPTER
43

SHE CURSED AT ME. THEN SHE
passed out. When she roused, she cursed at me again, slur-
ring, though by then I'd packed the wound with spider-
web and honey from my sash and bound it, so the worst
of it was over. While Tom kept watch over our prisoners,
I found a pot in the kitchen and set it to boil so I could
make her the poppy infusion I'd promised. Though she
was in terrible pain, I kept the dose small; I didn't want her
getting too drowsy.

Now it was time to deal with Sir Edmund. He leaned
against the wall where Tom had propped him, hands and
feet tied behind him, legs tucked underneath. Julian lay

next to him, a swelling lump on one temple and blood in his hair where his head had slammed into the stone.

"You don't know what you've done," Sir Edmund said, voice trembling.

"I caught a kidnapper," I said.

He moaned, a sound of bitter despair. "You haven't stopped anything. You've only made it worse."

"How could anything be worse than you?"

"You don't understand. We were *saving* people. Why couldn't you leave it alone?"

I knelt close to Sir Edmund. "I know you've been working with Barbary pirates to kidnap children. I know your son tried to murder us yesterday, and your friend and colleague Álvaro would have murdered us tonight if we hadn't stopped him."

"You see?" Sir Edmund said. "You know *nothing*. Álvaro was *not* my friend. He's to blame for it all."

I remembered Moppet's terror. Even now, though Álvaro lay dead by the stairs, the girl still hid behind Tom's leg, holding him tight.

I finally realized what Sir Edmund was saying. "Álvaro was one of the pirates."

Sir Edmund nodded. "Their first mate."

"So . . . it's not Barbary pirates after all? The Spanish are attacking us?"

"No, they're Berbers."

"But Álvaro was a Spaniard."

"Many European converts have joined the corsairs. This whole plan was his idea. And now that he's dead . . . you've finished us all."

"What does that mean?"

Sir Edmund took a deep breath. "Two weeks ago, Álvaro arrived at my door. He told Cooper he was an old friend of mine from my witch-hunting days, and he'd come to visit. When I saw him in my drawing room, I had no idea who he was. I thought he'd come because of my reputation. I was quite famous, you see—"

"I don't care," I said.

"Right. Uh . . . anyway . . . once Cooper left, Álvaro let his disguise drop. He told me he was the first mate on the *Andalus*, a ship of a hundred Barbary pirates. He said fifty of his men were waiting, hidden in the woods outside my estate. They were going to ransack my home, then work their way back south, killing every man, burning every village, hamlet, and farm, until they had more plunder and slaves than they could carry.

"At first, I didn't believe him. So he dragged me to the window, where he used a mirror to flash sunlight toward the trees. Then I saw them." He shuddered. "They were waiting at the gates, Barbary pirates all. I thought we were doomed.

"I asked why he'd told me this. He said he could be persuaded not to raze the coast if I made it worth his while. I offered him all I had. Money's all they really care about, you see. When they take slaves, they always linger to ransom them back to their loved ones. They get their profit, and they don't have to worry about keeping the prisoners alive on the journey back to Africa.

"I thought this was the same. But once Álvaro had my money, he laughed. He said what I'd given him wasn't enough; he was going to take prisoners after all. I told him there was no more to be had. People here were poor; there would be no ransom. He said it made no difference. His captain had promised their pasha slaves.

"Again, I didn't understand why he was telling me this. Álvaro said he'd be willing to spare the villages if he could kidnap a few of the children. All I had to do was arrange for it to happen quietly."

I frowned. "Why quietly? Why not just raid the coast, like usual?"

"I asked him the same question. He said they'd raided the Dutch twice already on this trip, and the eastern shore of England after that, and they'd caused such havoc that both navies were after them. They needed to lay low, and they'd found a cove to hide in—but they still intended to find a way to profit. They didn't have much more room in their hold, so they only needed about a dozen more children. I could either help him capture them quietly, or his corsairs would slaughter everyone here, all the way down to Seaton. They'd take their slaves, one way or the other; they'd just rather do it without risk."

Tom glowered at him. "Better for your soul that you had fought them," he said.

"Fought them?" Sir Edmund cried. "Fifty men? With what? The handful of arms in my tower? My gout-cursed foot? Our servants, who flee at the first sign of danger? No, boy. I'm not your master's grandfather, and the people of Devonshire are not the King's Men. It was let them take a few—or have them kill *everyone*."

He drew a breath. "So I did what I was told. Álvaro had heard the legend of the White Lady—a legend believed here most seriously—so he knew any child's disappearance could be blamed on her, and in turn, on the witch in the woods. He forced me to send Julian to lead the children away quietly. And he made me teach him to write Leviathan's signature, to leave in the children's place."

"You claim you had no choice," I said. "Why not give up yourself? Your servants? Why other people's children? Why not your own?"

"If we were what he wanted, he could have taken us at any time. What could I have done to stop him? No, he said he would only accept little ones. They were easy to keep captive, easy to control. So that was our trade, Baron. Twelve children for the lives of hundreds. The Devil's bargain, yes. Perhaps I am damned for it. But I would make the same choice again. And so would you."

"Never," I said.

Tom was just as horrified. *"Never."*

Sir Edmund shook his head. "You judge so easily, because you never had to make the choice. But it wasn't your people staring down their guns. What would you do, Baron, if they came to Chillingham? If they told you everyone you loved, everyone you cared for, would all be slaughtered? Would you trade a dozen for the rest? Or would you condemn every man, woman, and child, just so you could keep your foolish pride?

"You've been surrounded your whole life by the safety

of soldiers, so you have the privilege of principles. You don't understand what it's like to live under the yoke of the strongest. There's a reason Barbary pirates have raided Devonshire for decades. These people have no one to defend them. You, you didn't even *think* about the choice, because you know you'd never have to make it. Well, think now! What would you do?"

I shuddered. I despised this man. And yet . . . what *would* I have done, given Álvaro's ultimatum? A dozen sold into torment—or hundreds dead?

"I'd *find* a way," I said, but my defiance sounded hollow, even to me.

I shook my head. It didn't matter what I'd have done in his place. We had *this* problem to solve, here and now. "How do we stop them?"

Sir Edmund looked at me incredulously. "You haven't heard a word. You've condemned us all."

"Why?"

"You killed Álvaro."

"It's not like he didn't deserve it."

"That's not the point."

"Look," I said, "we just need a little time. I've already sent a letter to Lord Ashcombe, asking for help. If he sends the King's Men, from what you said, the sight of them alone should scare the pirates off. All we have to do is stall until they arrive."

"*No,*" Sir Edmund said. "They're going to sack Seaton *tonight.*"

"But . . . you said they weren't going to raid the village. That was your deal."

"And you broke it when you killed Álvaro!" he cried. "Every night, one of the pirates comes to the garden. Álvaro confirms that the plan is still working. Then the pirate returns to the ship and tells the rest of them to remain hidden. That's why Álvaro stayed here: To ensure my compliance. To make certain I wouldn't betray him.

"Now Álvaro is dead. So there will be no meeting in the garden. The pirate will return to the *Andalus* and tell them the deal is broken. And Seaton—and the hundreds who live there—will fall."

He shook his head. "You see? You foolish boy. You thought you were saving the children. Instead, you've killed us all."

CHAPTER
44

WE STARED AT HIM IN HORROR.

"All right . . . then . . . we stop him," I said. "The pirate who's coming here. We lay a trap and—"

"Don't you think I thought of that?" Sir Edmund said. "It won't help. Either the man returns to the *Andalus* with the message that everything's all right, or he doesn't, and they sack the town. Preventing him from returning will delay them a few hours at most."

"Then . . ." I trailed off, heart sinking. What was there to say? I'd stumbled into this mess trying to help and instead had made the whole tower fall.

"What can we do?" Tom said.

"Nothing," Sir Edmund said.

Sally propped herself up, gritting her teeth. "There has to be something."

"Yes. We run."

Tom whirled on him, fists clenched. "Be quiet."

Sir Edmund shut his mouth, but his glance at me was knowing. *You see the truth of it.*

And I did. We couldn't fight a hundred men. We couldn't even fight a dozen. The people of Seaton weren't warriors. There *had* been fighters in the village—Captain Haddock's crew—but I'd sent them away. To bring soldiers who would come too late.

I couldn't see any way out of this. Every choice was bad. I thought once more about the Devil's bargain Sir Edmund had made with Álvaro. It made me want to crumble.

Don't despair, Master Benedict said. *Solve the problem.*

How? I said. *We can't possibly fight a hundred men.*

Who says you have to fight them?

Of course. "We'll go to Seaton," I said. "We'll warn the villagers of what's going to happen. Even with a few hours delay, that should be enough time to make for the woods. Everyone can hide in the neighboring hamlets."

"And if the pirates follow?" Tom said.

"Then we keep running. Go as far as we need to, until they give up."

"That won't work," Sir Edmund said. "It's not just Seaton that's in danger. It's *all* the villages. You can't warn every one."

"*We* can't," I said. "But in Seaton, we'll have hundreds more people on our side. They can fan out, run to every village, hamlet, and farm. Let the pirates come. They won't find anybody to take."

"The people will lose their homes," Sally said, "when the corsairs raid them."

"At least they'll be alive." Though for many that would be small comfort. The people here were poor. To lose their homes, their livelihoods . . . some of them wouldn't survive it. I didn't think my heart could sink any lower.

"What about the kidnapped children?" Tom said. "We have to get them back."

I wasn't sure how we could do that. "We don't even know where they are."

"They're on the *Andalus*," a groggy voice said.

It was Julian. He'd come to. Now he looked up at me with glassy eyes.

"Where's that?" I said.

"On the coast. East of Seaton, in a hidden cove.

About half a mile from the mouth of the river."

"You're sure the children are there?"

Julian nodded. "The pirates are living in the cave. They can keep a fire going, even so close to the village. They used to keep the children there, too, but one of them escaped a week ago, so they've locked them all back in the hold."

I glanced over at Moppet, who still hugged Tom's leg. "Are the children kept under guard?"

"One man walks the deck. The others stay in the cave; it's too cold."

Tom looked at me, hopeful. I thought about it.

"We might actually be able to do this," I said. "If we could sneak onto the ship, I could free the children from the hold."

"There's a padlock on their cell," Julian said.

"I can handle a lock. The real problem will be getting past the guard."

Tom loosened his sword in his scabbard, a haunted look in his eyes. "I'll take care of that."

"Not that way," I said, and Tom looked relieved. "It has to be done quietly; we can't risk a fight. Though we'll still need someone to warn Seaton."

Julian sat up. "I can do that."

I shook my head. Like his father, the boy might have thought kidnapping children was the righteous choice, but I didn't want him anywhere near the pirates.

"I'll warn Seaton," Sally said. She held up her bandaged hand. "I can't do much else anyway."

Tom nodded to the Darcys. "What about them?"

I wasn't sure. Leaving them behind would be a risk, but we couldn't take them with us. Beyond the fact they couldn't be trusted, Sir Edmund's gout would slow us down. "We'll have to leave them here."

Tom didn't like that. "What if they tell the pirate who comes what we're doing?"

Sir Edmund, quieted earlier by Tom's threat, stiffened. "I only made a deal with those blackguards because I had no other choice," he said. "Though you may think otherwise, I am not a monster."

But he is a monster, Master Benedict said, and the truth in his words made me stop.

Sir Edmund didn't realize it, but I knew. Twenty years ago, he'd murdered eleven girls by falsely proving them witches. And I'd seen the scars on Julian's back.

And as I remembered that, I noticed his eyes. They were searching me. Trying to see if I believed him.

What do I do? I asked my master. *Do I confront him as an Ashcombe?*

You don't need to. He's already lied to you.

About what?

Think, my master said. *Something he told you is clearly not true.*

I didn't know what he meant. Did Sir Edmund not do a deal with Álvaro after all?

No, he must have. But what did Sybil say about him? I'd asked her, *Even if Edmund Darcy was a fraud, why would he steal children now?*

And she'd answered, *I don't know. All I can tell you is that it must be for money. All Edmund Darcy is loyal to, all he believes in, is money.*

That was it. The *money.* Sir Edmund said he gave them money. But his house was still full of valuable things.

Yes, Master Benedict said. *He gave them something far more valuable than baubles.*

The children, I said.

Even more than that. Why did the pirates offer the deal at all? Barbary pirates have been raiding the coast for decades. Why not this time?

He said they were hiding from the Royal Navy.

So what's wrong with that story?

I frowned. I couldn't see anything wrong with that story. The navy would certainly chase the pirates; the pirates would certainly want to hide; and it would certainly be less risk to steal children secretly than to raid.

Unless? my master asked.

Unless the navy *wasn't* chasing them. But why would the navy stop—

"The storm," I said suddenly.

"What storm?" Tom said.

"The one that wrecked us. The one that started this whole thing. It was almost three weeks ago. Just before Sir Edmund claims the pirates came to him."

"They *did* come to me," Sir Edmund protested.

Tom ignored him. "The storm was three weeks ago. So what?"

"So why are the pirates still here?"

I looked at Sir Edmund. He looked back, puzzled.

But you saw it, Master Benedict said, and I had. For a moment, Sir Edmund had looked *scared.*

I knelt in close again. "Well?"

He shied away from me, no longer hiding his fear. "Well what?"

"Why are the pirates still here?"

"I . . . I told you. They demanded twelve children. We've only given them five—"

"No," I said. "You said the pirates were hiding from the navy, and it was less risky for them to steal the children in secret. But if the navy wasn't out there, it would have been *far* less risky for them to just raid Seaton, take whomever they pleased, then flee for the Barbary Coast."

"But the navy *is* out there—"

"No. It isn't." I turned to Tom and Sally. "You remember what Captain Haddock said? No one would sail in that storm. The navy would have put into dock."

I turned back to Sir Edmund. "The pirates are sailors; they'd know this as well as Captain Haddock. So when the first clear morning came, they could have raided Seaton, taken what they wanted, and set off long before the navy could relaunch. Certainly long enough to round the coast of France, and leave England behind for good. But the pirates are still here. Why are they still here?"

Sir Edmund stared back, but he didn't say anything.

I believed I already knew the answer. "Julian? How many pirates have you seen?"

"I told you," Sir Edmund began, "it's a hundred—"

"Tom," I said. "If Sir Edmund opens his mouth again, cut off his head."

Slowly, deliberately, Tom drew Eternity and placed the blade under Sir Edmund's chin. I knew he wouldn't do it, but, like me, he was angry enough to pretend. And he pretended very well.

Julian looked confused. "Father?"

"Just tell me, Julian," I said. "How many pirates have you seen?"

"I don't know. A lot."

"How many? A number."

"Well . . . there were the fifty who showed up here."

"That's what your father said. Did you see them come here yourself?"

"No. But—"

"What about their cave?" I said. "You must have seen them then, when you brought them the children. You saw the *Andalus*."

"Yes."

"So how many pirates were there?"

"I . . . don't know. A dozen? Maybe more?"

"And each time you went back to their ship. Did you always see the same pirates? Or were they different?"

Julian frowned.

"They were the same ones, weren't they?"

Now Julian looked even more confused. "I don't understand."

"But your father does. Don't you, Sir Edward?"

The baronet looked terrified now, and not because of the blade at his throat. I pushed Tom's sword away.

"I didn't know," Sir Edmund said, panicked. "I didn't know. He *tricked* me."

"How?"

"When Álvaro showed me the men at the gates, I only saw a few. But he said a hundred more were waiting at the coast. I believed him. Why wouldn't I? How was I to know?"

"Know what? What did you find out?"

"He told me one night, how he'd tricked me. How it was just a small band of them after all. They'd set sail with a hundred, yes, but they got caught near Antwerp by the Dutch. They won the battle, and took the Dutch ship as a prize, but the fight had cost them dearly. Their own ship had been holed by cannon, and was sinking. Worse, they'd lost nearly their entire crew.

"Their captain meant to cut his losses, to flee back to the Barbary Coast with the stolen ship. But all they were able to salvage from their own hold were a few children they'd captured in the Netherlands. Their pasha had ordered this expedition; if they returned empty-handed, they'd be finished.

"So Álvaro came up with a plan. He knew Devonshire; he'd raided here before. The coast had coves where they could hide. Even with such a small crew, using the legend of the White Lady, he could steal children without ever being suspected. That was their plan all along. He told me, like it was some grand joke. But I didn't know until then! I swear it!"

Julian was stunned. "They . . . tricked us?"

"Why didn't you tell somebody?" I said. "When you found out how small the pirates' crew was, why didn't you tell the people of Seaton? They could have done something to stop it."

"How could I tell anyone?" Sir Edmund said. "Álvaro was always here, by my side."

His words had the ring of truth. And yet . . .

You still don't believe him, my master said.

No.

Why not?

Because if it was true, why did he lie to me about the number of men at the start? He was trying to manipulate me. He still is.

Yes. The question is: Why?

And I realized why—for there could only be one reason.

"It was *your* plan," I said.

"No," Sir Edmund said. But the fear in his eyes spoke differently.

"Father?" Julian said. "What's he talking about?"

"That's why you lied to me about seeing fifty men," I said. "You knew if you told me there were only a handful, we might confront them. And you couldn't risk that. Because then *they* might tell us the truth."

Sir Edmund floundered for an answer. "Th-that's absurd. I was just ashamed. I didn't want you to know how foolish I'd been. How badly I'd been duped."

"No. You *wanted* us to fail. You wanted us to never get the children back. You knew that, if we did, we'd learn the truth. It was never Álvaro's plan to use the legend of the White Lady. It was *yours*."

"Father?" Julian's voice trembled. "Is this true?"

"Of course not," Sir Edmund said, his own voice shaking. "He's just trying to divide us—"

"But it *is* true." I turned to Julian. "Maybe Álvaro already knew the legend of the White Lady. But he couldn't have known your father had the only person who could allow his plan to succeed: you."

Julian's voice was a whisper. "Me?"

"Yes," I said. "For the White Lady to be blamed, someone had to lead the children away without causing a stir. Álvaro's men couldn't do it; the children would run the moment they saw a corsair. Only you, Julian. Only you could make the plan work. Because only you—who knew the children, who could call to them as a friend, who could be tricked into believing he was saving the people of Devonshire—only you could make the plan succeed. Your father told you that you were saving innocent lives. In reality, you were only saving your fortune. *That* was the deal your father made with Álvaro. Let him keep his wealth, and he'd give them something better. The children, to sell as slaves."

"Lies," Sir Edmund said. But Julian was staring at him, shaking.

"You . . . ," Julian said, in barely a whisper. "You turned me into a monster."

Tom came closer, stood beside me, looming over Sir Edmund. I could *feel* his rage. It came off him in waves.

"You sold children into slavery," Tom said. "For money."

I stood. Tom gripped his sword so tightly his knuckles turned white.

"For *money*," he said.

He looked ready to thrash the man—or worse. I knew he was thinking of Moppet, and all the children like her that the pirates had taken, that Sir Edmund had helped them take. Even now, they must be so scared, so lost, so alone. Huddled somewhere in a dark, dank pirate hold, beaten, starving, freezing. A hairsbreadth away from a lifetime of torment, of endless abuse.

And though she couldn't understand us, I think Moppet saw it, too. She let go of Tom's leg and slipped her tiny hand into his.

Tom looked down at her. He drew a great, shuddering breath. Then he turned away.

Sir Edmund slumped, reprieved—at least for the moment. Julian, sitting next to him, rocked back and forth, seeing nothing. "A monster. I'm a monster," he said, over and over.

Sally stood. "What do we do now?" she asked quietly.

Tom wiped his eyes. "We go for the children."

"Shouldn't we stop at Seaton first? I know the village isn't in danger anymore, but maybe we could recruit some men to help us free the captives."

I wasn't sure. On the one hand, I'd love to have more men to face the pirates. On the other hand, I didn't want to face the pirates at all. If we were successful, they wouldn't even know we'd come until they discovered the children were missing.

The others had looked to me for answers ever since they found me—even when I couldn't remember. This wasn't a decision I could make for anyone else.

"We can get help if you want," I said. "But one way or another, we're going to have to sneak into the cove. The more people we bring, the more likely it is we'll be spotted. And once the pirates are alerted, all they'll have to do is get into their boat and sail away.

"That's the choice," I said. "More men makes it safer for us, but less likely we'll save the children. So: Do we go for Seaton, or straight to the cove?"

Tom spoke without thinking. "The cove."

Sally hesitated, but in the end she said the same. "The cove."

That was settled, then. Though it still left us one problem. Sally motioned to the Darcys. "What are we going to do with them?"

That wasn't clear, either. Though both were culpable for

terrible crimes, Julian, at least, had been duped. I wasn't sure I could trust him, but I *knew* I couldn't trust Sir Edmund.

I pointed at the baronet. "Gag him," I said to Tom, "and take him to the top of the tower."

Sir Edmund pleaded for clemency, until Tom silenced him with a strip of linen torn from the man's own shirt. Even then, he mumbled desperately through the gag until Tom carried him out of earshot. As for Julian, I knelt beside him. He was still rocking back and forth.

I feared his mind had snapped. "Julian?"

The boy was crying, tears tracking silently down his cheeks. "I'm a monster, Christopher."

"You haven't killed anyone yet," I said.

"I tried to kill you. And the children . . . the children are gone."

"No, they're still here. And we're going to get them back."

"We are?"

"*We* are. Tom, and Sally, and me. I need you to do something else."

He looked at me, hopeful.

"Your father is going to betray us to the pirates," I said. "One of them is coming here tonight, and your father will tell him we're going to free the children. I need you to not let that happen. Whatever you do, don't let the two of them speak. Do you understand?"

Julian sniffled. "Yes."

"Good. Do this, and you'll be redeemed."

He shook his head sadly. "No, Christopher," he said. "I'll never be redeemed."

We waited for Tom to come back downstairs. In the meantime, I made Julian give me every detail he could think of regarding the pirates: their ship, the cave, how to get there. He was giving me directions when Tom returned.

"Is Sir Edmund secured?" I said.

Tom nodded. "*Very* tightly."

"So what's the plan?" Sally said.

I shook my head, motioning toward Julian. *Not here.*

I cut the boy loose, then went upstairs to the armory. I took the firearms: the musket for Tom, the pistols for me and Sally. I took a sword for myself as well, buckling it around my waist. I wasn't sure what I was going to do with it—I had no training—but I felt better with it hanging at my side.

Outside, the sun had already set. I could see the tracks Sir Edmund's servants had left in the snow. Apparently fleeing into the dark was safer than facing an Ashcombe's wrath.

Now that we were alone, I could speak. "All right. Here's what we're going to do—"

Tom grabbed my arm. "Christopher!"

He pointed. I turned to see a single flame, a lantern bobbing among the trees. Someone was coming.

My heart sank, even as my blood began to race. *The pirate messenger already?* I'd hoped for at least a few more hours.

I ducked, the other three crouching beside me. Sally peered into the distance.

"Can we sneak around him?" Tom whispered. "Or do we have to fight?"

"Wait," Sally said, and she stood.

"What are you doing?"

"It's not a pirate." She waved at him. "Wise!"

In the dim glow of the lantern, I saw Wise's lanky form emerge from the trees, longbow slung across his back. He stopped at Sally's call and raised his hand.

We went to him. "You came," I said, grateful.

He bowed his head. He cupped his hand against his heart, then held it palm up.

"Don't be sorry," I said. "You have no idea how glad we are you're here. We could really use your help. Do you know the coves east of Seaton?"

He nodded. I gave him Julian's directions, and he tapped his chest confidently. *I can take you there.*

"All right, then. Let's go," I said, "and I'll tell you how we're going to save the children."

CHAPTER
45

WISE LED US THROUGH THE FOREST
like it was his home—which, I supposed, in a way, it was.
He knew the land so well, we didn't even have to hug the
riverbank. That saved us, because an hour after we left the
Darcy estate, he suddenly blew out our lantern.

The forest turned pitch black. "Wh—*mmph*!"

Wise clamped his hand over my mouth. I fell silent. He
let me go and turned my head.

There. In the distance, flickering beside the river, I saw
a pinpoint of light: A torch. The pirate, on his way to meet
Álvaro.

"What do we do?" Tom whispered.

"Let him go," I whispered back. We'd have to leave him to Julian—and trust the boy wouldn't betray us.

Wise kept us still. We watched the light until it passed. Then we went forward, even more worried than before.

Wise guided us all the way there. Shuttering our lantern, he navigated our party around the lights that dotted Axmouth and Seaton and led us to the coast. High atop a cliff, he pointed.

Though the clouds let through no moonlight, by now my eyes had adjusted well enough to the darkness that I could see the beach. A crescent of sand curved outward, a hundred feet from the foot of the cliffs. At high tide, the sand would lie hidden below the surface and snare ships that sailed it unawares.

I whispered to Wise. "Julian said the cove was about half a mile east."

Wise nodded, and we moved on. Carefully, carefully he stepped, as the cliffs rose and fell; one wrong foot, and we'd tumble over the edge. It had taken us hours to travel miles; these last few steps seemed to stretch for days. I shuddered, and not from the cold.

Suddenly Wise stopped. He held up a hand, head cocked to the side.

I listened with him. All I could hear was the waves, lapping against the sand.

Or . . . was that a voice?

And . . . there. Faint, mingled with the salt scent of the ocean. I smelled smoke. A campfire.

Wise motioned for us to stay. Then he got on his knees and crawled through the snow to a ridge, twenty feet away. I blinked. In the darkness, I hadn't even seen it. If it hadn't been for Wise, I'd have stepped into space.

Wise peeked his head over the edge. He watched for a moment, then beckoned us forward. Crawling, we joined him and looked down.

And there, as Julian had said we would, we found the pirates.

The cove cut deeply into the shoreline, the cliffs curving around it, as if a giant had gouged an opening in the coast. The water formed a pool in the center. In it, the captured Dutch yacht—renamed by the pirates as the *Andalus*—bobbed gently in the shallows, sails furled. The boat was anchored; a rope ladder at the stern dangled from the rail, just touching the water. The timbers creaked with the ebb and flow of the waves that lapped against the hull.

A single torch at the prow lit the deck. One of the pirates, draped in a cloak of fur, leaned on the rail and huddled next to the flame, warming his hands.

Faint light spilled from a hollow at the far end of the cove. I could just make out the base of a campfire. Here, too, a man waited, pacing in front of the flames, stamping his feet to keep warm. Beyond him slept the rest of the crew, shapeless lumps buried under their blankets.

The shadows cast by the flames made it hard to number them. Still, the count left me deflated. With the man on the *Andalus*, I made it at least fifteen pirates, possibly more hidden farther inside the cave.

I pushed back from the edge. The pirates had picked the perfect spot: Sheltered from land and sea, their fire barely brightened the sky. They could have stayed here, safe, forever.

That would work to our advantage. Their feeling of security meant they'd only left a pair of sentries, one guarding the cave, the other on the boat; and both seemed far less concerned with keeping watch than keeping warm. My stomach fluttered. We might just pull this off.

"All right," I whispered, my voice barely higher than the surf. "Tom and I will climb down the cliff near the ship's stern. We'll swim to the boat and use the rope ladder to get on board. Once we're on deck, Tom will choke the guard until he passes out. Remember: no swords, no guns. If we make a sound, we're finished."

Tom nodded.

"Sally and Wise will keep watch from above. I'll go belowdecks and free the children. Tom and I will send them up the cliff, then follow once the last one's safe. Sally, as soon as the children reach the top, you and Wise run with them toward Seaton. Some of them will be Dutch, so hopefully Moppet will understand and can let them know what to do."

She'd already helped me a little. As we'd hurried through the woods, after much gesturing and confusion, I'd got her to teach me a word of Dutch, one I thought I might need in the hold.

Wise nocked an arrow in his longbow. Sally drew the pistol I'd given her from her belt. Tom gave her the musket, too, for all the good it might do. An extra shot wouldn't help much against fifteen.

· · ·

The climb down was terrifying. Not because it was slippery—if anything, the pressure from our boots formed little steps in the snow, making it easier to find my footing than I'd dared hope—but because the whole way, we were exposed. The path we took down, opposite the cave, allowed the boat to shield us from the pirate at the fire, but left us totally visible to the man on deck. All he had to do was look behind him, and he'd see us, black shapes against the cliff.

I never thought I'd pray for the cold to turn even more bitter. But I did, and whether it was my prayers or simple luck, the sentries remained huddled around their flames, and we made it to the beach undiscovered.

Now we had to board the ship. Slowly, slowly, slowly, I put a boot into the water.

My whole body tightened with the chill—and I'd barely touched it. When I waded in knee high, I prayed again, this time that the cords I'd tied around my deerskin breeches would keep the water from seeping underneath.

The seal worked—yet still I froze. The shock of the cold made my breath rattle and my head swim. Images filled my mind. I remembered my nightmare: caught in the ice of Cocytus, the ninth circle of hell, under the terrible glare of the Raven. But another memory came, too. It struck me like a cannonball, and I couldn't stop thinking about

the trip. We were on the ship, on our way back from France, when the storm came. Hail pounded the deck, scarred the wood, pelted my head. The boat heaved in the swells, ten feet high.

"Christopher!"

A wave crashed over the rail, driving me into the fo'c'sle.

"Christopher! Christopher! Over here!"

Tom. That was Tom's voice. Sally added her own as a second wave smashed me into the deck.

"The yawl! Christopher! We're in the yawl!"

I could just make them out through the rain. Jagged hailstones scoured my skin, and I could feel the soul of the storm. It wasn't just angry. It was angry at me.

I gripped the rail with the crook of my arm, terrified to move, cupping something warm and trembling to my chest. A bird. I knew her now. It was Bridget.

"Christopher!" Sally screamed. "Look out!"

I turned to see the wave. It was a wall of water, twenty feet high. It picked me up, threw me down—and then I was flying

backward. The memory shattered as my boot slipped on

a slime-covered rock. I lost my footing, and my windmilling arms made a splash.

The liquid ice made my muscles seize, but the shock of it barely registered. Something much worse had happened than getting wet.

I'd made a noise.

CHAPTER
46

TOM FROZE, EYES WIDE WITH TERROR.

A voice called. The pirate, on the deck of the *Andalus*. The words were harsh, guttural. I didn't understand them; I'd never even heard the language. But I could guess what he'd said.

Who's there?

A second voice came from the cave, questioning.

The first man called back, wary. The light shifted as he pulled the torch from the prow. I heard footsteps on the deck, coming closer.

Tom grabbed my collar. *What do we do?* he mouthed, panicked.

I didn't know. If we ran, we'd make noise in the water.

If we stayed, he'd see us. He'd have to, unless something else came—

Something else *did* come. From the darkness, Bridget swooped down. Her wings slapped together, echoing in the quiet, as she landed on the rail of the ship. She cooed.

The man on the *Andalus* called to his friend, sounding exasperated. The man in the cave replied, laughing. *It's just a pigeon.*

I sent a silent thanks up to Sally. But then the light came forward again. I could see the pirate on the ship now, his head covered by his fur hat. He approached Bridget, clucking at her. From the cave came another call, a question. *What are you doing?*

The pirate pulled a pistol from his belt.

No! I thought, but it was the other man who saved her. What sounded like a curse came from the cave. The pirate on deck cursed back, but he relaxed his aim, swatting the barrel at Bridget instead. She flapped away, back into the darkness.

It took me a moment to remember: The pirates had to stay silent, too. A gunshot in the dead of night would carry a long way in the cold. This close to Seaton, the report would give them away.

The light faded, returning to the prow, and I could

breathe again. Slowly, so slowly, I pushed myself out of the water. My skin, wet, stung brutally in the chill of the air. If I didn't soon find warmth, I'd freeze to death.

The pool in the cove deepened, and we had to swim the rest of the way to the ship. At the rope ladder, I motioned for Tom to go first. Once he was on deck, I began my own climb.

Tom disappeared beyond the rail, moving cautiously, his footsteps blending in with the creaking of the timbers. I didn't hear him grab the pirate, but by the time I got to the deck, Tom was already lying on his back, choking the man with his massive forearm, legs wrapped around him, pinning his arms to his chest. The pirate wriggled, trying to free himself from Tom's grip, until his eyes went glassy and rolled back in his head. Tom didn't let go until he was sure the man was completely out.

I looked toward the cave. The other sentry stood with his back to us, hands held over the fire.

Tom lifted the unconscious pirate and carried him into the shadows cast by the fo'c'sle, where he pulled the man's pistol from his belt, then used the belt itself to bind the pirate's hands and feet together. Tom would stay here, keeping watch to see the man didn't wake. As for me, I needed to hurry. If the sentry turned from the campfire, his companion's absence might be noticed.

Julian had said the children were being kept in the hold, through the hatch behind the mainmast, near the aftcastle. I crept toward it, crouched, one eye on the deck, the other on the man by the cave.

I slid out the bar that held the hatch in place and opened it. A reek of waste and body odor rose from below. A ladder led down into the dank.

The hold was tight and damp, the only light a dim, hooded lantern hanging from a hook next to the entrance. I could make out two doors on either side of me, a third behind the ladder. In the other direction, a corridor led away.

I lifted the lantern from its hook and checked the doors. None of them were locked. The one on my right opened to the smell of salt, overpowering even the scent of the ocean. I thought I smelled stale bread, too; their room for provisions. I also smelled spices: part of their booty, I guessed. I left it behind. I was only here for the children.

The door behind the ladder opened to a scent I knew well. Pungent, penetrating, the stench filled the air.

Gunpowder.

I'd found their magazine, where the ship's weapons were stored. A dozen barrels stood stacked against the far wall, held fast with rope nets. More netting lay beside them, pinning a pyramid of cannonballs to the floor. There was enough gunpowder and shot to start my own war.

But a war was the last thing I wanted right now. I needed quiet. So I closed the door to the magazine—carefully—and moved on to the third. And I found something even more interesting.

There was a small desk in here, papers scattered around like it had been ransacked. A leather volume lay atop it. The notes inside were in Dutch—the former captain's ship's log, I guessed. Above that, tacked to the wall, were a pair of maps. One was a navigational chart of the waters of northern Europe, marked everywhere with rhumb lines, the crisscross of bearings that allowed a navigator to follow a straight course between ports. The markings here were Dutch, too.

The other map showed only the Channel. Here were no rhumb lines. Instead, the southern coast of England was marked everywhere with Xs. Little notes had been scribbled in Spanish beside each one, marking coves and hidden outposts.

A pirate's map. That's what this was, a guide to the places an outlaw ship could find safe harbor.

This must have been Álvaro's. I stared at the map, and everywhere there was an *X*, all I could see was more misery. More men to be murdered, more children to be kidnapped, more lives to be ruined. My heart sank with the futility of our quest. After all, even if we saved these children, the pirates could always find new ones to take.

Well, I wouldn't make it easy for them. I tore the maps from the wall, stuffed them into my breeches. I might not be able to stop the pirates, but I could prevent a raid or two. With Álvaro *and* his map gone, let them try to find safe coves now.

In the meantime, I still had the children to find. The only place left to check was down the passage. I didn't think the stench belowdecks could get more foul, but it did. And when I turned the corner, and I saw the brig, I understood why.

CHAPTER
47

I'D FOUND THEM.

Filthy and ragged, freezing and starving, twenty children huddled behind the iron bars. They were crammed together so thick, so still, my guts dropped.

I'm too late, I thought in despair. The room was like ice, the only warmth provided by a single brazier, the flame low, capped with a plate of holed iron. *They've already frozen to death.*

But they shifted as I brought my lantern close to the bars. Twenty terrified faces looked back at me, and their pain made my heart break.

I whispered to them. "My name is

and the truth of it came like a thunderbolt: I knew my name, knew *it, deep in my bones*

Christopher Rowe," I said, and I swelled at the sound of it. "I work for King Charles. He sent me to free you."

Five of the children stared at me, barely daring to hope. These must have been the English children, who understood my words.

A boy spoke, his voice trembling. "The king? He really sent you?"

"Absolutely." I drew a vial from the sash under my shirt. "You're all so important to him. Emma Lisle"—a girl sat up—"and David Cavill"—now a boy joined her—"and Little Jack"—the boy who spoke smiled shyly—"he sent me for all of you. Your families are waiting for you to come home."

They scrambled toward the bars. I held out my hands.

"Shhh," I whispered. "You have to be quiet, all right? We're going to sneak out of here, and we can't let the pirates hear us. This means you can't make any sound, not even a peep, no matter what. You need to be brave. Can you be brave for the king?" They nodded, and I was so proud of their courage.

Now I needed to deal with the Dutch children. There were fifteen of them, all looking confused but hopeful from the way the English had rushed toward me. I put my finger to my lips and spoke the word Moppet had taught me.

"*Stil,*" I said. "*Stil.*" Quiet.

They all copied me, every one of them, fingers on their lips. I couldn't help but smile.

But we weren't free yet. Little Jack came forward and grabbed the bars. His hands, so small, couldn't wrap all the way around them. "The door is locked," he whispered. "Do you have the key?"

"I don't need a key," I said. "My master taught me about a very special liquid that melts iron." I showed him the vial I held. "It's called oil of vitriol, and when I pour it on the padlock—like this—it will dissolve."

The children clustered around the bars as the iron of the padlock began to fizz. Then they coughed at the acrid stink coming from the bubbles. I shooed them back, nervous. I doubted the guard by the cave could hear their coughing, but I didn't want to take any chances.

I waited for the vitriol to stop fizzing, then dripped more on the padlock. The children huddled against the far wall, keeping their distance from the smell that made them choke. At their feet, I saw how badly the pirates had been starving them. There were four empty bowls and three tin cups, not nearly enough to feed this group. As the lock burned, so, too, I burned with hatred for the pirates above.

The padlock wasn't very strong—it didn't take much to imprison five-year-olds, I thought bitterly—but this was our good fortune, because it only took a few minutes for the lock to snap. I opened the brig, cringing at the creak of the iron door. The children followed me down the passage like lambs, silent as could be.

We reached the hatch. "Tom," I whispered. "Tom! Are you there?"

He loomed above us. The children pulled back, scared.

"It's all right," I said. "That's

and I knew him, too; I knew him

my best friend, Tom." I knelt next to the children. "He's really big and really strong, and he's never, ever let me down. He's going to show you the way back home."

One by one, they climbed up to the deck. Tom led them to the rail. We didn't know if they could swim, so we decided not to chance it. Tom went into the water first and swam to shore with each one on his back.

I watched the cave to make sure we hadn't been spotted. I tried to keep my mind focused, but more memories flooded in, coming in waves. And then, suddenly, they were all there. Tom and Sally, Master Benedict and Isaac, Lord Ashcombe and Simon Chastellain. All my friends, all of them, all. Even my enemies returned to me: the Raven in Paris, the Cult of the Archangel—

I froze.

The Cult of the Archangel, I thought.

The whisper came from the water. "Christopher. Christopher!"

It was Tom, waiting for me to send the last child down—a little Dutch girl, just like our Moppet. I helped her onto the ladder, then turned away.

"Where are you going?" Tom said.

"I have an idea," I said.

His whisper carried just far enough for me to hear it. "Oh *no.*"

By the time I returned to the rail, Tom was ushering the last of the children up the cliff. I couldn't believe how courageous they'd been. In the faint light of the pirates' flames, I could just see the ridge where Sally waited, pulling the children up the last few inches and sending them scurrying toward Seaton, Wise leading the way.

I lowered myself into the water and prayed. *A few more minutes. Just a few more minutes, please. And we'll have pulled off the impossible.*

But this prayer was not to be answered. As I reached the foot of the cliff, I heard a groan from behind me, coming from the deck of the ship.

"Hurry," I whispered to Tom, who climbed ahead of me. "The pirate's waking."

Suddenly Tom gasped. "I forgot," he said in despair.

"Forgot what?"

The groan came again. From the cave echoed a call. A question.

"His pistol," Tom said. He climbed more frantically now. "I left it on the deck when I went into the water to carry the children. I forgot to pick it up."

I scrambled behind Tom, my rising panic making me clumsy. My hands, already burning with frost, slipped in the snow.

Come on, I begged my fingers. *Oh, please, come on.*

The guard by the cave called again, sharply. The man on deck didn't answer, but I could hear his shuffling.

I risked a glance back. With horror, I saw the pirate had managed to slip free of the belt that had bound him. Now he staggered over to the rope ladder. Confused, he stared at his feet, where the stolen pistol rested.

I crawled. Tom reached the top and hauled himself over the ridge.

The pirate picked up the pistol.

Just a few feet more. I crawled.

A call came again from the cave, no longer with any attempt to mute his voice. This time, the call was returned. A shout.

We'd been spotted.

Up I went. I heard a snap behind me. My heart skipped as I recognized the sound. A trigger, pulled; a flintlock, hammering down.

I crawled, ears buzzing with the sparkling fizz of gunpowder.

And then he shot me.

CHAPTER

48

PAIN.

A spear, driven into my shoulder. A dagger, deep in my flesh. The slug slammed me into the cliff, and suddenly I was slipping, my left arm hot and numb.

The shot echoed in the cavern, rang through the night, so loud I thought they'd hear it in London. Even in the dim light, I could see my blood as I fell. It streaked across the white, leaving a trail where my shoulder dragged against the snow. I smelled it, too, hot, metallic, and then I tumbled the rest of the way down.

I lay there, breathing. Still the shot seemed to echo.

Now voices came, too, not a pair but a chorus, their song alarmed and angry.

I felt my master standing over me. *Get up, Christopher,* he said.

My shoulder screamed. My head swam with the pain. Still I heard his plea. *I need you to get up.*

I rose, shoulder burning. I went to the cliff and again began to crawl. My arm howled—oh, merciful Savior, how it howled. Only instinct and terror kept me going—so much terror, so much pain, tears blinding me so badly I couldn't see.

Another shot cracked into the night, and a slug punched into the cliff. Another, and my cheek stung, a puff of bloody snow spraying my face.

I couldn't help it; I turned to look. Half the pirates were rising; half had already thrown off their furs. All had pistols; all drew them; all of them aimed right at me.

I was too easy a target against the snow. I had to let go. I fell.

Thunder rolled as their bullets thudded into the cliff. I rolled, too, head over heels back to the beach. My shoulder screamed with every bump, and I screamed with it, all the way down. I hit the ground, sliding until my face splashed in the icy pool. It roused me, the shock of the chill numbing the shock of the pain.

"Christopher!"

Tom's horrified cry came from overhead. He leaned over the ridge, looking desperately down at me.

Three more shots barked. Snow kicked up beside Tom, and he disappeared. I couldn't see if he'd been hit; I prayed he wasn't. My prayers were answered when Tom returned the shot, his musket booming, sending its own lead back in response.

He didn't hit anyone—I heard the bullet crack as it punched into wood, saw splinters fly from the ship—but suddenly the angry alarm of the pirates became less angry and more alarmed. They scattered for cover.

Tom's shot had bought me a moment. I pushed myself to my feet, and the agony of it made my head spin. *Help me, Master,* I prayed, as I climbed the cliff once more. Slowly, so slowly, so slowly I went, fire burning inside.

And then someone gripped my leg.

My panic pushed away the pain as the fingers around my ankle dragged me down. I began to slip—one foot, two feet, three.

I looked to see who had me. It was the pirate who'd been guarding the deck. The closest of the villains, he'd caught up as I'd tried to get away. Now he glared at me as he pulled, hatred in the darkness of his eyes.

There was nothing for it. If he dragged me back down, I was finished. So I reached for my belt, pulled out my pistol, and aimed it at him.

His eyes went wide. He cried out, that same, strange language I didn't know—though this word I understood well enough.

No!

It made me hesitate. But I had no choice. I thought of the children he'd stolen as I pulled the trigger.

Clack.

The flintlock struck. I saw the spark. But there was no fizz of powder, no burst of smoke.

Horrified, I realized: the powder. It was wet. When we'd gone into the water, I'd forgotten to plug the barrel.

The pirate blinked, stunned. Then he, too, realized what had gone wrong. He grinned and drew his own weapon: a double-bladed hand ax.

He reared back, aiming at my leg. There was only one thing left I could do.

I threw the pistol at him.

It cracked him right in the teeth. He cried out, dropping his ax as his hand flew to his mouth. I tried to drag my ankle from his grasp, but still he held me fast.

And then Bridget returned.

She swooped in and landed right on his face. He cried out again in surprise as she smacked him with her wings, drove her beak into his eyes. He released me, trying to swat her away; his grip lost, he tumbled down the cliff. Bridget tumbled, too, end over end, bumping across the snow.

She righted herself near the bottom and, with a flustered flapping of wings, flew back into darkness. I followed her up, desperation muting the pain.

And then I heard someone else scrambling behind me.

It was the sentry from the cave. He'd made it around the pool, sword already in hand. Inside, I wailed with despair.

Then, suddenly, came a roar. I looked up just in time to see Tom sliding down, feetfirst. He skidded past me and smashed both heels right into the pirate's cheeks. Back down all of us went.

I sprawled in the snow beside the water. Tom shook flakes from his face. The pirate lay groaning, barely conscious, out of the fight.

Tom hauled me up. "Are you—"

He cried out, crumpling to one knee in the snow.

My blood froze. Had he been shot? I hadn't heard another shot.

Tom gripped his right leg. "My ankle," he said, terrified. "I can't move it."

My guts dropped. "Come on." I tugged on his arm. "I'll help you."

He looked up to the ridge. "I can't make that."

"I got shot," I said, "and *I* did it."

"Christopher—"

"You can. I'm here. I'll help you."

I yanked him up. He could barely place any weight on his right foot at all. We hurried, three-legged, to the cliff. "You go first," I said.

But it was hopeless. Facing no more bullets from above, their own ammunition spent, the pirates sprang from cover and charged around the pool, swords, axes, clubs held aloft. They cursed at us, vicious guttural promises, and I was grateful I didn't know what they were saying.

Then, from above, I heard a *twang*. And then, from behind me, I heard a scream.

The lead pirate fell, an arrow in his chest. The pirates skidded to a stop as a second man gasped, another arrow driving him into the snow.

I looked up. It was Wise, returned. He stood atop the ridge, calmly nocking arrows, letting them loose.

The pirates scrambled back to safety as Wise took his vengeance. With each shot, I felt the pain of decades of nightmares, of memories he wished he could forget. The pirates continued to pay for it: A third man took an arrow in the back, a fourth in the leg, and one more—I heard the howl—I know not where. We used our reprieve to creep up the cliff, me behind Tom, pushing on his thigh, giving his leg the support his wounded ankle couldn't.

I was sure I would faint. Every inch was excruciating. But slowly, slowly, we went. And all the while, Wise gave us cover, arrows buzzing down to greet any pirate who dared poke his head from the cave.

Finally we made it to the top. Sally grabbed Tom's hand, helping him over, then she took my hand, too. Wise grabbed the back of my collar, and together they pulled me the rest of the way.

I lay in the snow, gasping, trying to stomach the pain. Sally tugged at me. "Come on," she said, near panic. "We have to go."

She was right. Wise, looking worried, showed me his quiver; it was empty. Soon the pirates would realize the rain of arrows had ended. And we had nothing left with which to stop them.

"Where are the children?" I said.

Sally pointed. A furrow of tracks led through the snow, toward Seaton, village lights winking beneath the glow of the lighthouse on the coast.

"Go with them," I told Wise. "Make sure they get safely to town, that no pirates try to flank them."

He nodded and gripped my uninjured shoulder. Then he ran into the darkness, toward the light.

I scrambled to my feet, and put Tom's arm around me. "Come on," I said to Sally. "We have to help him."

She took his other arm. Together we all took a step toward Seaton, but Tom cried out and fell.

"What happened?" Sally said.

My eyes met Tom's. I'd never seen him so scared.

"I can't," he whispered.

And I knew it was true. "Sally."

She looked at me quizzically.

"Go with Wise," I said. "Help the children. When you get to town, tell everyone you see what's happening. They'll have already heard the shots. I know they're not soldiers, but if enough of them come, maybe they'll scare the pirates away—"

"Why are you telling me this?" she said. "You're coming with me."

"Tom's twisted his ankle. He can't run."

She looked at me, then at Tom, horrified. "But . . . so . . . we'll help him."

"We can't," I said. "Once the pirates realize we're out of arrows, they'll swarm over that ridge. If we try to help Tom walk, we'll move too slowly. They'll catch up to us well before Seaton."

"You can't mean to stay here!" she said, angry and scared. "They'll kill you!"

"Of course we're not going to stay here," I said, like the idea was madness. "But Tom can't run, so we're going to hide. We're going to climb down to the coast, then find a cove to stay in until help comes."

"They'll follow you," she said. "They'll see your tracks."

"They won't," I said, "because we're going to use Julian's trick. We'll walk into the water, then double back and hide where they won't expect."

"And if they keep searching?"

"They won't," I said pointedly, "if you get men from Seaton *and hurry back*. So go."

She looked torn. She knew what I said was the only possible way out for Tom. But still . . . "I'll stay with you," she said.

"Two will be easier to hide than three. Besides, we need you to tell the villagers to come get us. Wise can't speak."

Her lip trembled. "I'm coming back for you. Don't you dare die on me."

"Who, us?" I said. "We've been shot, stabbed, strangled, poisoned, burned, bludgeoned, and blown up. Twice."

"Three times, actually," Tom said.

"You see?" I forced a smile. "We're invincible."

"Oh . . . ," she said, and she wrapped Tom in a hug. Then she threw her arms around me. She lingered, holding me close, her cheek pressed to mine. If I could have, I'd have stayed like that forever.

But I couldn't. I pushed her away. "Now go."

"Don't you *dare* die on me," she said. Then she turned and disappeared into the darkness.

And I knew I'd never see her again.

CHAPTER
49

I JUST STOOD THERE, WATCHING her go.

"Christopher," Tom said.

A strange sort of calm had come over me. "Yes?"

"Your memories came back, didn't they? You remember us now."

"I do."

I turned. He stood in the snow, his right foot barely holding any weight.

"Your plan won't work," he said.

"I know."

"I can't climb down with this ankle. Not fast enough to avoid the pirates."

"I know."

"And there's nowhere around for us to hide."

"I know that, too."

"But then . . . you have to go."

"No," I said.

"You *have* to. If you stay, you're going to die."

I shrugged. "You don't know that."

"Of course you will!" He was angry now. "Don't be stupid. Please. I'm begging you to go."

"I can't."

"But why?"

"Because I *remember*," I said. "I remember all the times you stayed, when *you* shouldn't have. I remember every ludicrous scheme we tried. I remember meeting you on the green when we were eleven, and hitting you with that ridiculous catapult, and I remember finding the best friend I'll ever have." My words caught in my throat. "I remember everything, Tom. And I can't leave you behind to die."

"I'm going to die, anyway," he said, his own voice cracking. "You don't have to."

"Maybe not." I wiped my eyes on my sleeve. "If I go,

I might survive. But I'd always wonder if there was something I might have done that could have saved you. And that I just couldn't live with."

"Christopher—"

"No one knows the future," I said. "We saw a genuine miracle in Paris. Maybe we'll see another one here. Maybe God will send His avenging angel on blessed wings, and we'll make jokes about his hair on our way to London. Or maybe we'll fall beneath the pirates' swords, and we'll stand tonight before Saint Peter. It doesn't matter. Whatever happens, wherever we go, we'll face it together."

Tom bowed his head. Then he turned toward the cove and drew his sword. He stripped off the sheath covering the hilt, and thrust Eternity into the ground so it stood upright, a holy cross.

Light glowed over the ridge. The pirates, coming with their torches. I could hear their curses—and now thunder, too, in the distance, a low, rolling rumble.

"Storm's back," I said.

"I hear it."

"Hey," I said suddenly, "did you see me hit that pirate in the face with my pistol?"

Tom nodded. "That was funny."

"I've been thinking. Homemade cannons, two-hundred-year-old arquebuses, pistols with wet powder . . . I'm pretty good with guns, aren't I? When we get back to London, I think I should learn to use one properly."

Tom shook his head. "God help us all."

I drew my sword, held it loose in my right hand. Left shoulder still burning, I pulled the vial of aqua fortis from my sash and yanked the cork out with my teeth. It would stop one of the pirates, at least.

Rough hands reached over the ridge, finding a hold in the matted snow.

Tom's voice trembled. "Christopher?"

"Yes?"

"I'm scared."

"Me, too," I said.

And then the pirates swarmed over the edge.

CHAPTER
50

I FINALLY GOT A DECENT LOOK AT them, illuminated now by their torchlight. Their outfits were an unsightly mix, stolen from their victims during their travels: Ottoman *shalvars* under Dutch linen shirts under English sheepskin coats, all stained and filthy. But their weapons—swords, axes, clubs, a flail, a spear—would do the job well enough.

They seemed surprised to see us, waiting. They were even more surprised when Tom pointed at them and shouted.

"STOP."

They did, eyes wide.

"This is England," Tom said. "And no man who serves

the king can ever be a slave. Go. Go home. Or this land will be your grave."

I don't know who was more shocked, them or me. They stared at this strange boy, twice the size of any of them, and they hesitated. A man in the center said something harsh—a command—and they put aside their surprise and advanced.

"I don't think they speak English," I said.

"I didn't suppose they would." Tom sighed. "I just always wanted to say something like that."

The thunder rumbled, getting closer. Tom pulled his sword from the ground—and this made them pause once again.

The moonstone glowed red in the light of the pirates' torches. One of them muttered something as he stared at the blade. I didn't understand the word, but it spread like ripples through the ranks.

I felt the tiniest thrill of hope. "Maybe they'll understand Eternity," I said.

Tom raised his sword high. Slowly, he started to whirl it about. The blade rang as it sliced the air, and Eternity began to sing.

The pirates' muttering grew louder. Where the blade and its moonstone had made them nervous, its song sparked genuine fear. Two of them actually backed away, and, for a moment, I really thought they might flee.

Then the same man as before—he had to be the captain—cursed at them. He barked a string of alien words, and it stopped the pirates in their tracks. One of them, wielding a wickedly curved blade, gathered his courage, stepped forward, and shouted a challenge at Tom.

Tom stayed where he was; his twisted ankle wouldn't let him advance, anyway. He just whirled Eternity faster, her song ringing in our ears.

The pirate paled. His challenge faltered.

The captain screamed at him. The man steeled himself, raised his cutlass overhead, and charged.

Tom stood his ground. He leaned forward as he spun his blade, as if to rush to meet his attacker. Then, just as the pirate came within range, Tom dropped, cutting downward.

The pirate angled his cutlass into a high parry, expecting to block the blade coming from above. But Tom's arms heaved, and his mighty strength twisted Eternity as he fell to his knees. Her path curved, and she sang in triumph as she sliced across the man's chest. The pirate stopped in his tracks.

Eternity's song faded, and all we heard was rolling thunder. Tom remained on his knees, panting. The pirate stood there, looking puzzled.

Then he fell.

The pirates gasped. The magic blade had defeated their champion with ease. Tom said nothing. He just pushed himself up with his one good leg and began to whirl Eternity again.

This time, all the pirates backed away—all but one. Their captain cursed at them. One of them cursed back and turned, ready to bolt.

The captain didn't scream at him anymore. He simply thrust his sword through his crewman's back. Then he kicked the body off his blade, into the snow.

His men froze. The captain said nothing more; he didn't have to. Their choice was clear: Fight the English giant with the singing sword, or die by their own captain's hand.

In the end, they stayed. Though they didn't try to charge us again. Instead, they fanned out, encircling us.

I pivoted with them, my back against Tom's. My sword was nothing holy, so I just gripped it, praying it wouldn't slip in the sweat of my palm. I raised the vial of aqua fortis, ready to cast it in the face of the first man who attacked.

"Don't worry about the men behind you," I said to Tom. I had to force my voice to stop shaking. "I have them."

I hoped the pirates couldn't hear my fear. But Tom did. He brought Eternity down, gripped her hilt with both hands. Her song faded, until there was only thunder and wind.

"Thank you," he said.

"Always," I said.

And we readied for their final attack.

CHAPTER
51

THE THUNDER ROLLED EVER CLOSER.

So did the pirates. Their circle was complete; there was nowhere to run. Everything would end here.

I'm going to die, I thought, and I couldn't believe my own calm. *Master?*

He came to me. *I am here.*

I could see his face again. I sent a prayer of thanks heavenward. I'd so wanted to see him one more time.

I thought you'd gone, I said. *I thought I'd lost you forever.*

Never, he said, and he echoed my words to Tom. *I am with you always.*

The pirates pressed closer. So did the thunder, a long, steady rumble—

I frowned.

The thunder. It *was* steady—*too* steady. And there were no lightning flashes. It was the earth itself that began to shake.

The pirates stopped their advance, uncertain of what strange new magic they were facing. Tom and I were just as confused.

"What *is* that?" Tom said.

An earthquake, I thought.

But it wasn't an earthquake. I looked past the pirates to the lights of Seaton—and I saw those lights were dancing.

I blinked. Had I gone mad? No, I was certain of it: The lights were dancing. And they were coming closer, rising up and down like—

Torches.

And the sound. It wasn't thunder. It was . . .

"Horses," I said.

And the first of them came into view.

I stared as the figures rode down on us. In the lead was a man in furs, all black, a terrifying scowl on his face. He wore a patch over his left eye and a three-fingered glove on his right hand.

Impossible. It was impossible. "It *can't* be," Tom said.

Lord Ashcombe roared as he rode toward us, forty of the King's Men thundering behind. He dropped his reins, drawing two pearl-handled pistols from his belt. He aimed them and fired, and the pirate in front of me flew backward into the snow.

The pirates broke and ran. Their captain sprinted after them, terror finally etched on his face. They made for the cliff, flowing past us like we weren't even there.

Lord Ashcombe roared again as he drew his sword, left handed. *"For the king!"* he howled, and he swung his blade. A fleeing pirate's head left his shoulders, gathering snow as it bounced away. Lord Ashcombe rode a second man beneath his warhorse's churning hooves, then chased a third to the ridge. He wheeled to the right, swung a steel-studded boot, and kicked the man over the side.

Lord Ashcombe pointed to the cove with his sword as the King's Men reined in. *"Take no prisoners!"* he cried, and forty English soldiers jumped from their mounts and swung over the edge, weapons waving, battle cries echoing into the night.

Lord Ashcombe watched them go, then flicked his reins. His warhorse plodded toward us, head bobbing. The King's Warden looked down from his mount as we gaped up at him in astonishment.

"Everywhere you go," he said, "there's trouble."

I flushed.

He spotted the blood on the shoulder of my coat, saw Tom leaning on me, limping. "Do you need a surgeon?"

What I really need, I thought, *is sleep.* Or maybe I already was asleep. This had to be a dream. "Who . . . what . . . how did you find us?"

Lord Ashcombe frowned. "You sent me a letter."

"Yes, but how did you get all the way here from Oxford?"

"I wasn't in Oxford." He explained as we stood there, dumbfounded. "After the storm, a courier brought news that your ship never made it to Dover. Other boats were lost that day, and their wrecks were washing up on shore, so we rode down from Oxford to look for you. We knew the storm blew ships west, so I moved our command to Southampton.

"I've had men scouring the coast for a fortnight, but we were looking too close to the port. I never imagined you'd be carried this far. Regardless, when your courier arrived in Southampton, he spotted the King's Men at the docks, and they brought him to me with your letter. I conscripted Captain Haddock to return to Seaton immediately."

"But how did you know we were *here*?" Tom asked.

"The gunfire," he said. "The innkeeper at the Blue Boar told me you hadn't yet returned. It was too dark to go searching for you, but when I heard the shots, I knew: Follow the explosions, and you'll find Christopher Rowe."

I flushed even deeper as Tom glared at me. "But . . . *you* came to look for me?" I said.

Lord Ashcombe regarded me sternly. "You did His Majesty a great service in Paris. And we don't abandon our friends."

I shrank under his gaze. "Right. Sorry."

"Now. Your letter was somewhat vague." He pointed behind him. "Do you mind telling me whose head that is?"

"A Barbary pirate's," I said.

He scowled. "Foul beasts. I've been pressing His Majesty to deal with them. When the war with the Dutch has ended, we'll rid our waters of them once and for all."

Some of the King's Men began climbing back over the ridge, puffing in their heavy leather armor. One of Lord

Ashcombe's pistols had fallen from his belt; a King's Man found it and brought it to him.

Lord Ashcombe brushed off the snow. "Did you finish them?"

The soldier shook his head. "Sorry, General. They got away."

Lord Ashcombe reined his horse over to the edge. I helped Tom hobble over, and we stood beside him.

The *Andalus* had already cleared the cove. It appeared that as soon as the gunfire had started, the captain had ordered a few of his men to push the ship out to sea. The mainsail unfurled, billowing in the wind, speeding them away from the coast.

Smoke rose from the beach, pistols thundering as the King's Men emptied their guns at the departing ship. "I could ride to Seaton, General," the soldier with us said. "Order Captain Haddock to sail after them."

Lord Ashcombe shook his head. "No use. That yacht will outrun the *Manticore*." He cursed. "How I'd love to sink that boat."

"Actually, my lord—" I began.

Suddenly the sky filled with light. A second later came a massive *BOOM*—and the *Andalus* exploded.

Fire ripped it apart from inside the hold, casting flaming timbers off in glowing arcs. The mainmast shot into the sky like a spear, the sail burning on its ropes. It tumbled end over end before splashing down a hundred yards away. We ducked as a beam of wood whistled past, bouncing a fiery path through the snow.

The remains of the *Andalus* glowed brightly as it sank beneath the waves. Tom and Lord Ashcombe turned to stare at me.

I flushed so deeply I stopped freezing. "I can explain."

"Perhaps you'd better," Lord Ashcombe said.

"I found a map," I said, and I handed him the pirate chart I'd stuffed in my breeches. "It made me realize that even if we rescued *these* children, the pirates could always lay in somewhere else and kidnap more. I knew we had to stop them for good. I just didn't know how.

"But then my memories returned, and I recalled how we'd stopped the Cult of the Archangel. I didn't have any Archangel's Fire, of course, but I'd seen the pirates' gunpowder, in the magazine, in their hold."

"You set a fuse?" Lord Ashcombe said.

I shook my head. "The fuses they had were too short. The ship would have exploded before we'd climbed out of the cove. Instead, I used nitrum flammans. It's this powder—if you mix it with zincum india, then add some spirit of salt, it makes a flame, all on its own. It's really something to see. I can show you—"

He raised an eyebrow.

"Uh . . . right. Anyway, like oil of vitriol, spirit of salt dissolves metals. So I took one of the tin cups from the brig and filled it with all the spirit I had. Then I put the cup on top of the nitrum, which I'd dumped inside one of the barrels. I knew it would take several minutes for the spirit to eat through the tin, which gave us time to escape. Then, once the tin was finally eaten through, the spirit of salt would drip down, and . . . well . . ." I motioned to the burning water. "That."

Tom buried his face in his hands. I couldn't read Lord Ashcombe's expression. Finally, he spoke.

"You're like a cannon," he said. "In human form."

Tom moaned. "Oh, please, my lord. Don't give him any more ideas."

DECEMBER 25–31, 1665

Nihil autem opertum est, quod non reveletur;
neque absconditum, quod non sciatur.

CHAPTER
52

WITH THE DANGER PASSED, THE pain, the cold, and my exhaustion finally overwhelmed me. I collapsed in the snow. I have only vague memories of what happened next: Tom and me being lifted into saddles by the King's Men, a bone-rattling gallop back to Seaton, and a blessed blast of warmth at the Blue Boar Inn. I was carried to my room, laid facedown on the bed, then pinned to the mattress by a pair of soldiers.

I was only vaguely aware of why—until a hot lance burned my shoulder. I screamed, then passed out, and by the time I awoke, the King's Men had removed the bullet and bound the wound tight.

Tom sat next to me, his ankle wrapped snugly. Sally was there, too, pacing, chewing on a fingernail, cradling her own bandaged hand against her chest.

Oh, how I hurt. "Poppy," I croaked.

"It's already boiling—" Tom began, and then Sally flung herself onto me and held me close.

"Ow."

"Sorry," she said. She let me go, shaking. "But . . . the explosion. When I heard it . . . I thought . . ."

Tom spared me the effort of telling the story. He explained what had happened on the ridge after she left— well, *almost* everything. He thought it prudent to leave out the part where I'd lied to her so she'd get to safety. I mouthed to him a silent and deeply grateful thanks.

She still wasn't pleased. She stared at us, first incredulous, then angry. By the end, she was just flummoxed. "You're *both* mad."

"Don't look at me," Tom said. "This is all *his* fault."

That was so unfair. "I noticed," I said, "you left out the part with the whole 'Stop, pirates, this is England' speech."

"*That* was mad? You threw a pistol at them. A pistol!"

"Well, it worked, didn't it?"

We were still arguing when Sally stomped off, shaking her head in disgust.

Blessedly, the poppy infusion took the edge off the pain. Once it finally began to work, Lord Ashcombe sent everyone out of my room. He listened grimly as I told him all that had happened since I'd washed up on the beach. I fell asleep promptly after that, but Tom and Sally told me that the moment the dawn lightened the sky, a dozen of the King's Men rode furiously to the Darcy estate, with orders to bring Sir Edmund and Julian in chains.

Lord Ashcombe nearly spat with contempt when I mentioned the man's name. "I knew he was a fraud," he said. "I tried to warn His Majesty not to give him a baronetcy."

"Then how did he get it?"

"The usual way. Money. It costs a great deal to run a kingdom, and we were in particular need of coin when Charles returned to his throne."

"Sir Edmund said he knew you. He said you discussed cavalry charges."

Lord Ashcombe snorted. "*He* talked. *I* wondered how

angry the king would be if I ran my sword through his newest baronet." He shrugged. "Opportunities missed, I suppose."

I awoke to a chorus, singing.

At first, I thought I was still dreaming. It was coming from outside my window. I blinked and sat up, wincing with the pain. Tom lay sleeping on the palliasse, Moppet hanging half off his back as usual, Bridget resting on top of her. Sally, dozing in the chair next to me, woke when I did.

"Careful," she said, and she rose to check my bandage. The wound underneath was swollen—and agonizing—so she slathered it in honey and set more poppy to boil.

I nodded toward the window. "What's going on?"

"It's Christmas," Sally said.

I'd forgotten completely. Now I heard the songs more clearly: carols, sung by roving bands of merrymakers.

"Joyous Yuletide," Sally said, and, despite my pain, it really was. At least for a while.

The King's Men returned that afternoon—alone. Lord Ashcombe came to my room to tell me the news.

"The men found one of the pirates at the Darcy estate,"

he said. "His body, anyway. It was riddled with arrows."

That would have been Julian's doing. I was heartened that he'd kept his word. "And the Darcys?"

"Dead."

I went very still. "How?"

"Hanged," Lord Ashcombe said. "They were strung from the top of their tower. My guess is some of the locals discovered what the Darcys had done, and decided to mete out justice before the courts did."

I didn't tell him, but I didn't think that was true. I remembered Julian's last words to me.

No, Christopher. I'll never be redeemed.

I wondered if, in his own sad way, he'd tried. I wondered, and my heart lay heavy.

The news from the Darcy estate was bleak, but everything else was warmth. Word had spread at first light to the nearby hamlets and farms, ringing in Christmas with the news their children were alive and safe in Seaton. Two by two, the parents stumbled panting through the snow into town, scooping their little ones into their arms, weeping, as what was forever lost was found.

The Dutch children, of course, would have to wait a

little longer to see their parents, but they were no less over-joyed to realize they were finally safe. They were promised that they would be returned to their families, too, by—of all people—Lord Ashcombe, who spoke Dutch fluently. I was surprised, until I remembered that he'd stayed for years in the Netherlands with King Charles when His Majesty was still in exile.

"It looks like Álvaro told Darcy the truth," Lord Ashcombe said after speaking with the children. "The pirates raided the Dutch coast, but when their own ship was sunk, they had to shelter here. Would have been smarter for them if they'd just laid low until the storm blew over."

Despite the torment the English children had faced, I sent God a prayer of thanks for the pirates' greed. If they hadn't tried to fill their brig, these fifteen Dutch little ones would have been lost.

Lord Ashcombe's fearsome scars notwithstanding, the Dutch children clung to him like he was their father. It was understandable; though the pirates were gone, the children were still strangers in a strange land—and one at war with the Netherlands. Lord Ashcombe reassured them that the war had nothing to do with them, and they had our king's promise that they'd all get home safely. He spent the lion's share of his time with Moppet. Now that the pirates were gone, and she was with someone who spoke her language, she wouldn't stop talking.

"Her name's Katrijn," Lord Ashcombe told us. "That's Dutch for Catherine."

She spoke animatedly, pointing over and over at Tom. I couldn't understand most of it, but I heard two words quite clearly. One I already knew: *Piraten*. The other we'd heard before, but never understood.

"Monmon," I said. "That's what she said the first time she saw Tom. What does it mean?"

"It's not 'Monmon,'" Lord Ashcombe said. "It's *Maanman*. It means 'Moon Man.'" He turned to Tom, frowning. "She thinks you're an angel."

Tom's jaw dropped. "I'm a *what*?"

"She says . . ." He listened as she spoke. "She says you look like an ordinary boy, but you're really an angel in disguise. She knows this because . . . what?"

He frowned again. She repeated what she'd said, insistent.

"She says she knows this because when you came down from heaven, you plucked the Moon from the sky. And you used it to save them."

Tom looked at me, confused. I was just as puzzled—until I realized what she meant.

"Your *sword*," I said. "The moonstone on your sword. She thinks it's the real thing."

Stunned, Tom drew Eternity from her scabbard and pulled the sheath from her hilt. I hadn't ever seen the King's Warden startled before. In the darkness outside the pirate's cove, he hadn't got a good look at the blade. Now he stared at it in disbelief.

Moppet—Katrijn—came over to Tom. And as he knelt to greet her, I finally saw what the girl had seen that day in the woods. The stone really *did* look like the Moon. It even glowed with its own inner light. If I'd been five years old, and alone and scared, and this giant came to save me . . . wouldn't I think Tom was an angel? I half believed it already.

She spoke to him. Lord Ashcombe translated.

"She wants to thank you for saving her. And she thanks your earthly servants, too."

Tom grinned at me, and I sighed. I'd be hearing this one for a while.

"She says she misses her family," Lord Ashcombe continued, "and she can't wait to see them again. Do angels have families, too?"

Tom's smile faded. "Yes."

"Do you miss them?"

"Every day," he said.

She looked at him shyly and spoke again.

"She wants to know if she can touch the Moon."

Wordlessly, Tom balanced the blade on his palms. The moonstone glowed.

Katrijn reached out for the pommel. Ever so lightly, she touched the tip of her finger to the gem. Then she cupped it, gently, in her palm, before pulling away. She looked up at him.

"When you go home to your family, will you put the Moon back in the sky?"

"I will," Tom said. "And every night, when you look up and see it, you'll know I'm thinking of you."

She flung herself at him. She wrapped her arms tightly around his neck and whispered in his ear. *Ik hou van je, Tom.*

He closed his eyes and held her. "I love you, too, Katrijn."

With the children rescued, and the pirates defeated, we were finally granted a few days' rest. Which was good, because, with our injuries, we couldn't have taken another step. Sally spent so much time caring for me that I almost forgot she had her own injury, nearly as bad as mine.

The wound in her hand swelled. We both took the poppy now for our pain, and we became reliant on Tom to keep our wounds clean, Sally's especially. If the infection got too great, she'd lose the hand.

She didn't seem to care about that. I spoke to her sternly. "Believe it or not, the pain is good. It's a sign that you'll be able to use the hand, once it gets better. It'll be a lot of hard work, but I'll be there. I'll help you."

She shrugged. "All right," she said, and I could tell she didn't really believe it. But she didn't fight me, and I thought that maybe, for a moment, I saw a glimmer of hope in her eyes.

Thankfully, my shoulder didn't get infected too badly. Lord Ashcombe, more than experienced with the wounds of battle, noted the bullet had injured only flesh. "Another inch to the right and you'd have lost the arm."

I shuddered. "That's good to know."

"Two inches and you'd be dead."

I didn't think I wanted to know any more.

Tom, as usual, fared the best of us. Though his ankle swelled so badly it was two days before he could put any weight on it, none of his bones were broken, so in a couple of weeks, he'd be fully healed.

Fortunately, we wouldn't have to walk anywhere for a while. With the English children returned to their families, we'd be leaving Seaton, once again on the conscripted *Manticore*. The plan was to sail to Southampton; from there, Lord Ashcombe would send the Dutch children on to the Netherlands, while we rode in a carriage back to Oxford. The day we left, Robert and Wise came to see us off.

"Thank you," I said, "Thank you both. Robert, you took me in and kept me safe. And Wise . . ."

He waved away my thanks.

"No," I said. "I know how scared you were. To face down Barbary pirates, after what they did to you . . . not many men would have had that kind of courage. You saved us. You saved the children. I'll always be grateful."

Wise touched his hand to his heart, then held it out to me.

"He says—" Robert began.

"I know," I said, and I hugged them both. "I understand every word."

The night before we left, I didn't sleep. I didn't want to. I was afraid.

Everyone had paid for their crimes: the Darcys by their own hands; the pirates by ours. The White Lady, Sybil as a witch, Sir Edmund as witchfinder . . . all had been exposed as lies. Fear had ruled these hills—had ruled me, too. Fear, played upon and used, a weapon for the wicked to corrupt the truth.

It made me wonder: What other things, too, might be false?

The storm. Was it really the work of evil, or just a storm? My memories. Had they fallen prey to the Raven's hand, or were they simply taken by an illness?

My master had never taught me of such an affliction. Yet he *had* taught me that, just because I've never seen a thing, doesn't mean it cannot be.

And my dreams. Was the Raven really visiting me, or were they just dreams?

Just dreams, I told myself.

So why was I so afraid to sleep?

I closed my eyes, and in my mind I stood frozen in the icy plain, the hollow black bird above me.

I know you, I said. *I know you now. You are nothing but a dream.*

The Raven turned to look at me. His eyes glittered, pulling me inside his malevolent mind. And there I heard his voice—not in my dreams, but awake.

DO YOU THINK THAT WILL SAVE YOU

?

I opened my eyes, trembling. The fire burned low in the hearth, and its flickering shadows looked like wings. I was awake. I *had* to be awake. But I could still hear that terrible voice. It taunted me, corrupting my master's words.

I AM WITH YOU ALWAYS

it said.

"Go away," I whispered

and I sat alone in my bed. Tom lay asleep by the fire, Katrijn curled, dozing, on his back.

My friends. Tom. Sally. Even little Katrijn. They'd stood by me when I'd thought I'd lost everything. They'd nearly died because of me.

"It'll be safer," I whispered, "if I leave. Then the Raven won't come after you. Then he might leave you alone."

Tom spoke, startling me. "I found you once," he said quietly. "I can do it again."

I guess he was awake after all. "If you stay with me," I said, "you'll die."

"Maybe. Maybe not. Either way, I'm not going anywhere, and neither are you. I told you: We're friends forever." He paused. "It's easy to be brave in a nice warm room, isn't it?"

"Tom—"

"Go to sleep, Christopher."

But I couldn't. My friends had already been taken from me once. This time, I got them back. The next time, if the Raven came for them, there wouldn't be any return.

I couldn't let that happen. If we were going to stop him, we needed to do what he didn't expect: Take the fight to *him*. And we couldn't do that by ourselves. We needed the help of everyone we knew.

No more hiding, no more secrets. It was time for the truth.

I waited until Tom was asleep—really asleep, this time—then crept from my room. I went down the hall, to where two of the King's Men stood guard. Though the hour was late, Lord Ashcombe was still awake, poring over reports at his desk in the candlelight.

He looked up as I closed the door behind me. If he was surprised to see me, he didn't say so. He just regarded me for a moment. Then he motioned to the chair by the fire.

I took it. He waited. And we sat there, in silence, until I spoke.

"I need to tell you a story," I said.

We rode the waves back to Southampton, Bridget flying overhead. I had all my memories now, including the terrifying moment I'd been thrown into the sea. That fear returned as the boat bobbed on the water.

I was tired, so tired, of being afraid. So I forced myself to stand at the prow, next to the figurehead of the manticore. I trembled, hands gripping the rail, sweat running down my face, but there I stood, and there I remained. *I won't let you rule me,* I said to the sea, and I thought I could see Master Benedict smile.

Tom, Sally, and Katrijn, all fighting their own fears, stood with me. We felt the salty chill of the water's spray.

"Oh, look," a voice grumbled. "It's the source of my misery."

We turned. Captain Haddock lumbered toward us, looking dreadfully unhappy.

"What's the matter, Captain?" I said.

"Do you know what your grandfather ordered? He's making *me* take the children back to the Netherlands."

"Surely you wouldn't want them abandoned?" Sally said.

"Of course not. But why does it have to be me? Does the marquess not know what I do for a living?"

"He already sent a message to their king," I said. "Their navy has orders not to attack you."

"That's not the point. I *take* things from the Dutch. I don't return them." He looked at me sorrowfully. "Your grandfather's a hard man."

I couldn't resist. "Can you keep a secret?"

"Probably not," he admitted.

I told him anyway. "Lord Ashcombe's not really my grandfather. I'm not even a baron. My name is Christopher Rowe, and I'm an apothecary's apprentice. I only pretended to be an Ashcombe so people would help me."

He stared at me. "By Neptune's crusted . . . you *tricked* me!"

"Sorry."

"You deceitful . . . little . . ." He thought about it. "Do you want a job?"

"Me? On the *Manticore*? As a *pirate*?"

"I'm a privateer," he said testily. "And I could use an apothecary. Especially one that lies so well."

I shuddered at the thought. "Thank you, Captain, but no. I don't think the sea life is for me."

"How can anyone not want to live out here?"

"The ocean tried to drown me," I pointed out.

"That's just her way of saying she loves you."

I shook my head. "I already have Bridget. If I need any more love, I'll get a dog."

We disembarked at Southampton. Captain Haddock looked at us forlornly, hoping Lord Ashcombe would change his mind about sending him to the Netherlands. He didn't. The captain's eyes did light up, though, as his men carried a fresh crate of rum up the gangplank.

Tom and Katrijn clung to each other, until the *Manticore* could wait no longer. They spoke in quiet voices, and I supposed it didn't matter that they couldn't understand each other's language. Sometimes, the words themselves are the least important things to say.

We stayed on the dock, watched the *Manticore* sail away. The children waved at us from the rail—except for Katrijn. She just watched Tom, and he watched her back, until the ship disappeared beyond the waves.

I stood by his side. "Are you all right?"

"Can we go home now?" he said. "I think I'd like to go home."

I slung my arm around him and walked him to the carriage.

A FEW MATTERS OF
HISTORICAL NOTE

The 1600s were the peak of witchcraft hysteria. Starting with the very first witch trial (in Ireland, in 1324), the next five centuries would see an estimated 100,000 people across Europe tried for malevolent sorcery.

Our stereotypical image of a witch is a woman living in isolated poverty, and there is some reason for this: the poor were far more likely to be convicted, and the majority of the accused were female. In truth, however, anyone could have been charged. One-quarter of all accused witches were male, and in countries such as France, Russia, Finland, Iceland, and Estonia, the majority of the defendants were men. Age was no barrier, either;

in the Salem, Massachusetts, witch trials of 1692, four-year-old Dorothy Good was arrested and imprisoned for nearly nine months.

The trials themselves were terrible affairs, full of fear, confusion, and sometimes outright lies. Around half of all trials ended in execution (strangulation was the most common punishment in England, not burning, as is commonly believed). Even at the time, however, there were protests against the unfairness of the trials, and by the 1700s witch hunting was viewed with deep skepticism. In England, the Witchcraft Act of 1735 put an end to legal witch trials for good.

Superstitions die hard, however, and there remain places in the world today where being accused of witchcraft remains a death sentence. In Tanzania, for example, between 2005 and 2011, an estimated three thousand suspected witches were lynched by angry mobs.

If the seventeenth century was the age of witchcraft, so, too, was it the golden age of piracy. The discovery of the New World and the expansion of global commerce meant there was a great deal of money to be made on the seas—and where some chose trade, others chose murder and theft. No pirates were more feared than those from the Barbary Coast.

Though the Barbary pirates' main targets were in the Mediterranean, they raided nearly every coastal country in Europe, attacking as far away as Iceland. In addition to the countless lives lost, between 1530 and 1780 corsairs kidnapped and sold into slavery as many as 1.25 million Europeans. The southwest of England was a favorite target, and would remain so until Charles II finally built up his navy and drove them from English waters, some ten years or so after Christopher was shipwrecked in Devon.

Even then, the threat of the Barbary pirates remained. Their actions were so damaging to the fledgling United States of America that, in 1794, the United States Navy was founded, specifically to deal with corsairs. After two wars, the first started when President Thomas Jefferson refused to pay tribute to the Barbary nations, the pirates were defeated. Their threat would end for good when France finally conquered Algiers in 1830.

Yet, just as with accusations of witchcraft, on the high seas pirates still remain. As of this writing, around two hundred pirate attacks occur each year, the majority around Indonesia and Africa, costing shippers an estimated 4 to 8 billion dollars—to say nothing of those poor souls lost at sea.

ACKNOWLEDGMENTS

It's my privilege to have so many talented folks helping put these books together. I'd like to say thank you to the following:

To Liesa Abrams, Tricia Lin, and Suri Rosen, all of whom offered insights that made this story immeasurably better.

To Mara Anastas, Chriscynethia Floyd, Jon Anderson, Katherine Devendorf, Karin Paprocki, Julie Doebler, Jodie Hockensmith, Christina Pecorale, Caitlin Sweeny, Anna Jarzab, Michelle Leo, Greg Stadnyk, Hilary Zarycky, Laura Lyn DiSiena, Victor Iannone, Gary Urda, and Stephanie Voros at Aladdin.

To Kevin Hanson, Felicia Quon, Sheila Haidon, Jacquelynne Lennard, and Rita Silva at Simon & Schuster Canada.

To Dan Lazar, Cecilia de la Campa, Torie Doherty-Munro, and James Munro at Writers House.

To the publishers around the world who have embraced the Blackthorn Key series.

To Ingrid van der Mooren, to Terry Bailey, and to Alma, for their assistance with translation. Any errors remaining are my own.

And, as always, to you, dear reader: Thank you for joining Christopher on this adventure. While the Raven remains at large, more are sure to come. . . .